Philippine Folktales

Philippine Folktales

Introduction by
by Gabriela Lee

General Editor: Jake Jackson

FLAME TREE
PUBLISHING

This is a FLAME TREE Book

FLAME TREE PUBLISHING
6 Melbray Mews
Fulham, London SW6 3NS
United Kingdom
www.flametreepublishing.com

First published 2025

25 27 29 28 26
1 3 5 7 9 8 6 4 2

ISBN: 978-1-83562-258-2
ebook ISBN: 978-1-83562-494-4

The text in this book is selected and edited from the following original sources: *Philippine Folk-Tales* by Clara Kern Bayliss, et al.; *Philippine Folk Tales* by Mabel Cook Cole, 1916 (Chicago: A.C. McClurg & Company); *Filipino Popular Tales* by Dean S. Fansler, 1921 (New York: The American Folk-Lore Society); and *Philippine Folklore Stories* by John Maurice Miller, 1904 (Boston: Ginn & Company).

Designed and created in the UK | Printed and bound in China

Contents

Series Foreword

STRETCHING BACK to the oral traditions of thousands of years ago, tales of heroes and disaster, creation and conquest have been told by many different civilizations in many different ways. Their impact sits deep within our culture even though the detail in the tales themselves are a loose mix of historical record, transformed narrative and the distortions of hundreds of storytellers.

Today the language of mythology lives with us: our mood is jovial, our countenance is saturnine, we are narcissistic and our modern life is hermetically sealed from others. The nuances of myths and legends form part of our daily routines and help us navigate the world around us, with its half truths and biased reported facts.

The nature of a myth is that its story is already known by most of those who hear it, or read it. Every generation brings a new emphasis, but the fundamentals remain the same: a desire to understand and describe the events and relationships of the world. Many of the great stories are archetypes that help us find our own place, equipping us with tools for self-understanding, both individually and as part of a broader culture.

For Western societies it is Greek mythology that speaks to us most clearly. It greatly influenced the mythological heritage of the ancient Roman civilization and is the lens through which we still see the Celts, the Norse and many of the other great peoples and religions. The Greeks themselves learned much from their neighbours, the Egyptians, an older culture that became weak with age and incestuous leadership.

It is important to understand that what we perceive now as mythology had its own origins in perceptions of the divine and the rituals of the sacred. The earliest civilizations, in the crucible of the Middle East, in the Sumer of the third millennium BC, are the source to which many of the mythic archetypes can be traced. As humankind collected together in cities for the first time, developed writing and industrial scale agriculture, started to irrigate the rivers and attempted to control rather than be at the mercy of its environment, humanity began to write down its tentative explanations of natural events, of floods and plagues, of disease.

Early stories tell of Gods (or god-like animals in the case of tribal societies such as African, Native American or Aboriginal cultures) who are crafty and use their wits to survive, and it is reasonable to suggest that these were the first rulers of the gathering peoples of the earth, later elevated to god-like status with the distance of time. Such tales became more political as cities vied with each other for supremacy, creating new Gods, new hierarchies for their pantheons. The older Gods took on primordial roles and became the preserve of creation and destruction, leaving the new gods to deal with more current, everyday affairs. Empires rose and fell, with Babylon assuming the mantle from Sumeria in the 1800s BC, then in turn to be swept away by the Assyrians of the 1200s BC; then the Assyrians and the Egyptians were subjugated by the Greeks, the Greeks by the Romans and so on, leading to the spread and assimilation of common themes, ideas and stories throughout the world.

The survival of history is dependent on the telling of good tales, but each one must have the 'feeling' of truth, otherwise it will be ignored. Around the firesides, or embedded in a book or a computer, the myths and legends of the past are still the living materials of retold myth, not restricted to an exploration of origins. Now we have devices and global communications that give us unparalleled access to a diversity of traditions. We can find out about Native American, Indian, Chinese and tribal African mythology in a way that was denied to our ancestors, we can find connections, match the archaeology, religion and the mythologies of the world to build a comprehensive image of the human experience that is endlessly fascinating.

The stories in this book provide an introduction to the themes and concerns of the myths and legends of their respective cultures, with a short introduction to provide a linguistic, geographic and political context. This is where the myths have arrived today, but undoubtedly over the next millennia, they will transform again whilst retaining their essential truths and signs.

Jake Jackson
General Editor

Introduction to Philippine Folktales

Charting an Ocean of Stories

WITH OVER 7,600 islands and more than 130 language groups, the Philippines is a country in Southeast Asia that is filled with oceans of stories. The archipelago is geographically located in the western Pacific Ocean southeast of China, and sits in what is known as the Pacific Ring of Fire. The country is divided into three main island regions: Luzon in the north, Mindanao in the south and the different islands in the middle, collectively known as the Visayas. Many of the folk narratives in the Philippines were intertwined with precolonial belief systems from different indigenous groups, as well as hybrid folk practices that were the results of uneven colonial influences. Because the Philippines has a long and complicated colonial history, this influenced the kinds of folk narratives that have survived until the present day.

Pre-Colonial Philippines

The first indigenous communities that settled in the Philippines were known collectively as the Philippine Negrito groups. The name refers to communities such as the Aetas and Agtas in Luzon, the Ati and Iraya Mangyans in the Visayas and the Mamanwa in Mindanao. They still remain there today, living in roughly the same regions where their ancestors settled. Many of the islands were also settled by various Austronesian groups, travelling across the Pacific Ocean in *balangays*, long lashed-lug boats that functioned as trading ships in precolonial Philippines. The Filipino term *barangay*, meaning 'village', can be etymologically traced to these precolonial seafaring vehicles. Remains of the oldest *balangays* were excavated in Butuan alongside trade goods from East Asia and the Middle East, and have been carbon dated to as far back as 689 CE. In fact, archeological evidence exists of a lively trade route that originated in China and passed through the Philippines and other Southeast Asian kingdoms, bringing different religious and cultural influences – such as Islam, Hinduism, Buddhism and animism – that were adapted by the various island societies or complemented existing beliefs. The societies of these islands were usually divided into three levels: the nobility, the general free populace and bondsmen or dependents. They were usually ruled by a *datu*, sultan or rajah. Because of the archipelagic nature of the country, many communities asserted independence from each other and established their own kingdoms. They constantly established alliances with, or waged war against, their neighbours.

Many of the narrative traditions during the precolonial period were unwritten, passed down orally from generation to generation. Indigenous groups often had a designated individual or a group of learned elders who also maintained their tribe's collective narratives, social practices and religious beliefs: for instance, they were called the *mombaki* among the Ifugaos in northern Luzon or the *gurungan* among the Mangyans in Mindoro. Perhaps the best-known example of this was done by the Panay Bukidnon tribe in the Visayas. Here they practised a custom involving the veiling of a young woman, known as a *binukot*, who was kept away from society in order to raise her bride price. The young woman was shaded from the sun and maintained her modesty by bathing in the evening, away from prying eyes. As the *binukot*, she was the only one allowed to memorize the Panay Bukidnon epics, the *sugidanon*, with the intention of raising her status in the community. The last living *binukot*, Lucia Caballero, is married to Federico Caballero, the son of a former *binukot* and a Gawad Manlilikha ng Bayan (National Living Treasure) awardee, which is awarded to individuals or groups recognized by the Philippines government for their contributions to the intangible cultural heritage of the country.

Spanish Colonial Period in the Philippines

The Portuguese explorer Ferdinand Magellan arrived in the islands in 1521, attempting to claim the country for Spain. He was killed by warriors led by the *datu*, or indigenous leader, Lapu-Lapu in the Battle of Mactan, during an early-morning skirmish between Lapu-Lapu's men and Magellan's indigenous allies and European naval company. In 1565 Miguel Lopez de Legazpi brought more ships, with more military forces and religious clergy, and successfully declared the Philippines to be a colony under the Spanish empire. Using divide-and-conquer tactics learned from quelling indigenous rebellions in South America, de Legazpi was able to bring the country under a unified government administered in Manila by the Viceroy of New Spain, which was based in Mexico.

The Philippines was then transformed into a trans-Pacific hub through the establishment of the Manila galleon trade between the two Spanish colonies. This brought the country to international prominence as a vital aspect of the expanding global economy of empires. Both the Dutch and the British, at one point in time or another, attempted to wrest control of Manila from Spain, but their forces were successfully repelled.

Part of Spain's enduring presence in the Philippines was because of the integration of Catholicism with folk religions across the archipelago – with the exception of Southern Mindanao, where many of the indigenous groups managed to repel the Spanish armies and retain their independence. However, many Catholic orders were able to establish a strong presence in increasingly urban areas, while simultaneously reaching out to rural communities and establishing centres of learning and worship. Churches were not only spaces of prayer, but functioned as the town's social centre. Families were encouraged to bring their children in to learn their letters and prayers using Spanish syllabaries called *catons*, while young people mingled and flirted demurely under the watchful eyes of their elderly guardians. In many rural towns established by the Spanish clergy, this can be easily seen in the town's urban planning, with the town plaza or public square usually flanked by the parish church on one side and the town's government offices on the other. Embedding themselves in the daily lives of Filipinos, the Catholic Church was able to dismantle the power of indigenous beliefs by painting them as pagan and demonic, and insisting that the keepers and practitioners of these belief systems were destined for eternal torment and damnation.

However, many of these folk narratives and practices did persist, albeit informally. They were either syncretized with Catholicism, producing variations of Catholic and folk beliefs, or passed on through informal oratory means. For instance, the roots of the *pasyon*, a religious chant usually recited during Holy Week, lie in the practice of performing indigenous epic songs, in which the heroic figure is celebrated by a detailed retelling of their life and deeds. In this case, versions of the *pasyon* detail the creation of the world and the birth, life and death of Jesus Christ, usually in five-line stanzas and accompanied by a melody or a chanted *capella*. The *pasyon* may involve anywhere from 18 to 30 hours of continuous singing by an individual or a group of singers; it is performed in public as part of the general *pabasa* rites practised by religious devotees during Lent.

Usually seen as a sign of devotion, *pasyon* performances are normally sponsored by families or religious brotherhood/sisterhood groups. These sponsorships are signified by the presence of the *poon*, a religious statue of the Christ-figure usually passed down from one generation to the next. The oldest version of the *pasyon* is dated 1703, but the most popular one, by an unknown author, was written in Tagalog and published in 1814. It is commonly known as the *Pasiong Mahal* or *Pasyong Pilapil*.

Similarly, metrical romances such as the Tagalog *awit* and *korido* were instrumental in preserving many folk narratives, providing a formal poetic structure used to retell these stories. The *korido* was derived from the Spanish musical form *corrido*, in which the performer sings narrative verses accompanied by a guitar. However, in Philippine metrical romance the *korido* referred to long verse narratives, usually centred around stories concerning heroism, legends and folktales or religious figures. The *awit* is a subset of the *korido*, referring to the syllabic count of a particular korido form; it has been arguably the most popular form of the *korido* among the Tagalogs. Similar lengthy verse narratives existed among other indigenous groups, for example the *biag* in Ilocos and the *sugilanon* in

Ilonggo. However, the *awit* is distinguished by its material presence: there are about 229 recorded instances of Tagalog metrical romances, most of which are in *awit* forms.

By the nineteenth century, the most popular tales included adaptations of European metrical romances, as well as Philippine romances like the *Ibong Adarna* and *Florante at Laura*, legendary figures such as Bernardo Carpio and folktales such as *Mariang Alimango* and *Eliseo at Felisa*. Considered to be popular literature, many of these metrical romances were published as chapbooks by 1815 and sold outside the church after Sunday mass. They were deemed simple, disposable forms of entertainment; most of these *koridos* were unsigned and anonymous, although some authors did sign their initials or use pseudonyms at the end of the poems to lay ownership of the tale. By the early twentieth century, these poets sometimes used their real names to claim authorship of the verses, but the genre was still held in low regard, as noted by Damiana L. Eugenio and Ma. Cecilia Locsin-Nava in their journal article 'Metrical Romance': 'at the turn of the century, serious writers…looked down upon the metrical romance as a debased form' (2020). Nevertheless, these metrical romances bridged the distance between the intangible and the tangible versions of folk narratives, making it possible to trace the provenance of many Philippine folktales to their collective or individual sources.

Furthermore, despite a dearth of print materials about folk narratives during the three centuries of Spanish colonial rule in the Philippines, two men attempted to elevate Philippine folk narratives to an international audience. Isabelo de los Reyes, sometimes referred to as the father of Philippine folklore, was one of the first Filipinos who compiled folktales and practices in a two-volume manuscript called *El Folk-Lore Filipino*. The work was awarded the silver medal at the Madrid Exposition in 1887 and subsequently published in Spanish in 1890 and 1891. In 1994 it was translated into English by Salud C. Dizon and Maria Elinora P. Imson and published by the University of the Philippines Press.

Reyes' collection contained information on the folk beliefs and narratives of people living in the provinces of Malabon, Zambales and Ilocos Sur, as well as records of customs, traditions and even folk literature and poetry from Ilocos Sur, where de los Reyes originally came from. As

Benedict Anderson observed in 'The Rooster's Egg: Pioneering Folklore in the Philippines' (2000), de los Reyes

> *made clear what he thought folklore was about, and how he saw its social value...It offered an opportunity for a reconstruction of the indigenous past which was impossible in the Philippines by any other means, given the absence of pre-Spanish monuments, inscriptions or, indeed, of any written records at all.*

In fact, one of the motivating influences for de los Reyes was to show Spanish authorities that Filipinos, especially the indigenous groups never fully subsumed into the colonial system of governance, were already civilized before the arrival of Spain. In his introduction for *El Folk-Lore Filipino*, de los Reyes referred to himself as '*hermano de los selváticos, aetas, igorrotes y tinguianes* (brother of the forest-peoples, the Aeta, the Igorots and the Tinguians)' (Anderson), acknowledging that their indigenous knowledge systems, in some way, undergirded his own self-identity. In this way:

> *[F]olklore – comparative folklore – enabled [Isabelo] to bridge the deepest chasm in colonial society...the abyss between [people in urbanized spaces] and those whom we would today call 'tribal minorities'...There thus emerged a strange new brotherhood, and an adored father/motherland. (Anderson)*

Alongside the work of de los Reyes in *El Folk-lore Filipino*, Jose Rizal also contributed to a nascent attempt at placing Philippine folktales on a level with European ones. A contemporary of de los Reyes, Rizal is perhaps best known as the official national hero of the Philippines. His two novels, *Noli Me Tangere* and *El Filibusterismo*, ignited the nationalist passions of Filipinos, inspiring the 1898 Philippine Revolution that sought to remove the Spanish colonial government. However, during Rizal's time in Europe, he was also inspired to translate and illustrate several fairy tales by Hans Christian Andersen into Tagalog, and to send these to his nephews and nieces as a Christmas gift in 1886. Rizal's own attempts at bringing international attention to Philippine folklore were revealed in the 1889 publication of 'Specimens of Tagalog Folklore'; the work was published in *Trubner's Oriental Record*, a journal published in England that specialized in Asian cultural studies.

In the same year, Rizal also contributed an illustrated retelling of 'The Monkey and the Turtle', a fable with multiple versions that can be found all over the Philippines. Another Tagalog folktale, 'Mariang Makiling', was published in 1890 in *La Solidaridad*, the revolutionary newspaper in which many Filipino intellectuals published their scathing opinions about the abuses conducted in the Philippines by the Spanish government. Rizal also formed a deep friendship with the Austrian schoolteacher Ferdinand Blumentritt. He was inspired to catalogue what he learned about Philippine folklore through his interactions with Rizal and other Filipino contemporaries in the book *Diccionario Mitológico De Filipinas*, published in Madrid in 1895.

Both de los Reyes and Rizal were intent on introducing Philippine folklore to audiences outside the Philippines, responding directly to the colonial notion that Filipinos were uncivilized savages. For these two men, privileged enough to be able to study in Europe and to be introduced to the ideals of the Enlightenment, folk narratives and beliefs became a way for them to prove that civilized thought and practices were well established among the Filipinos, predating the arrival of Spanish colonizers.

American Colonial Period in the Philippines

When the United States defeated Spain in the Spanish-American War of 1898, one of the conditions of Spanish surrender was the turnover of the Philippines to American governance, alongside other Spanish colonies such as Puerto Rico and Guam. Under the Treaty of Paris, the United States 'purchased' the Philippines for $20 million – a decision to which the Philippines did not consent. Then-president William McKinley wrote down the 'Benevolent Assimilation' Proclamation of 1898 over the Philippines, which he detailed in a letter to his Secretary of War. In this proclamation, McKinley declared that

> *the mission of the United States is one of benevolent assimilation, substituting the mild sway of justice and right for arbitrary rule. In the fulfillment of this high mission...there must be sedulously maintained the strong arm of authority, to repress disturbance and to overcome all obstacles to the bestowal of the blessings of good and stable government upon the people of the Philippine Islands under the free flag of the United States.*

One of the first things that McKinley did upon assuming sovereignty over the Philippines was to send over the First Philippine Commission. It was led by Dr Jacob Schurman, who was instructed to observe Filipino society and report back on how to proceed with governance. Based on the observations of the five-member Commission, the Philippines was unprepared for independence and needed tutelage from an American-led democratic government. However, this did not go over well with the Filipinos; they had already fought for independence from Spain in 1898 and were now preparing to install an independent Philippine government in 1899. The resulting Philippine-American War was fought from 1899 until 1902. Although the first Filipino president, Emilio Aguinaldo, was captured by US forces in 1901, his guerrilla forces continued to push back against the American army for another year.

Once the United States had a firm foothold on the Philippines, one of the first things they did was to record and systematize information found across the archipelago. In doing so, they set up a robust public school system, partially modelled on the Native American boarding school system in the United States. English became the dominant language of instruction, with books for learning and for leisure imported from America to the Philippines to teach Filipino children their ABCs. Folklore studies flourished under the American colonial system. Initially spearheaded by American academics – mostly anthropologists and schoolteachers – folklore studies became embedded in the Philippine university system through undergraduate classes introduced at the University of the

Philippines in 1910, when folklorist and English professor Dean S. Fansler joined the faculty at the College of Liberal Arts.

Even before instituting these college courses, however, the folk narratives of indigenous groups were already being recorded. The work conducted by people such as Fletcher Gardner, Lucetta Kellenbarger, Mabel Cook Cole and Clara Bayliss in recording and compiling Filipino folktales, mostly for younger readers but also for academic folklore journals, was a large step in codifying Philippine folktales. Under their influence, the process shifted from a largely oral and informal system to a more systematized way of organizing folk narratives.

In an article titled 'Folklore in Philippine Schools' (1987), the notable Filipino folk scholar Damiana L. Eugenio provided a brief historical overview of how Philippine folktales were disseminated within the American-led public school system in the country. She names Camilo O. Osias's *Philippine Readers* series, first published in 1920 as supplementary material for Filipino elementary students, as a valuable way of introducing students to 'authentic folklore' collected by academics, as well as highlighting the fact that 'Philippine tales were presented side by side with foreign tales'. Such testimony shows why stories such as 'Why the Sky is High' and 'The Legend of the First Bananas' were etched in the memories of Filipino schoolchildren in the early twentieth century. Another collection that made its way into the classroom was the *Philippine National Literature* series. This three-volume supplementary set, published around 1921, was edited by Harriet Ely Fansler and Isidoro Panlasigui. Its aim, according to the editors, was to

> *afford the people of the Philippine Islands access to their own literature in a common tongue [i.e. English]…The Philippine is to be congratulated on possessing such a rich store, notable in variety, strength, and charm. (Eugenio)*

One highly influential figure during this time was Dean S. Fansler, whose *Filipino Popular Tales* was perhaps the most robust collection of Philippine folk narratives prior to the Second World War. Featuring over 82 folk narratives collected from and annotated by Fansler's students at the University of the Philippines between 1908 and 1914, the stories were, according to Eugenio, 'carefully chosen to display to advantage the richness of tale types in the Christian Filipino folk narrative traditions'. Fansler's unpublished manuscript collection amounted to about 4,000 folk narratives, collected over 28 years of field research and organized into 76 volumes. Unfortunately only about 23 volumes have survived at the University of the Philippines' Main Library. Similarly Fansler's academic contemporary, archaeologist H. Otley Beyer, had a more modest collection of about 20 volumes of largely unpublished folk narratives, titled *Philippine Folklore, Customs and Beliefs*, culled from Beyer's ethnographic data research of over 150 volumes. No longer in the Philippines, the Beyer collection resides instead at the National Library of Australia.

Beyond the collection, publication and distribution of Philippine folktales by scholars and hobbyists, the introduction of college-level courses in folklore studies, taught by actual practitioners and researchers such as Fansler, Beyer and their protégés, meant that there was now at least a generation of Filipino students well-versed in the systems and protocols of ethnographic field research and comparative folklore studies. Well-read and well-trained, this new generation of folklorists were ready to take on the world.

And then the Second World War reached the Philippine shores.

Post-War Independence and Contemporary Folklore Studies in the Philippines

Soon after the liberation of Manila from Japanese forces in 1946, the United States granted the Philippines independence. In the 1950s and 1960s a new crop of Filipino folklore scholars emerged, many of whom had been trained under Fansler and Beyer. Perhaps at the forefront of this new generation of folklorists was E. Arsenio Manuel, who undertook the work of collecting and organizing the scattered remnants of folktales to bring them into the twentieth century. Manuel's work on Philippine folk epics stands as one of the enduring studies on the subject matter, earning him the nickname 'Dean of Philippine Anthropology'. Similarly, Fr. Francisco Demetrio's work on Philippine mythology, eventually collected into two massive volumes called *Encyclopedia of Philippine Folk Beliefs and Customs*, also proved a significant step forward in providing access to Philippine folk stories.

A number of graduate dissertations also focused on comparative folklore studies that defined the widening scope of engagement with Philippine folk practices. As well as contributing to an expanding academic field, these studies also illuminated what Joseph Baumgarten describes as

> *[embodying] all the elements that have gone into the make-up of Filipino culture...[and serving] as a mirror that shows us the major lineaments of the Filipino soul. ('Folklore: The Forgotten Mirror of Philippine Culture', 1980)*

Many of these scholars from the 1950s, 1960s and 1970s contributed to a more systemic and comparative approach towards folklore studies in the Philippines. In so doing they linked what was otherwise a largely textual study to other fields such as history, ethnography, anthropology and archaeology. The First National Folklore Conference was held in 1972. It provided a platform for folklorists from across the Philippines, as well as other Asian Studies scholars outside the country, to exchange methods and insights about their work. Similarly, special journal issues of *Studies in Philippine Linguistics* in 1978 and the *Philippine Quarterly of Culture and Society* in 1980 served to highlight ongoing research in Philippine folklore studies.

Much of the work had also been towards creating accessible materials for young readers. An important figure here was Maximo Ramos, whose ten-volume series, *Realms of Myths and Reality*, was instrumental in cataloguing the distinctions and folk stories surrounding creatures of Philippine lower mythology. Drawing upon his 1965 PhD dissertation 'The Creatures of Philippine Lower Mythology', Ramos produced several other volumes that tracked the provenance of mythical and monstrous creatures in the Philippines. His seminal article, 'The Aswang Syncrasy in Philippine Folklore', was published in 1969 by the journal *Western Folklore*. Ramos's research as a scholar and a teacher earned him a position as the first editor-in-chief for Phoenix Publishing House, a pioneering producer of textbooks and other learning materials for Filipino schoolchildren.

In a similar vein, Damiana L. Eugenio's work on the multi-volume *The Philippine Folk Literature* series stands as a testament to her decades-long commitment to uplifting Philippine folk narratives. It also earned her the moniker 'Mother of Philippine Folklore'. In her research, she divides Philippine folk narratives into proverbs, epics, myths and legends. Eugenio also compiled representative examples of folk narratives, folk speech and folk songs in an anthology that could be easily used in the classroom. The first volume of the series was published by the University of the Philippines Press in 1981, and still continues to be reprinted.

Other scholars such as William Henry Scott, Felipe Jocano Sr. and Resil Mojares, among others, were also instrumental is contributing to the growth of Philippine folklore studies in the mid- to late twentieth century. Other notable books published in the 1980s and 1990s were Gilda Cordero-Fernando's *The Soul Book* and Herminia Meñez Coben's *Explorations in Philippine Folklore*. In 2017 appeared the long-awaited first book of the Panay epics, *Tikum Kadlum: Sugidanon (Epics) of Panay* (Book 1), translated by Alicia P. Magos. Magos spent 25 years recording, transcribing and translating what turned out to be the ten-volume folk epics of the Panay-Bukidnon indigenous group.

Philippine folklore also seeped into popular culture throughout most of the twentieth and twenty-first centuries, adapting and influencing everything from theatre and film adaptations to television shows with characters culled straight from folk epics and legends, to comics and graphic novels, to stories for children and adults alike. As the folklore scholar Erlinda K. Alburo says, reading Philippine folktales 'is not just the final product, but also the doing, and the experiences and symbols involved, which are deemed equally important' ('Continuing and Emerging Directions in Contemporary Philippine Folklore Studies', 1992).

The internet, social media and the advent of digital archiving also played into the dissemination and accessibility of Philippine folklore to a global audience, although it also lost much of the scholarly rigour that characterized its growth in the university setting. As a result, the Filipino diasporic communities were able to find diverse ways to learn more about their home cultures, and how these play into the formation of their identities. As folktales were circulated and embedded themselves in the public consciousness, they also inspired new generations of creators – writers, illustrators, game designers, musicians and others – to grow new stories from the seeds of the old.

Gabriela Lee (Introduction) is a faculty member in the Department of English and Comparative Literature at the University of the Philippines, Diliman, where she teaches creative writing and children's literature. Lee's research sits at the intersections of postcolonial children's literature, genre studies and creative writing studies. Her works of short fiction and academic scholarship have been published in the Philippines and abroad. Most recently, she is the co-editor of *Mapping New Stars: A Sourcebook on Philippine Speculative Fiction*, published by the University of the Philippines Press.

Quests & Adventures

MANY OF THE STORIES that are considered quests and adventures in Philippine folktales are undertaken for honour, for loyalty or for revenge. They frequently have a supernatural or magical cast, but more often than not the heroic deeds and actions they contain are meant to be examples of how to behave in one's community. In fact, the hero is not usually royalty, but an ordinary person able to perform extraordinary deeds. For instance, 'Gawigawen of Adasen' is a Tingguian tale that emphasizes family loyalty and honouring the dead. Meanwhile, 'The Story of Carancal' is a Tagalog tale that emphasizes the heroism of Carancal, a small Tom Thumb-esque character who overcomes his parents' abuse and becomes a hero in his own right, before returning home laden with wealth and forgiving his parents.

Perhaps one of the most famous tales in this collection is 'Ang Ibong Adarna' (The Adarna Bird), a Philippine metrical romance written in verse and collected in three volumes. The earliest published version of this quest narrative is traced back to 1900, when it was anonymously published in the Tagalog language in Manila; there are also versions in other Philippine languages such as Ilocano and Bikolano. Eugenio describes this tale as 'one of the greatest favourites among Philippine metrical romances' (2020). 'Ang Ibong Adarna' has been adapted into films, a ballet, a puppet play and many children's books. Adarna Books, Inc, the well-known Philippine children's book publisher, is named after this mythical bird.

The Aderna Bird

THERE WAS ONCE a king who greatly desired to obtain an aderna bird, which is possessed of magical powers, has a wonderful song, and talks like men. This king had a beautiful daughter, and he promised her to anyone who would bring him an aderna bird. Now the quest for the aderna bird is very dangerous, because, if the heart is not pure, the man who touches the bird becomes stone, and the bird escapes.

There were in that country three brothers, Juan, Diego and Pedro, and they all agreed to set out together to catch the aderna bird. Afar in the mountains they saw him, and Diego, being the eldest, had first chance, and he caught the aderna bird, but being of impure life he became a stone, and the bird flew away over the mountains.

Juan and Pedro pursued it over the rocky way till at last they saw it again, and Pedro, being the next eldest, essayed to catch it. He, too, being a bad man, was turned into stone and the aderna bird flew over another mountain, and Juan, undaunted, followed alone.

When at last he saw the aderna bird he made a trap with a mirror with a snare in front and soon caught the bird. He made a cage for it and started on his homeward journey. When he reached the stone which was his brother Pedro, he begged the bird to undo its work and make him a man again, and the bird did so. Then the two went on to where Diego was, and again Juan entreated the bird to set the other brother free, and the bird did so.

But Pedro and Diego, far from being grateful for what Juan had done for them, bound him, choked him, beat him and left him for dead far from any road or any habitation, and went on their way to the king with the aderna bird, expecting for one the hand of the princess and for the other a rich reward.

But the aderna bird would not sing. Said the king, "O Aderna Bird, why do you not sing?" The bird replied, "O Mighty King, I sing only for him who caught me." "Did these men catch you?" "No, O King, Juan caught me, and these men have beaten him and stolen me from him." So the king had them punished, and waited for the coming of Juan.

Juan meanwhile had freed himself from his bonds, and wandered sore and hungry and lame through the forest. At last he met an old man who said to him, "Juan, why do you not go to the king's house, for there they want you very much?" "Alas," said Juan, "I am not able to walk so far from weakness, and I fear I shall die here in the forest." "Do not fear," said the old man, "I have here a wonderful hat that, should you but whisper to it where you wish to go, in a moment you are transported there through the air."

So the old man gave him the hat, and Juan put it on and said, "Hat, if this be thy nature, carry me across the mountains to the king's palace." And the hat carried him immediately into the presence of the king. Then the aderna bird began to sing, and after a time Juan married the princess, and all went well for the rest of their lives.

Adventures of the Tuglay

IT WAS EIGHT MILLION (kati) years ago, in the days of the Mona, that the following events took place.

The Tuglay lived in a fine house the walls of which were all mirrored glass, and the roof was hung with brass chains. One day he went out into the woods to snare jungle-fowl, and he slept in the woods all night. The next day, when he turned to go home, he found himself puzzled as to which trail to take. He tried one path after another, but none seemed to lead to his house. At last he said to himself, "I have lost my way: I shall never be able to get home."

Then he walked on at random until he came to a vast field of rice, where great numbers of men were cutting the palay. But the rice field belonged to Buso, and the harvesters were all buso-men. When they saw Tuglay at the edge of their field, they were glad, and said to one another, "There's a man! We will carry him home."

Then the buso caught Tuglay, and hastened home with him. Now, the great Buso's mansion stretched across the tops of eight million mountains, and very many smaller houses were on the sides of the mountains, all around the great Buso's house; for this was the city of the buso where they had taken Tuglay. As he was carried through the groves of coconut palms on Buso's place, all the coconuts called out, "Tuglay, Tuglay, in a little while the Buso will eat you!"

Into the presence of the great chief of all the buso, they dragged Tuglay. The Datto Buso was fearful to look at. From his head grew one great horn of pure ivory, and flames of fire were blazing from the horn. The Datto Buso questioned the man.

"First of all, I will ask you where you come from, Tuglay."

"I am come from my house in T'oluk Waig," replied the man.

And the great Buso shouted, "I will cut off your head with my sharp kris!"

"But if I choose, I can kill you with your own sword," boldly answered Tuglay.

Then he lay down, and let the Buso try to cut his neck. The Buso swung his sharp sword; but the steel would not cut Tuglay's neck. The Buso did not know that no knife could wound the neck of Tuglay, unless fire were laid upon his throat at the same time. This was eight million years ago that the Buso tried to cut off the head of Tuglay.

Then another day the Tuglay spoke to all the buso, "It is now my turn: let me try whether I can cut your necks."

After this speech, Tuglay stood up and took from his mouth the chewed betel nut that is called isse, and made a motion as if he would rub the isse on the great Buso's throat. When the Buso saw the isse, he thought it was a sharp knife, and he was frightened. All the lesser buso began to weep, fearing that their chief would be killed; for the isse appeared to all of them as a keen-bladed knife. The tears of all the buso ran down like blood; they wept streams and streams of tears that all flowed together, forming a deep lake, red in colour.

Then Tuglay rubbed the chewed betel on the great Buso's throat. One pass only he made with the isse, and the Buso's head was severed from his body. Both head and body of the mighty Buso rolled down into the great lake of tears, and were devoured by the crocodiles.

Now, the Tuglay was dressed like a poor man in bark (bunut) garments. But as soon as he had slain the Buso, he struck a blow at his own legs, and the bark trousers fell off. Then he stamped on the ground, and struck his body, and immediately his jacket and kerchief of bark fell off from him. There he stood, no longer the poor Tuglay, but a Malaki T'oluk Waig, with a gleaming kampilan in his hand.

Then he was ready to fight all the other buso. First he held the kampilan in his left hand, and eight million buso fell down dead. Then he held the kampilan in his right hand, and eight million more buso fell down dead. After that, the Malaki went over to the house of the Buso's daughter, who had but one eye, and that in the middle of her forehead. She shrieked with fear when she saw the Malaki coming; and he struck her with his kampilan, so that she too, the woman-buso, fell down dead.

After these exploits, the Malaki T'oluk Waig went on his way. He climbed over the mountains of benati, whose trees men go far to seek, and then he reached the mountains of barayung and balati wood. From these peaks, exultant over his foes, he gave a good war cry that echoed through the mountains, and went up to the ears of the gods. Panguli'li and Salamia'wan heard it from their home in the Shrine of the Sky (Tambara ka Langit), and they said, "Who chants the song of war (ig-sungal)? Without doubt, it is the Malak T'oluk Waig, for none of all the other malaki could shout just like that."

His duty performed, the Malaki left the ranges of balati and barayung, walked down towards the sea, and wandered along the coast until he neared a great gathering of people who had met for barter. It was market day, and all sorts of things were brought for trade. Then the Malaki T'oluk Waig struck his legs and his chest, before the people caught sight of him; and immediately he was clothed in his old bark trousers and jacket and kerchief, just like a poor man. Then he approached the crowd, and saw the people sitting on the ground in little groups, talking, and offering their things for sale.

The Malaki Lindig Ramut ka Langit and all the other malaki from the surrounding country were there. They called out to him, "Where are you going?"

The Tuglay told them that he had got lost, and had been travelling a long distance. As he spoke, he noticed, sitting among a group of young men, the beautiful woman called Moglung.

She motioned to him, and said, "Come, sit down beside me."

And the Tuglay sat down on the ground, near the Moglung. Then the woman gave presents of textiles to the Malaki Lindig Ramut ka Langit and the other malaki in her crowd. But to the Tuglay she gave betel nut that she had prepared for him.

After that, the Moglung said to all the malaki, "This time I am going to leave you, because I want to go home."

And off went the Moglung with the Tuglay, riding on the wind. After many days, the Moglung and the Tuglay rested on the mountains of barayung, and, later, on the mountains of balakuna trees. From these heights, they looked out over a vast stretch of open country, where the deep, wavy meadow grass glistened like gold; and pastured there were herds of cows and carabao and many horses. And beyond rose another range of mountains, on the highest of which stood the Moglung's house. To reach it they had to cross whole forests of coconut and betel nut trees that covered eight million mountains. Around the house were all kinds of useful plants and trees. When they walked under the floor of the house, the Moglung said, "My grandmother is looking at me because I have found another grandchild for her."

Then the grandmother (Tuglibung) called to them, saying, "Come up, come up, my grandchildren!"

As soon as they entered the house, the Tuglay sat down in a corner of the kitchen, until the grandmother offered him a better place, saying, "Do not stay in the kitchen. Come and sleep on my bed."

The Tuglay rested eight nights in the grandmother's bed. At the end of the eight nights the Moglung said to him, "Please take this betel nut that I have prepared for you."

At first Tuglay did not want to take it; but the next day, when the Moglung again offered the betel, he accepted it from her and began to chew. After that, the Tuglay took off his trousers of bark and his jacket of bark, and became a Malaki T'oluk Waig. But the Moglung wondered where the Tuglay had gone, and she cried to her grandmother, "Where is the Tuglay?"

But the Malaki stood there, and answered her, "I am the Tuglay." At first the Moglung was grieved, because the Malaki seemed such a grand man, and she wanted Tuglay back.

But before long the Malaki said to her, "I want you to marry me." So they were married. Then the Moglung opened her gold box, and took out a fine pair of trousers (saroa'r) and a man's jacket (umpak ka mama), and gave them to the Malaki as a wedding gift.

When they had been living together for a while, there came a day when the Malaki wanted to go and visit a man who was a great worker in brass, the Malaki Tuangun, and the Moglung gave him directions for the journey, saying, "You will come to a place where a hundred roads meet. Take the road that is marked with the prints of many horses and carabao. Do not stop at the place of the crossroads, for if you stop, the Bia who makes men giddy will hurt you."

Then the Malaki went away, and reached the place where a hundred roads crossed, as Moglung had said. But he stopped there to rest and chew betel nuts. Soon he began to feel queer and dizzy, and he fell asleep, not knowing anything. When he woke up, he wandered along up the mountain until he reached a house at the border of a big meadow, and thought he would stop and ask his way. From under the house he called up, "Which is the road to the Malaki Tuangun?"

It was the Bia's voice that answered, "First come up here, and then I'll tell you the road."

So the Malaki jumped up on the steps and went in. But when he was inside of her house, the Bia confessed that she did not know the way to the Malaki Tuangun's house.

"I am the woman," she said, "who made you dizzy, because I wanted to have you for my own."

"Oh! that's the game," said the Malaki. "But the Moglung is my wife, and she is the best woman in the world."

"Never mind that," smiled the Bia. "Just let me comb your hair." Then the Bia gave him some betel nut, and combed his hair until he grew sleepy. But as he was dropping off, he remembered a certain promise he had made his wife, and he said to the Bia, "If the Moglung comes and finds me here, you be sure to waken me."

After eight days had passed from the time her husband left home, the Moglung started out to find him, for he had said, "Eight days from now I will return."

By and by the Moglung came to the Bia's house, and found the Malaki there fast asleep; but the Bia did not waken him. Then the Moglung took from the Malaki's toes his toe-rings (paniod), and went away, leaving a message with the Bia:

"Tell the Malaki that I am going back home to find some other malaki: tell him that I'll have no more to do with him."

But the Moglung did not go to her own home: she at once started for her brother's house that was up in the sky-country.

Presently the Malaki woke up, and when he looked at his toes, he found that his brass toe-rings were gone.

"The Moglung has been here!" he cried in a frenzy. "Why didn't you waken me, as I told you?" Then he seized his sharp-bladed kampilan, and slew the Bia. Maddened by grief and rage, he dashed to the door and made one leap to the ground, screaming, "All the people in the world shall fall by my sword!"

On his war shield he rode, and flew with the wind until he came to the horizon. Here lived the Malaki Lindig Ramut ka Langit. And when the two malaki met, they began to fight; and the seven brothers of the Malaki Lindig that live at the edge of the sky, likewise came out to fight. But when the battle had gone on but a little time, all the eight malaki of the horizon fell down dead. Then the angry Malaki who had slain the Bia and the eight young men went looking for more people to kill; and when he had shed the blood of many, he became a buso with only one eye in his forehead, for the buso with one eye are the worst buso of all. Everybody that he met he slew.

After some time, he reached the house of the great priest called "Pandita," and the Pandita checked him, saying, "Stop a minute, and let me ask you first what has happened to make you like this."

Then the Buso-man replied sadly, "I used to have a wife named Moglung, who was the best of all the Bia; but when I went looking for the Malaki Tuangun, that other Bia made me dizzy, and gave me betel, and combed my hair. Then she was my wife for a little while. But I have killed her, and become a buso, and I want to kill all the people in the world."

"You had better lie down on my mat here, and go to sleep," advised the Pandita. While the Buso slept, the Pandita rubbed his joints with betel nut; and when he woke up, he was a malaki again.

Then the Pandita talked to him, and said, "Only a few days ago, the Moglung passed here on her way to her brother's home in heaven. She went by a bad road, for she would have to mount the steep rock terraces. If you follow, you will come first to the Terraces of the Wind (Tarasu'ban ka Kara'mag), then you reach the Terraces of Eight-fold Darkness (Walu Lapit Dukilum), and then the Terraces of the Rain (Tarasuban k'Udan).

Eagerly the Malaki set out on his journey, with his kabir on his back, and his betel nut and buyo leaf in the kabir. He had not travelled far, before he came to a steep ascent of rock terraces: the Terraces of the Wind, that had eight million steps. The Malaki knew not how to climb up the rocky structure that rose sheer before him, and so he sat down at the foot of the ascent, and took his kabir off his back to get out some betel nut. After he had begun to chew his betel, he began to think, and he pondered for eight days how he could accomplish his hard journey. On the ninth day he began to jump up the steps of the terraces, one by one. On each step he chewed betel, and then jumped again; and at the close of the ninth day he had reached the top of the eight million steps, and was off, riding on his shield.

Next he reached the sharp-edged rocks called the "Terraces of Needles" (Tarasuban ka Simat), that had also eight million steps. Again he considered for eight days how he could mount them. Then on the ninth day he sprang from terrace to terrace, as before, chewing betel nut on each terrace, and left the Tarasuban ka Simat, riding on his shield. Then he arrived at the Terraces of Sheet-Lightning (Tarasuban ka Dilam-dilam); and he took his kabir off his back, and prepared a betel nut, chewed it, and meditated for eight days. On the ninth day he jumped from step to step of the eight million terraces, and went riding off on his war shield. When he reached the Terraces of Forked-Lightning (Tarasuban ka Kirum), he surmounted them on the ninth day, like the others.

But now he came to a series of cuestas named "Dulama Bolo Kampilan," because one side of each was an abrupt cliff with the sharp edge of a kampilan; and the other side sloped gradually downward, like a blunt-working bolo. How to cross these rocks, of which there were eight million, the Malaki did not know; so he stopped and took off his kabir, cut up his betel nut, and thought for eight days. Then on the ninth day he began to leap over the rocks, and he kept on leaping for eight days, each day jumping over one million of the cuestas. On the sixteenth day he was off, riding on his shield. Then he reached the Terraces of the Thunder (Tarasuban ka Kilat), which he mounted, springing from one terrace to the next, as before, after he had meditated for eight days. Leaving these behind him on the ninth day, he travelled on to the Mountains of Bamboo (Pabungan Kawayanan), covered with bamboo whose leaves were all sharp steel. These mountains he could cross without the eight days' thought, because their sides sloped gently. From the uplands he could see a broad sweep of meadow beyond, where the grass glistened like gold. And when he had descended, and walked across the meadow, he had to pass through eight million groves of coconut trees, where the fruit grew at the height of a man's waist, and every coconut had the shape of a bell (korung-korung). Then he reached a forest of betel nut, where again the nuts could be plucked without the trouble of climbing, for the clusters grew at the height of a man's waist. Beyond, came the meadows with white grass, and plants whose leaves were all of the rare old embroidered cloth called tambayang. He then found himself at the foothills of a range of eight million mountains, rising from the heart of the meadows, and, when he had climbed to their summit, he stood before a fine big house.

From the ground he called out, "If anybody lives in this house, let him come look at me, for I want to find the way to the Shrine in the Sky, or to the Little Heaven, where my Moglung lives."

But nobody answered.

Then the Malaki sprang up the bamboo ladder and looked in at the door, but he saw no one in the house. He was weary after his journey, and sat down to rest in a chair made of gold that stood there. Soon there came to his ears the sound of men's voices, calling out, "There is the Malaki T'oluk Waig in the house."

The Malaki looked around the room, but there was no man there, only a little baby swinging in its cradle. Outside the house were many malaki from the great town of Lunsud, and they came rushing in the door, each holding a keen blade without a handle (sobung). They all surrounded the Malaki in the gold chair, ready to fight him. But the Malaki gave them all some betel nut from his kabir, and made the men friendly towards him. Then all pressed around the Malaki to look at his kabir, which shone like gold. They had never before seen a man's bag like this one. "It is the kabir of the Malaki T'oluk Waig," they said. The Malaki slept that night with the other malaki in the house.

When morning came, the day was dark, like night, for the sun did not shine. Then the Malaki took his kampilan and stuck it into his belt, and sat down on his shield. There was no light on the next day, nor on the next. For eight days the pitchy darkness lasted; but on the ninth day it lifted. Quick from its cradle jumped the baby, now grown as tall as the bariri plant; that is, almost knee-high.

"Cowards, all of you!" cried the child to the Malaki Lunsud. "You are no malaki at all, since you cannot fight the Malaki T'oluk Waig." Then, turning to the Malaki T'oluk Waig, the little fellow said, "Please teach me how to hold the spear."

When the Malaki had taught the boy how to make the strokes, the two began to fight; for the boy, who was called the Pangalinan, was eager to use his spear against the Malaki. But the Malaki had magical power (matulus), so that when the Pangalinan attacked him with sword or spear, the blades of his weapons dissolved into water. For eight million days the futile battle went on. At last the Pangalinan gave it up, complaining to the Malaki T'oluk Waig, "How can I keep on fighting you, when every time I hit you my knives turn to water?"

Disheartened, the Pangalinan threw away his spear and his sword. But the Malaki would not hurt the Pangalinan when they were fighting; and as soon as the boy had flung his weapons outside the house, the Malaki put his arm around him and drew him close. After that, the two were friends.

One day the Pangalinan thought he would look inside the big gold box that stood in the house. It was his mother's box. The boy went and raised the lid, but as soon as the cover was lifted, his mother came out from the box. After this had happened, the Pangalinan got ready to go and find the Moglung whom the Malaki had been seeking. The boy knew where she lived, for he was the Moglung's little brother (tube'). He took the bamboo ladder that formed the steps to the house, and placed it so that it would reach the Shrine in the Sky, whither the Moglung had gone. Up the bamboo rounds he climbed, until he reached the sky and found his sister. He ran to her crying, "Quick! come with me! The great Malaki T'oluk Waig is down there."

Then the Moglung came down from heaven with her little brother to their house where the Malaki was waiting for her. The Moglung and the Malaki were very happy to meet again, and they slept together that night.

Next day the Moglung had a talk with the Malaki, and said, "Now I want to live with you; but you remember that other woman, Maguay Bulol, that you used to sleep with. You will want her too, and you had better send for her."

So the Malaki summoned Maguay Bulol, and in a few minutes Maguay Bulol was there. Then the Malaki had two wives, and they all lived in the same house forever.

Benito, the Faithful Servant

ON A TIME THERE lived in a village a poor man and his wife, who had a son named Benito. The one ambition of the lad from his earliest youth was that he might be a help to the family in their struggle for a living.

But the years went by, and he saw no opportunity until one day, as they sat at dinner, his father fell to talking about the young King who lived at a distance from the village, in a beautiful palace kept by a retinue of servants. The boy was glad to hear this, and asked his parents to let him become one of the servants of this great ruler. The mother protested, fearing that her son could not please his Royal Majesty; but the boy was so eager to try his fortune that at last he was permitted to do so.

The next day his mother prepared food for him to eat on the journey, and he started for the palace. The journey was tiresome; and when he reached the palace he had difficulty in obtaining an audience with the King. But when he succeeded and made known his wish, the monarch detected a charming personality hidden within the ragged clothes, and, believing the lad would make a willing servant, he accepted him.

The servants of his Majesty had many duties. Theirs was not a life of ease, but of hard work. The very next day the King called Benito, and said, "I want you to bring me a certain beautiful princess who lives in a land across the sea; and if you fail to do it, you will be punished."

Benito did not know how he was to do it; but he asked no questions, and unhesitatingly answered, "I will, my lord."

That same day he provided himself with everything he needed for the journey and set off. He travelled a long distance until he came to the heart of a thick forest, where he saw a large bird which said to him, "Oh, my friend! please take away these strings that are wrapped all about me. If you will, I will help you whenever you call upon me."

Benito released the bird and asked it its name. It replied, "Sparrow-hawk," and flew away. Benito continued his journey until he came to the seashore. There he could see no way of getting across, and, remembering what the King had said would happen if he failed, he stood looking out over the sea, feeling very sad. The huge King of the Fishes saw him, and swam towards him. "Why are you so sad?" asked the Fish.

"I wish to cross the sea to find the beautiful Princess," replied the youth.

"Get on my back and I will take you across," said the King of the Fishes.

Benito rode on the back of the Fish and crossed the sea. As soon as he reached the other side, a fairy in the form of a woman appeared to him, and became a great aid to him in his adventure. She knew exactly what he wanted; so she told him that the Princess was shut up in a castle guarded by giants, and that he would have to fight the giants before he could reach her. For this purpose she gave him a magic sword, which would kill on the instant anything it touched.

Benito now felt sure he could take the Princess from her cruel guardsmen. He went to the castle, and there he saw many giants round about it. When the giants saw him coming, they went out to meet him, thinking to take him captive. They were so sure that they could easily do it, that they went forth unarmed. As they came near, he touched the foremost ones with his sword, and one after another they fell down dead. The other giants, seeing so many of their number slain, became terrified, and fled, leaving the castle unguarded.

The young man went to the Princess and told her that his master had sent him to bring her to his palace. The young Princess was only too glad to leave the land of the giants, where she had been held captive. So the two set out together for the King's palace.

When they came to the sea they rode across it on the back of the same Fish that had carried Benito. They went through the forest, and at last came to the palace. Here they were received with the greatest rejoicings.

After a short time the King asked the Princess to become his wife. "I will, O King!" she replied, "if you will get the ring I lost in the sea as I was crossing it."

The monarch called Benito, and ordered him to find the ring which had been lost on their journey from the land of the giants.

Obedient to his master, Benito started, and travelled on and on till he came to the shore of the sea. There he stood, gazing sadly out over the waters, not knowing how he was to search for what lay at the bottom of the deep ocean.

Again the King of the Fishes came to him, asking the cause of his sadness. Benito replied, "The Princess lost her ring while we were crossing the sea, and I have been sent to find it."

The King-Fish summoned all the fishes to come to him. When they had assembled, he noticed that one was missing. He commanded the others to search for this one, and bring it to him. They found it under a stone, and it said, "I am so full! I have eaten so much that I cannot swim." So the larger ones took it by the tail and dragged it to their King.

"Why did you not come when summoned?" asked the King-Fish. "I was so full I could not swim," replied the Fish.

The King-Fish, suspecting that it had swallowed the ring, ordered it to be cut in two. The others cut it open, and, behold I there was the lost ornament. Benito thanked the King of the Fishes, took the ring, and brought it to the monarch.

When the great ruler got the ring, he said to the Princess, "Now that I have your ring, will you become my wife?"

"I will be your wife," replied the Princess, "if you will find the earring I lost in the forest as I was journeying with Benito."

Instantly Benito was called, and was ordered to find the lost jewel. He was very weary from his former journey; but, mindful of his duty, he started for the forest, reaching it before the day was over. He searched for the earring faithfully, following the road which he and the Princess had taken; but all in vain. He was much discouraged, and sat down under a tree to rest. To his surprise a mouse of monstrous size appeared before him. It was the King of the Mice.

"Why are you so sad?" asked the Mouse.

"I am searching for an earring which the Princess lost as we passed through the forest, but am unable to find it."

"I will find it for you," said the King-Mouse.

Benito's face brightened at hearing this. The King-Mouse called all his followers, and all but one little mouse responded. Then the King of the Mice ordered some of his subjects to find the absent one. They found him in a small hole among the bamboo trees. He said he could not go because he was so satisfied (sated). So the others pulled him along to their master; and he, finding that there was something hard within the little mouse, ordered him to be cut open. It was done; and there was the very earring for which the tired servant was looking. Benito took it, thanked the King of the Mice, and brought the earring to his own King.

When the monarch received it, he immediately restored it to its owner and asked, "Will you now become my wife?"

"Oh, dear King!" responded the Princess, "I have only one more thing to ask of you; and if you will grant it, I will be your wife forever."

The King, pleased with his former successes, said, "Tell me what it is, and it shall be granted."

"If you will get some water from heaven," said the Princess, "and some water from the netherworld, I will become your wife. That is my last wish."

The King called Benito, and commanded him to get water from these two places. "I will, my King," said Benito; and he took some provisions and started. He came to the forest; but there he became confused, for he did not know in which direction to go to reach either of the places. Suddenly he recalled the promise of the bird he had helped the first time he entered the wood. He called the bird, and it soon appeared. He told it what he wanted, and it said, "I will get it for you."

He made two cups of bamboo, and tied one to each of the bird's legs. They were very light, and did not hinder the bearer at all. Away the bird flew, going very fast. Before the day was ended, it came back with each cup full of water, and told Benito that the one tied to its right leg contained water from heaven, and the one tied to its left leg contained water from the netherworld.

Benito untied the cups, taking great care of them. He was about to leave, when the bird asked him to tarry long enough to bury it, as the places to which it had been were so far away that it was weary unto death.

Benito did not like to bury the bird, but he soon saw that it really was dying, so he waited; and when it was dead, he buried it, feeling very sorry over the loss of so helpful a friend.

He went back to the palace and delivered the two kinds of water to his master. The Princess then asked the King to cut her in two and pour the water from heaven upon her. The King was not willing to do it, so she did it herself, asking the King to pour the water. This he did, and, lo! the Princess turned into the most beautiful woman that ever the sun shone on.

Then the King was desirous of becoming handsome; so he asked the Princess to pour the other cup of water over him after he cut himself. He cut himself, and she poured over his body the water from the netherworld; but from him there arose a spirit more ugly and ill-favoured than imagination could picture. Fortunately, it soon vanished from sight.

The Princess then turned to Benito, and said, "You have been faithful in your duties to your master, kind to me in restoring the jewels I lost, and brave in delivering me from the cruel giants. You are the man I choose for my husband."

Benito could not refuse so lovely a lady. They were married amid great festivities, and became the King and Queen of that broad and fertile land.

Benito gave his parents one of the finest portions of his kingdom, and furnished them with everything they could desire. From that time on they were all very happy, so happy that the story of their bliss has come down through the centuries to us.

Gawigawen of Adasen

APONIBOLINAYEN WAS SICK with a headache, and she lay on a mat alone in her house. Suddenly she remembered some fruit that she had heard of but had never seen, and she said to herself, "Oh, I wish I had some of the oranges of Gawigawen of Adasen."

Now Aponibolinayen did not realize that she had spoken aloud, but Aponitolau, her husband, lying in the spirit house outside, heard her talking and asked what it was she said. Fearing to tell him the truth lest he should risk his life in trying to get the oranges for her, she said, "I wish I had some biw" (a fruit).

Aponitolau at once got up, and, taking a sack, went out to find some of the fruit for his wife. When he returned with the sack full, she said:

"Put it on the bamboo hanger above the fire, and when my head is better I will eat it."

So Aponitolau put the fruit on the hanger and returned to the spirit house, but when Aponibolinayen tried to eat, the fruit made her sick and she threw it away.

"What is the matter?" called Aponitolau as he heard her drop the fruit.

"I merely dropped one," she replied, and returned to her mat.

After a while Aponibolinayen again said:

"Oh, I wish I had some of the oranges of Gawigawen of Adasen," and Aponitolau, who heard her from the spirit house, enquired:

"What is that you say?"

"I wish I had some fish eggs," answered his wife; for she did not want him to know the truth.

Then Aponitolau took his net and went to the river, determined to please his wife if possible. When he had caught a nice fish he opened it with his knife and took out the eggs. Then he spat on the place he had cut, and it was healed and the fish swam away.

Pleased that he was able to gratify his wife's wishes, he hastened home with the eggs; and while his wife was roasting them over the fire, he returned to the spirit house. She tried to eat, but the eggs did not taste good to her, and she threw them down under the house to the dogs.

"What is the matter?" called Aponitolau. "Why are the dogs barking?"

"I dropped some of the eggs," replied his wife, and she went back to her mat.

By and by she again said:

"I wish I had some of the oranges of Gawigawen of Adasen."

But when her husband asked what she wished, she replied:

"I want a deer's liver to eat."

So Aponitolau took his dogs to the mountains, where they hunted until they caught a deer, and when he had cut out its liver he spat on the wound, and it was healed so that the deer ran away.

But Aponibolinayen could not eat the liver any more than she could the fruit or the fish eggs; and when Aponitolau heard the dogs barking, he knew that she had thrown it away. Then he grew suspicious and, changing himself into a centipede, hid in a crack in the floor. And when his wife again wished for some of the oranges, he overheard her.

"Why did you not tell me the truth, Aponibolinayen?" he asked.

"Because," she replied, "no one who has gone to Adasen has ever come back, and I did not want you to risk your life."

Nevertheless Aponitolau determined to go for the oranges, and he commanded his wife to bring him rice straw. After he had burned it he put the ashes in the water with which he washed his hair. Then she brought coconut oil and rubbed his hair, and fetched a dark cloak, a fancy belt, and a headband, and she baked cakes for him to take on the journey. Aponitolau cut a vine which he planted by the stove, and told his wife that if the leaves wilted she would know that he was dead. Then he took his spear and head-axe and started on the long journey.

When Aponitolau arrived at the well of a giantess, all the betel nut trees bowed. Then the giantess shouted and all the world trembled. "How strange," thought Aponitolau, "that all the world shakes when that woman shouts." But he continued on his way without stopping.

As he passed the place of the old woman, Alokotan, she sent out her little dog and it bit his leg.

"Do not proceed," said the old woman, "for ill luck awaits you. If you go on, you will never return to your home."

But Aponitolau paid no attention to the old woman, and by and by he came to the home of the lightning.

"Where are you going?" asked the lightning.

"I am going to get some oranges of Gawigawen of Adasen," replied Aponitolau.

"Go stand on that high rock that I may see what your sign is," commanded the lightning.

So he stood on the high rock, but when the lightning flashed Aponitolau dodged.

"Do not go," said the lightning, "for you have a bad sign, and you will never come back."

Still Aponitolau did not heed.

Soon he arrived at the place of Silit (loud thunder), who also asked him:

"Where are you going, Aponitolau?"

"I am going to get oranges of Gawigawen of Adasen," he replied.

Then the thunder commanded:

"Stand on that high stone so that I can see if you have a good sign."

He stood on the high stone, and when the thunder made a loud noise he jumped. Whereupon Silit also advised him not to go on.

In spite of all the warnings, Aponitolau continued his journey, and upon coming to the ocean he used magical power, so that when he stepped on his head-axe it sailed away, carrying him far across the sea to the other side. Then after a short walk he came to a spring where women were dipping water, and he asked what spring it was.

"This is the spring of Gawigawen of Adasen," replied the women. "And who are you that you dare come here?"

Without replying he went on towards the town, but he found that he could not go inside, for it was surrounded by a bank which reached almost to the sky.

While he stood with bowed head pondering what he should do, the chief of the spiders came up and asked why he was so sorrowful.

"I am sad," answered Aponitolau, "because I cannot climb up this bank."

Then the spider went to the top and spun a thread, and upon this Aponitolau climbed up into town.

Now Gawigawen was asleep in his spirit house, and when he awoke and saw Aponitolau sitting near, he was surprised and ran towards his house to get his spear and head-axe, but Aponitolau called to him, saying:

"Good morning, Cousin Gawigawen. Do not be angry; I only came to buy some of your oranges for my wife."

Then Gawigawen took him to the house and brought a whole carabao for him to eat, and he said:

"If you cannot eat all the carabao, you cannot have the oranges for your wife."

Aponitolau grew very sorrowful, for he knew that he could not eat all the meat, but just at that moment the chief of the ants and flies came to him and enquired what was the trouble. As soon as he was told, the chief called all the ants and flies and they ate the whole carabao. Aponitolau, greatly relieved, went then to Gawigawen and said:

"I have finished eating the food which you gave me."

Gawigawen was greatly surprised at this, and, leading the way to the place where the oranges grew, he told Aponitolau to climb the tree and get all he wanted.

As he was about to ascend the tree Aponitolau noticed that the branches were sharp knives, so he went as carefully as he could. Nevertheless, when he had secured two oranges, he stepped on one of the knives and was cut. He quickly fastened the fruit to his spear, and immediately it flew away straight to his town and into his house.

Aponibolinayen was just going down the bamboo ladder out of the house, and hearing something drop on the floor she went back to look and found the oranges from Adasen. She eagerly ate the fruit, rejoicing that her husband had been able to reach the place where they grew. Then she thought to look at the vine, whose leaves were wilted, and she knew that her husband was dead.

Soon after this a son was born to Aponibolinayen, and she called his name Kanag. He grew rapidly, becoming a strong lad, and he was the bravest of all his companions. One day while Kanag was playing out in the yard, he spun his top and it struck the garbage pot of an old woman, who became very angry and cried:

"If you were a brave boy, you would get your father whom Gawigawen killed."

Kanag ran to the house crying, and asked his mother what the old woman meant, for he had never heard the story of his father's death. As soon as he learned what had happened, the boy determined to search for his father, and, try as she would, his mother could not dissuade him.

As he was departing through the gate of the town with his spear and head-axe, Kanag struck his shield and it sounded like a thousand warriors.

"How brave that boy is!" said the surprised people. "He is braver even than his father."

When he reached the spring of the giantess, he again struck his shield and shouted so that the whole world trembled. Then the giantess said:

"I believe that someone is going to fight, and he will have success."

As soon as Kanag reached the place where the old woman, Alokotan, lived, she sent her dog after him, but with one blow of his head-axe he cut off the dog's head. Then Alokotan asked where he was going, and when he had told her, she said:

"Your father is dead, but I believe that you will find him, for you have a good sign."

He hurried on and arrived at the place where lightning was, and it asked:

"Where are you going, little boy?"

"I am going to Adasen to get my father," answered Kanag.

"Go stand on that high rock that I may see what your sign is," said the lightning.

So he stood on the high rock, and when the bright flash came he did not move, and the lightning bade him hasten on, as he had a good sign.

The thunder, which saw him passing, also called to ask where he was going, and it commanded him to stand on the high rock. And when the thunder made a loud noise Kanag did not move, and it bade him go on, as his sign was good.

The women of Adasen were at the spring of Gawigawen dipping water, when suddenly they were startled by a great noise. They rose up, expecting to see a thousand warriors coming near; but though they looked all around they could see nothing but a young boy striking a shield.

"Good morning, women who are dipping water," said Kanag. "Tell Gawigawen that he must prepare, for I am coming to fight him."

So all the women ran up to the town and told Gawigawen that a strange boy was at the spring and he had come to fight.

"Go and tell him," said Gawigawen, "that if it is true that he is brave, he will come into the town, if he can."

When Kanag reached the high bank outside the town, he jumped like a flitting bird up the bank into the town and went straight to the spirit house of Gawigawen. He noticed that the roofs of both the dwelling and the spirit houses were of hair, and that around the town were many heads, and he pondered:

"This is why my father did not return. Gawigawen is a brave man, but I will kill him."

As soon as Gawigawen saw him in the yard he said:

"How brave you are, little boy; why did you come here?"

"I came to get my father," answered Kanag; "for you kept him when he came to get oranges for my mother. If you do not give him to me, I will kill you."

Gawigawen laughed at this brave speech and said:

"Why, one of my fingers will fight you. You shall never go back to your town, but you shall stay here and be like your father."

"We shall see," said Kanag. "Bring your arms and let us fight here in the yard."

Gawigawen was beside himself with rage at this bold speech, and he brought his spear and his head-axe which was as big as half the sky. Kanag would not throw first, for he wanted to prove himself brave, so Gawigawen took aim and threw his head-axe at the boy. Now Kanag used magical power, so that he became an ant and was not hit by the weapon. Gawigawen laughed loudly when he looked around and could not see the boy, for he thought that he had been killed. Soon, however, Kanag reappeared, standing on the head-axe, and Gawigawen, more furious than ever, threw his spear. Again Kanag disappeared, and Gawigawen was filled with surprise.

Then it was Kanag's turn and his spear went directly through the body of the giant. He ran quickly and cut off five of the heads, but the sixth he spared until Gawigawen should have shown him his father.

As they went about the town together, Kanag found that the skin of his father had been used for a drumhead. His hair decorated the house, and his head was at the gate of the town, while his body was put beneath the house. After he had gathered all the parts of the body together, Kanag used magical power, and his father came to life.

"Who are you?" asked Aponitolau; "how long have I slept?"

"I am your son," said Kanag. "You were not asleep but dead, and here is Gawigawen who kept you. Take my head-axe and cut off his remaining head."

So Aponitolau took the head-axe, but when he struck Gawigawen it did not injure him.

"What is the matter, Father?" asked Kanag; and taking the weapon he cut off the sixth head of Gawigawen.

Then Kanag and his father used magic so that the spears and head-axes flew about, killing all the people in the town, and the heads and valuable things went to their home.

When Aponibolinayen saw all these come into her house, she ran to look at the vine by the stove, and it was green and looked like a jungle. Then she knew that her son was alive, and she was happy. And when the father and son returned, all the relatives came to their house for a great feast, and all were so happy that the whole world smiled.

Juan and His Adventures

ONCE IN A CERTAIN village there lived a couple who had three daughters. This family was very poor at first. Near the foot of a mountain was growing a tree with large white leaves. Pedro the father earned their living by selling the leaves of that tree. In time he got so much money from them that he ordered a large house to be built. Then they left their old home, and went to live in the new house. The father kept on selling the leaves. After a year he decided to cut down the tree, so that he could sell it all at

once and get much money. So he went to the foot of the mountain one day, and cut the tree down. As soon as the trunk had crashed to the ground, a large snake came out from the stump. Now, this snake was an enchanter, and was the friend of the kings of the lions, eagles and fishes, as we shall see.

The snake said to Pedro, "I gave you the leaves of this tree to sell; and now, after you have gotten much money from it, you cut it down. There is but one suitable punishment for you: within three days you must bring all your daughters here and give them to me." The man was so astonished at first, that he did not know what to do. He made no reply, and after a few minutes went home. His sadness was so great that he could not even eat. His wife and daughters, noticing his depression, asked him what he was thinking about. At first he did not want to tell them; but they urged and begged so incessantly, that finally he was forced to do so.

He said to them, "Today I cut down the tree where I got the leaves which I sold. A snake came out from the stump, and told me that I should bring you three girls to him or we should all die."

"Don't worry, Father! we will go there with you," said the three daughters.

The next day they prepared to go to the snake. Their parents wept very much. Each of the three girls gave her mother a handkerchief as a remembrance. After they had bidden goodbye, they set out on their journey with their father.

As soon as they reached the foot of the mountain, the three daughters disappeared at once, and the poor father returned home cheerless. A year had not passed by before a son was born to the old couple. They named him Juan. When the boy was about eighteen years old, his mother showed him the handkerchiefs of his sisters.

"Have I any sister?" said Juan to his mother.

"Yes, you have three; but they were taken away by a snake," she told him. Juan was so angry that he asked his parents to give him permission to go in search of his sisters. At first they hesitated, but at last they gave him leave. So, taking the three handkerchiefs with him, Juan set out, and went to the mountain.

After travelling for more than ten days, Juan came across three boys quarrelling over the possession of a cap, a pair of sandals and a key. He went near them, and asked them why they all wanted those three things. The boys told him that the cap would make the person who wore it invisible, the sandals would give their owner the power to fly, and that the key would open any door it touched.

Juan told the three boys that it would be better for them to give him those articles than to quarrel about them; and the boys agreed, because they did not want either of the others to have them. So Juan put the key in his pocket, the cap on his head, and the sandals on his feet, and flew away. After he had passed over many mountains, he descended. Near the place where he alighted he saw a cave. He approached its mouth, and opened the door with his key. Inside he saw a girl sitting near a window. He went up to her and took off his cap.

"Who are you?" said the girl, startled.

"Aren't you my sister?" said Juan.

"I have no brother," said the lady, but she was surprised to see the handkerchiefs which Juan showed her. After he had told her his story, she believed that he was really her brother.

"You had better hide," said the lady, holding Juan's hand, "for my husband is the king of the lions, and he may kill you if he finds you here."

Not long afterwards the lion appeared. She met him at the door. "You must have some visitors here," said the lion, sniffing the air with wide-open nostrils.

"Yes," answered the lady, "my brother is here, and I hid him, for I feared that you might kill him."

"No, I will not kill him," said the lion. "Where is he?" Juan came out and shook hands with the lion. After they had talked for a few hours, Juan said that he would go to look for his other sisters. The lion told him that they lived on the next two mountains.

Juan did not have much trouble in finding his other two sisters. Their husbands were the kings of the fishes and the eagles, and they received him kindly. Juan's three brothers-in-law loved him very much, and promised to aid him whenever he needed their help.

Juan now decided to return home and tell his parents where his three sisters were; but he took another way back. He came to a town where all the people were dressed in black, and the decorations of the houses were of the same colour. He asked some people what had happened in that town. They told him that a princess was lost, and that he who could bring her back to the king should receive her hand in marriage and also half the property of the king. Juan then went to the king and promised to restore his daughter to him. The king agreed to reward him as the townspeople had said, if he should prove successful.

Early the next morning Juan, with his cap, sandals and key, set out to look for the princess. After a two days' journey he came to a mountain. Here he descended and began to look around. Finally he saw a huge rock, in which he found a small hole. He put the key in it, and the rock flew open. With his cap of invisibility on his head, he entered. There within he saw many ladies, who were confined in separate rooms. In the very last apartment he found the princess with a giant beside her. He went near the room of the princess, and opened the door with his key. The walls of all the rooms were like those of a prison, and were made of iron bars. Juan approached the princess, and remained near her until the giant went away.

As soon as the monster was out of sight, Juan took off his cap. The princess was surprised to see him, but he told her that he had come to take her away. She was very glad, but said that they had better wait for the giant to go away before they started. After a few minutes the giant went out to take a walk. When they saw that he had passed through the main door, they went out also. Juan put on his sandals and flew away with the princess. But when they were very near the king's palace, the princess disappeared: she was taken back by the giant's powerful magic. Juan was very angry, and he returned at once to the giant's cave. He succeeded in opening the main door, but he could not enter. After struggling in vain for about an hour, he at last determined to go to his brothers-in-law for help.

When he had explained what he wanted, the king of the eagles said to him, "Juan, the life and power of the giant are in a little box at the heart of the ocean. No one can get that box except the king of the fishes, and no one can open it except the king of the lions. The life of the giant is in a little bird which is inside the box. This bird flies very swiftly, and I am the only one who can catch it. The strength of the giant is in a little egg which is in the box with the bird."

When the king of the eagles had finished his story, Juan went to the king of the fishes. "Will you fetch me the box which contains the life and strength of the giant?" said Juan to the king of the fishes. After asking him many questions, his brother-in-law swam away, and soon returned with the box. When Juan had received it from him, he thanked him and went to the king of the lions.

The king of the lions willingly opened the box for him. As soon as the box was opened, the little bird inside flew swiftly away. Juan took the egg, however, and went back to the king of the eagles, and asked him to catch the bird. After the little bird had been caught, Juan pushed on to the cave of the giant. When he came there, he opened the door and entered, holding the bird in one hand and the egg in the other. Enraged at the sight of Juan, the giant rushed at him; and Juan was so startled, that he crushed the egg and killed the bird. At once the giant fell on his back, and stretched out his legs to rise no more.

Juan now went through the cave, opening all the prison doors, and releasing the ladies. He carried the princess with him back to the palace. As soon as he arrived, a great celebration was held, and he was married to the princess. After the death of the king, Juan became ruler. He later visited his parents, and told them of all his adventures. Then he took them to his own kingdom, where they lived happily together.

Juan and His Six Companions

NOT VERY LONG after the death of our Saviour on Calvary, there lived in a faraway land a powerful king named Jaime. By judicious usurpations and matrimonial alliances, this wise monarch extended his already vast dominions to the utmost limits. Instead of ruling his realm as a despot, however, he devoted himself to the task of establishing a strong government

based on moderation and justice. By his marvellous diplomacy he won to his side counts, dukes and lesser princes. To crown his happiness, he had an extremely lovely daughter, whose name was Maria. Neither Venus nor Helen of Troy could compare with her in beauty. Numerous suitors of noble birth from far and near vied with one another in spending fortunes on this pearl of the kingdom; but Maria regarded all suitors with aversion, and her father was perplexed as to how to get her a husband without seeming to show favouritism.

After consulting gravely with his advisers, the monarch gave out this proclamation: "He who shall succeed in getting the golden egg from the moss-grown oak on yonder mountain shall be my son-in-law and heir."

This egg, whose origin nobody knew anything about, rendered its possessor very formidable. When the proclamation had been made public, the whole kingdom was seized with wild enthusiasm; for, though the task was hazardous, yet it seemed performable and easy to the reckless. For five days and five nights crowds of lovers, adventurers and ruffians set sail for the "Mountain of the Golden Egg", as it was called; but none of the enterprisers ever reached the place. Some were shipwrecked; others were driven by adverse winds and currents to strange lands, where they perished miserably; and the rest were forced to return because of the horrible sights of broken planks and mangled bodies.

Some days after the return of the last set of adventurers, three brothers rose from obscurity to try their fortunes in this dangerous enterprise. They were Pedro, Fernando and Juan. They had been orphans since they were boys, and had grown up amid much suffering and hardship.

The three brothers agreed that Pedro should try first; Fernando second; and Juan last, provided the others did not succeed. After supplying himself with plenty of food, a good boat, a sword and a sharp axe, Pedro embraced his brothers and departed, never to return. He took a longer and safer route than that of his predecessors. He had no sooner arrived at the mountain than an old grey-headed man in tattered clothes came limping towards him and asking for help; but the selfish Pedro turned a deaf ear to the supplications of the old man, whom he pushed away with much disrespect. Ignorant of his doom, and regardless of his irreverence, Pedro walked on with hasty steps and high animal spirits. But lo! when his axe struck the oak, a large piece of wood broke off and hit him in the right temple, killing him instantly.

Fernando suffered the same fate as his haughty brother.

Juan alone remained. He was the destined possessor of the egg, and the conqueror of King Jaime. Juan's piety, simplicity and goodness had won for him the goodwill of many persons of distinction. After invoking God's help, he set sail for the mountain, where he safely arrived at noon. He met the same old man, and he bathed, dressed and fed him. The old man thanked Juan, and said, "You shall be amply requited," and immediately disappeared. With one stroke of his axe Juan broke the oak in two; and in a circular hole lined with down he found the golden egg. In the afternoon he went to King Jaime, to whom he presented the much-coveted egg.

But the shrewd and successful monarch did not want to have a rustic son-in-law. "You shall not marry my daughter," he said, "unless you bring me a golden ship."

The next morning Juan, very disconsolate, went to the mountain again. The old man appeared to him, and said, "Why are you dejected, my son?"

Juan related everything that had happened.

"Dry your eyes and listen to me," said the old man. "Not very far from this place you will find your ship all splendidly equipped. Go there at once!"

The old man disappeared, and Juan ran with all possible speed to where the ship was lying. He went on deck, and a few minutes later the ship began to move smoothly over stumps and stones.

While he was thus travelling along, Juan all of a sudden saw a man running around the mountain in less than a minute. "Corrin Corron, son of the great runner!" shouted Juan, "what are you doing?" The man stopped, and said, "I'm taking my daily exercise."

"Never mind that!" said Juan, "come up here and rest!" And Corrin Corron readily accepted the offer.

Pretty soon Juan saw another man standing on the summit of a high hill and gazing intently at some distant object. "Mirin Miron, son of the great Farsight!" said Juan, "what are you doing?"

"I'm watching a game of *tubigan* seven miles away," answered the other.

"Never mind!" said Juan, "come up here and eat with me!" And Mirin Miron gladly went on deck.

After a while Juan saw a hunter with gun levelled. "Puntin Punton, son of the great Sureshot!" said Juan, "what are you doing?"

"Three miles away there is a bat-fly annoying a sheep. I want to kill that insect."

"Let the creature go," said Juan, "and come with me!" And Puntin Punton, too, joined the party.

Not long after, Juan saw a man carrying a mountain on his shoulders. "Carguin Cargon, son of the great Strong-Back!" shouted Juan, "what are you doing?"

"I'm going to carry this mountain to the other side of the country to build a dam across the river," said the man.

"Don't exert yourself so much," said Juan. "Come up here and take some refreshment!" The brawny carrier threw aside his load; and, as the mountain hit the ground, the whole kingdom was shaken so violently that the inhabitants thought that all the volcanoes had simultaneously burst into eruption.

By and by the ship came to a place where Juan saw young flourishing trees falling to the ground, with branches twisted and broken. "Friends," said Juan, "is a storm blowing?"

"No, sir!" answered the sailors, amazed at the sight.

"Master Juan," shouted Mirin Miron, "sitting on the summit of yonder mountain," pointing to a peak three miles away, "is a man blowing with all his might."

"He is a naughty fellow," muttered Juan to himself; "he will destroy all the lumber trees in this region if we do not stop him." Pretty soon Juan himself saw the mischievous man, and said, "Soplin Soplon, son of the great Blast-Blower, what are you doing?"

"Oh, I'm just exercising my lungs and trumpeter's muscles," replied the other.

"Come along with us!" After blowing down a long line of trees like grain before a hurricane, Soplin Soplon went on board.

As the ship neared the capital, Juan saw a man lying on a bed of rushes, with his ear to the ground. "What are you doing, friend?" said Juan.

"I'm listening to the plaintive strains of a young man mourning over the grave of his deceased sweetheart, and to the touching love ditties of a moonstruck lover," answered the man.

"Where are those two men?" asked Juan.

"They are in a city twelve miles away," said the other. "Never mind, Oirin Oiron, son of the great Hear-All!" said Juan. "Come up and rest on a more comfortable bed! My divans superabound." When Oirin Oiron was on board, Juan said to the helmsman, "To the capital!"

In the evening the magnificent ship, with sails of silk and damask, masts of gold heavily studded with rare gems, and covered with thick plates of gold and silver, arrived at the palace gate.

Early in the morning King Jaime received Juan, but this time more coldly and arrogantly than ever. The princess bathed before break of day. With cheeks suffused with the rosy tint of the morning, golden tresses hanging in beautiful curls over her white shoulders, hands as delicate as those of a newborn babe, eyes merrier than the hummingbird, and dressed in a rich outer garment displaying her lovely figure at its best, she stood beside the throne. Such was the appearance of this lovely mortal, who kindled an inextinguishable flame in the heart of Juan.

After doffing his bonnet and bowing to the king, Juan said, "Will you give me the hand of your daughter?" Everybody present was amazed. The princess's face was successively pale and rosy. Juan immediately understood her heart as he stood gazing at her.

"Never!" said the king after a few minutes. "You shall never have my daughter."

"Farewell, then, until we meet again!" said Juan as he departed.

When the ship was beyond the frontier of Jaime's kingdom, Juan said, "Carguin Cargon, overturn the king's realm." Carguin Cargon obeyed. Many houses were destroyed, and hundreds of people were crushed to death. When the ship was within seven miles of the city, Oirin Oiron heard the king say, "I'll give my daughter in marriage to Juan if he will restore my kingdom." Oirin Oiron told Juan what he had heard.

Then Juan ordered Carguin Cargon to rebuild the kingdom; but when the work was done, Jaime again refused to fulfil his promise. Juan went away very angry. Again the kingdom was overturned, and more property and lives were destroyed. Again Oirin Oiron heard the king make a promise, again the kingdom was rebuilt, and again the king was obstinate.

Juan went away again red with anger. After they had been travelling for an hour, Oirin Oiron heard the tramp of horses and the clash of spears and shields. "I can see King Jaime's vast host in hot pursuit of us," said Mirin Miron.

"Where is the army?" said Juan. "It is nine miles away," responded Mirin Miron.

"Let the army approach," said Soplin Soplon. When the immense host was within eight hundred yards of the ship, Soplin Soplon blew forcible blasts, which scattered the soldiers and horses in all directions like chaff before a wind. Of this formidable army only a handful of men survived, and these were crippled for life.

Again the king sued for peace, and promised the hand of his daughter to Juan. This time he kept his word, and Juan and Maria were married amidst the most imposing ceremonies. That very day King Jaime abdicated in favour of his more powerful son-in-law. On the site of the destroyed houses were built larger and more handsome ones. The lumber that was needed was obtained by Soplin Soplon and Carguin Cargon from the mountains: Soplin Soplon felled the trees with his mighty blasts, and Carguin Cargon carried the huge logs to the city. Juan made Corrin Corron his royal messenger, and Soplin Soplon commander-in-chief of the raw troops, which later became a powerful army. The other four friends were assigned to high positions in the government.

The royal couple and the six gifted men led a glorious life. They conquered new lands, and ruled their kingdom well.

Juan the Blind Man

MANY YEARS AGO there lived in a little village near a thick forest eight blind men who were close friends. In spite of their physical defects, they were always happy, perhaps much happier than their fellow villagers, for at night they would always go secretly to one of the neighbouring coconut groves, where they would spend their time drinking *tuba* or eating young coconuts.

One evening a severe typhoon struck the little village, and most of the coconut trees were broken off at the top. The next afternoon the joyous party went to the coconut grove to steal fruits. As soon as they arrived there, seven of them climbed trees. Juan, the youngest of all, was ordered to remain below so as to count and gather in the coconuts his friends threw down to him. While his companions were climbing the trees, Juan was singing,

"Eight friends, good friends,
One fruit each eats;
Good Juan here bends,
Young nuts he takes."

He had no sooner repeated his verse three times than he heard a fall. "One," he counted; and he began to sing the second verse:

"Believe me, that everything
Which man can use he must bring,
No matter at all of what it's made;
So, friends, a counter you need."

Crrapup! He heard another fall, which was followed by three in close succession. "Good!" he said, "five in all. Three more, friends," and he raised his head as if he could see his companions. After a few minutes he heard two more falls.

"Six, seven – well, only seven," he said, as he began searching for the coconuts on the ground. "One more for me, friends – one more, and everyone is satisfied." But it was his friends who had fallen; for, as the trees were only stumps, the climbers fell off when they reached the tops.

Juan, however, did not guess what had happened until he found one of the dead bodies. Then he ran away as fast as he could. At last he met Justo, a lame man. After hearing Juan's story, Justo advised Juan not to return to his village, lest he be accused of murder by the relatives of the other men.

After a long talk, the two agreed to travel together and seek a place of refuge, for the blind man's proposal seemed a good one to the lame man:

"Blind man, strong legs;
Lame man, good eyes;
Four-footed are pigs;
Four-handed are monkeys.
But we'll walk on two,
And we'll see with two."

So when morning dawned, they started on their journey.

They had not travelled far when Justo saw a horn in the road, and told Juan about it. Juan said,

"Believe me, that everything
Which man can use he must bring,
No matter at all of what it's made;
So, friend, a horn too we need."

The next thing that Justo saw was a rusted axe; and after being told about it, Juan repeated his little verse again, ending it with, "So, friend, an axe too we need." A few hours later the lame man saw a piece of rope; and when the blind man knew of it, he said,

"Bring one, bring two, bring all,
The horn, the axe, the rope as well."

And last of all they found an old drum, which they took along with them too.

Soon Justo saw a very big house. They were glad, for they thought that they could get something to eat there. When they came near it, they found that the door was open; but when they entered it, Justo saw nothing but bolos, spears and shields hanging on the walls. After a warm discussion as to what they should do, they decided to hide in the ceiling of the house, and remain there until the owner returned.

They had no sooner made themselves comfortable than they heard some persons coming. When Justo saw the bloody bolos and spears of the men, and the big sack of money they carried, he was terrified, for he suspected that they were outlaws. He trembled; his hair stood on end; he could not control himself. At last he shouted, "Ay, here?"

The blind man, who could not see the danger they were in, stopped the lame man, but not before the owners of the house had heard them.

"Ho, you mosquitoes! what are you doing there?" asked the chief of the outlaws as he looked up at the ceiling.

"Aha, you rascals! we are going to eat you all," answered the blind man in the loudest voice he could muster.

"What's that you say?" returned the chief.

"Why, we have been looking for you, for we intend to eat you all up," replied Juan; "and to show you what kind of animals we are, here is one of my teeth," and Juan threw down the rusted axe. "Look at one of my hairs!" continued Juan, as he threw down the rope.

The outlaws were so frightened that they were almost ready to run away. The chief could not say a single word.

"Now listen, you ants, to my whistle!" said Juan, and he blew the horn. "And to show you how big our stomachs are, hear us beat them!" and he beat the drum. The outlaws were so frightened that they ran away. Some of them even jumped out of the windows.

When the robbers were all gone, Juan and Justo went down to divide the money; but the lame man tried to cheat the blind man, and they had a quarrel over the division. Justo struck Juan in the eyes with the palm of his hand, and the blind man's eyes were opened so that he could see. Juan kicked Justo so hard that the lame man rolled towards one corner of the house and struck a post. His lameness was cured, so that he could stand and walk.

When they saw that each had done the other a great service, they divided the money fairly, and lived ever after together as close friends.

Juan the Poor, Who Became Juan the King

ONCE UPON A TIME there lived in a small hut at the edge of a forest a father and son. The poverty of that family gave the son his name, Juan the Poor. As the father was old and feeble,

Juan had to take care of the household affairs; but there were times when he did not want to work.

One day, while Juan was lying behind their fireplace, his father called him, and told him to go to the forest and get some firewood.

"Very well," said Juan, but he did not move from his place.

After a while the father came to see if his son had gone, but he found him still lying on the floor. "When will you go get that firewood, Juan?"

"Right now, Father," answered the boy. The old man returned to his room. As he wanted to check, however, whether his son had gone or not, he again went to see. When he found Juan in the same position as before, he became very angry, and said,

"Juan, if I come out again and find you still here, I shall surely give you a whipping." Juan knew well that his father would punish him if he did not go; so he rose up suddenly, took his axe, and went to the forest.

When he came to the forest, he marked every tree that he thought would be good for fuel, and then he began cutting. While he was chopping at one of the trees, he saw that it had a hole in the trunk, and in the hole he saw something glistening. Thinking that there might be gold inside the hole, he hastened to cut the tree down; but a monster came out of the hole as soon as the tree fell.

When Juan saw the unexpected being, he raised his axe to kill the monster. Before giving the blow, he exclaimed, "Aha! Now is the time for you to die."

The monster moved backwards when it saw the blow ready to fall, and said,

"Good sir, forbear,
And my life spare,
If you wish a happy life
And, besides, a pretty wife."

Juan lowered his axe, and said, "Oho! is that so?"

"Yes, I swear," answered the monster.

"But what is it, and where is it?" said Juan, raising his axe, and feigning to be angry, for he was anxious to get what the monster promised him. The monster told Juan to take from the middle of his tongue a white oval stone. From it he could ask for and get whatever he wanted to have. Juan opened the monster's mouth and took the valuable stone. Immediately the monster disappeared.

The young man then tested the virtues of his charm by asking it for some men to help him work. As soon as he had spoken the last word of his command, there appeared many persons, some of whom cut down trees, while others carried the wood to his house. When Juan was sure that his house was surrounded by piles of firewood, he dismissed the men, hurried home, and lay down again behind the fireplace. He had not been there long when his father came to see if he had done his work. When the old man saw his son stretched out on the floor, he said, "Juan, have we firewood now?"

"Just look out of the window and see, Father!" said Juan. Great was the surprise of the old man when he saw the large piles of wood about his house.

The next day Juan, remembering the pretty wife of which the monster had spoken, went to the king's palace, and told the king that he wanted to marry his daughter. The king smiled scornfully when he saw the rustic appearance of the suitor, and said, "If you will do what I shall ask you to do, I will let you marry my daughter."

"What are your Majesty's commands for me?" said Juan.

"Build me a castle in the middle of the bay; but know that, if it is not finished in three days' time, you lose your head," said the king sternly. Juan promised to do the work.

Two days had gone by, yet Juan had not yet commenced his work. For that reason the king believed that Juan did not object to losing his life; but at midnight of the third day, Juan bade his stone build a fort in the middle of the bay.

The next morning, while the king was taking his bath, cannon shots were heard. After a while Juan appeared before the palace, dressed like a prince. When he saw the king, he said, "The fort is ready for your inspection."

"If that is true, you shall be my son-in-law," said the king. After breakfast the king, with his daughter, visited the fort, which pleased them very much. The following day the ceremonies of Juan's marriage with the princess Maria were held with much pomp and solemnity.

Shortly after Juan's wedding a war broke out. Juan led the army of the king his father-in-law to the battlefield, and with the help of his magical stone he conquered his mighty enemy. The defeated general went home full of sorrow. As he had never been defeated before, he thought that Juan must possess some supernatural power. When he reached home, therefore, he issued a proclamation which stated that anyone who could get Juan's power for him should have one-half of his property as a reward.

A certain witch, who knew of Juan's secret, heard of the proclamation. She flew to the general, and told him that she could do what he wanted done. On his agreeing, she flew to Juan's house one hot afternoon, where she found Maria alone, for Juan had gone out hunting. The old woman smiled when she saw Maria, and said, "Do you not recognize me, pretty Maria? I am the one who nursed you when you were a baby."

The princess was surprised at what the witch said, for she thought that the old woman was a beggar. Nevertheless she believed what the witch told her, treated the repulsive woman kindly, and offered her cake and wine; but the witch told Maria not to go to any trouble, and ordered her to rest. So Maria lay down to take a siesta. With great show of kindness, the witch fanned the princess till she fell asleep. While Maria was sleeping, the old woman took from underneath the pillow the magical stone, which Juan had forgotten to take along with him. Then she flew to the general, and gave the charm to him. He, in turn, rewarded the old woman with one-half of his riches.

Meanwhile, as Juan was enjoying his hunt in the forest, a huge bird swooped down on him and seized his horse and clothes. When the bird flew away, his inner garments were changed back again into his old woodcutter's clothes. Full of anxiety at this ill omen, and fearing that some misfortune had befallen his wife, he hastened home on foot as best he could. When he reached his house, he found it vacant. Then he went to the king's palace, but that too he found deserted. For his stone he did not know where to look. After a few minutes of reflection, he came to the conclusion that all his troubles were caused by the general whom he had defeated in battle. He also suspected that the officer had somehow or other got possession of his magical stone.

Poor Juan then began walking towards the country where the general lived. Before he could reach that country, he had to cross three mountains. While he was crossing the first mountain, a cat came running after him, and knocked him down. He was so angry at the animal that he ran after it, seized it, and dashed its life out against a rock. When he was crossing the second mountain, the same cat appeared and knocked him down a second time. Again Juan seized the animal and killed it, as before; but the same cat that he had killed twice before tumbled him down a third time while he was crossing the third mountain. Filled with curiosity, Juan caught the animal again: but, instead of killing it this time, he put it inside the bag he was carrying, and took it along with him.

After many hours of tiresome walking, Juan arrived at the castle of the general, and knocked at the door. The general asked him what he wanted. Juan answered, "I am a poor beggar who will be thankful if I can have only a mouthful of rice." The general, however, recognized Juan. He called his servants, and said, "Take this wretched fellow to the cell of rats."

The cell in which Juan was imprisoned was very dark; and as soon as the door was closed, the rats began to bite him. But Juan did not suffer much from them; for, remembering his cat, he let it loose. The cat killed all the rats except their king, which came out of the hole last of all. When the cat saw the king of the rats, it spoke thus: "Now you shall die if you do not promise to get for Juan his magical stone, which your master has stolen."

"Spare my life, and you shall have the stone!" said the king of the rats.

"Go and get it, then!" said the cat. The king of the rats ran quickly to the room of the general, and took Juan's magical stone from the table.

As soon as Juan had obtained his stone, and after he had thanked the king of the rats, he said to his stone, "Pretty stone, destroy this house with the general and his subjects, and release my father-in-law and wife from their prison."

Suddenly the earth trembled and a big noise was heard. Not long afterwards Juan saw the castle destroyed, the general and his subjects dead, and his wife and his father-in-law free.

Taking with him the cat and the king of the rats, Juan went home happily with Maria his wife and the king his father-in-law. After the death of the king, Juan ascended to the throne, and ruled wisely. He lived long and happily with his lovely wife.

The King, the Princess and the Poor Boy

THERE WAS ONCE A KING who loved his daughter very much, so much in fact that he did not wish her to marry; so he built for her a secret house or vault under the ground, and there he kept her away from all but her parents and her maidservants.

There was also an old man in the same city who had a son. The old man said to his son, "Come, lad, let us go into the country and plant crops that we may live," for they were very poor. After they had worked a short time in the country, the old man died and the boy returned to the king's city and then went up and down the street crying, "Oh! who will buy me for a slave, that I may bury my father?" A kind-hearted rich man saw him and enquired his troubles, and the boy told him that he was greatly grieved because his father was dead and he had no money for the funeral. The rich man told him not to grieve, that his father would be buried with all the ceremonies given to anyone. After the funeral the boy went to live with the rich man as his servant, and served him faithfully; so faithfully, indeed, that the rich man, who was childless, adopted him and gave him every advantage of education.

One day the boy wrote a sentence and placed it in the window: "You may hide your treasure with every care, and watch it well, but it will be spent at last." Now the boy had no idea of any hidden meaning in this sentence, but the king chanced to pass that way and read it. Angrily he called the rich man to his carriage, and demanded of him what it meant. "I do not know, most exalted king," said the rich man, "I have only now seen it. It must have been written by a poor boy to whom I have given shelter since his father died."

"Drive him away," said the king; "if he comes back he shall be put to death."

So the rich man, with a heavy heart, for he loved the boy, sent him out into the world. The boy wandered far and long, till at last he came to a house. He called out to those within, "Honourable people," and heard them answer, "Come in." Inside there was no one but only two statues, and one of these spoke, bidding him return to his own town and beg of his master princely clothing, a princely carriage, all gilt, and a music box that could play many tunes.

So the poor boy returned to his master, who sent for the tradesmen and tailors and had them make all manner of princely clothing.

Then he got into his carriage and drove around for a while, till he met a boy. To the boy he gave the music box and a piece of money and told him to play it everywhere but to sell it to nobody, and to report to him if anyone wanted it. So the boy got into the carriage and took the music box with him, while the poor boy went back to the rich man's house.

Soon the king saw the beautiful carriage and heard the sweet music of the music box. The king asked the boy who the owner was, and wished to buy them. The boy told the king that he must tell his employer, and soon the carriage and the music box were sent to the king for a present.

The king was much pleased, for he knew the princess would be delighted, so he had the carriage and the music box taken into her vault, and played on the music box a long time. After he had gone, out stepped the poor boy from a secret compartment of the carriage, and knelt before her telling his love in gentle tones. She listened to him, much frightened at first, but later more composedly, till at last she gave him her heart and promised him her hand.

When the king came in again he found them sitting holding each other's hands. He demanded in a loud voice, "Who are you? Why are you here? How did you come?" To this the boy modestly replied, saying that he had come concealed in the carriage, and told the king that "You may hide your treasure with every care, and watch it well, but it will be spent at last." But the princess entreated for him, and finally the king gave his consent to their marriage, and they lived happily ever after.

Lucas the Strong

ONCE THERE WAS A MAN who had three sons: Juan, Pedro and Lucas. His wife died when his children were young. Unlike most of his countrymen, he did not marry again, but spent his time in taking care of his children. The father could not give his sons a proper education, because he was poor; so the boys grew up in ignorance and superstition. They had no conception of European clothes and shoes. Juan and Pedro were hard workers, but Lucas was lazy. The father loved his youngest son Lucas, nevertheless; but Juan and Pedro had little use for their brother. The lazy boy used to ramble about the forests and along riverbanks looking for guavas and birds' nests.

One day, when Lucas was in the woods, he saw a boa constrictor. He knew that this reptile carried the centre of its strength in the horny appendage at the end of its tail. Lucas wished very much to become strong, because the men of strength in his *barrio* were the most influential. So he decided to rob the boa of its charm. He approached the snake like a cat, and then with his sharp teeth bit off the end of its tail, and ran away with all his might. The boa followed him, but could not overtake him; for Lucas was a fast runner, and, besides, the snake had lost its strength.

Lucas soon became the strongest man in his *barrio*. He surprised everybody when he defeated the man who used to be the Hercules of the place.

One day the king issued a proclamation: "He who can give the monarch a carriage made of gold shall have the princess for his wife." When Juan and Pedro heard this royal announcement, they were very anxious to get the carriage and receive the reward.

Juan was the first to try his luck. He went to a neighbouring mountain and began to dig for gold. While he was eating his lunch at noon, an old leper with her child approached him, and humbly begged him to give her something to eat.

"No, the food I have here is just enough for me. Go away! You are very dirty," said Juan with disgust.

The wretched old woman, with tears in her eyes, left the place. After he had worked for three weeks, Juan became discouraged, gave up his scheme of winning the princess, and returned home.

Pedro followed his brother, but he had no better luck than Juan. He was also unkind to the old leper.

Lucas now tried his fortune. The day after his arrival at the mountain, when he was eating, the old woman appeared, and asked him to give her some food. Lucas gave the woman half of his meat. The leper thanked him, and promised that she would give him not only the carriage made of gold, but also a pair of shoes, a coat and some trousers. She then bade Lucas goodbye.

Nine days passed, and yet the woman had not come. Lucas grew tired of waiting, and in his heart began to accuse the woman of being ungrateful. He repented very much the kindness he had shown the old leper. Finally she appeared to Lucas, and told him what he had been thinking about her. "Do not think that I shall not fulfil my promise," she said. "You shall have them all." To the great astonishment of Lucas, the woman disappeared again. The next day he saw the golden carriage being drawn by a pair of fine fat horses; and in the carriage were the shoes, the coat and the trousers. The old woman appeared, and showed the young man how to wear the shoes and clothes.

Then he entered the carriage and was driven towards the palace. On his way he met a man.

"Who are you?" said Lucas.

"I am Runner, son of the good runner," was the answer.

"Let us wrestle!" said Lucas. "I want to try your strength. If you defeat me, I will give you a hundred pesos; but if I prove to be the stronger, you must come with me."

"All right, let us wrestle!" said Runner. The struggle lasted for ten minutes, and Lucas was the victor. They drove on.

They met another man. When Lucas asked him who he was, the man said, "I am Sharpshooter, son of the famous shooter." Lucas wrestled with this man too, and overcame him because of his superhuman strength. So Sharpshooter went along with Lucas and Runner.

Soon they came up to another man. "What is your name?" said Lucas.

"My name is Farsight. I am son of the great Sharp-Eyes." Lucas proposed a wrestling match with Farsight, who was conquered, and so obliged to go along with the other three.

Last of all, the party met Blower, "son of the great blower." He likewise became one of the servants of Lucas.

When Lucas reached the palace, he appeared before the king, and in terms of great submission he told the monarch that he had come for two reasons: first, to present his Majesty with the golden carriage; second, to receive the reward which his Majesty had promised.

The king said, "I will let you marry my daughter provided that you can more quickly than my messenger bring to me a bottle of the water that gives youth and health to everyone. It is found at the foot of the seventh mountain from this one," he said, pointing to the mountain nearest to the imperial city. "But here is another provision," continued the king, "if you accept the challenge and are defeated, you are to lose your head." "I will try, O king!" responded Lucas sorrowfully.

The king then ordered his messenger, a giant, to fetch a bottle of the precious water. Lucas bade the monarch goodbye, and then returned to his four friends. "Runner, son of the good runner, hasten to the seventh mountain and get me a bottle of the water that gives youth and health!"

Runner ran with all his might, and caught up with the giant; but the giant secretly put a gold ring in Runner's bottle to make him sleep. Two days passed, but Runner had not yet arrived. Then Lucas cried, "Farsight, son of the great Sharp-Eyes, see where the giant and Runner are!"

The faithful servant looked, and he saw Runner sleeping, and the giant very near the city. When he had been told the state of affairs, Lucas called Blower, and ordered him to blow the giant back. The king's messenger was carried to the eighth mountain.

Then Lucas said, "Sharpshooter, son of the famous shooter, shoot the head of the bottle so that Runner will wake up!" The man shot skilfully; Runner jumped to his feet, ran and got the precious water, and arrived in the city in twelve hours. Lucas presented the water to the king, and the monarch was obliged to accept the young man as his son-in-law.

The wedding day was a time of great rejoicing. Everybody was enthusiastic about Lucas except the king. The third day after the nuptials, the giant reached the palace. He said that he was very near the city when a heavy wind blew him back to the eighth mountain.

Magbolotó

THERE WAS ONCE A MAN named Magbolotó who lived in the depths of the mountains. One day on going down to a brook he saw three goddesses bathing in the water. They had left their wings on the bank, and Magbolotó managed to slip down and steal one pair of them. When the goddesses had finished bathing and looked for their wings, they could not find those belonging to the youngest, Macaya. At last the two goddesses put on their wings and flew up to heaven, leaving behind them Macaya, who wept bitterly, since without her wings she could not go home. Then Magbolotó, feigning to have come from a distance, met her and asked, "Why do you weep, lady?"

"Why do you ask, if you will not help me in my trouble?" answered Macaya.

"I will do my best to help you," said Magbolotó, "if you will tell me about it."

So Macaya told him that she had lost her wings, and therefore could not return to her home in heaven.

"I am sorry not to be able to help you out of your trouble," said Magbolotó, "but we terrestrial people do not use wings, nor know where to get them. The only thing I can do for you is to offer you a home with me." Macaya was obliged to accept his offer, since there was nothing else for her to do.

About a year after Macaya became Magbolotó's wife they had a child. One day, as Magbolotó was making rice soup on the hearth, Macaya was swinging the child in a hammock. Accidentally, she noticed a bundle stuck into one of the bamboo posts in the partition. She withdrew the bundle, and upon unrolling it found, oh, joy! her long-lost wings, which Magbolotó had hidden in the hollow bamboo. She at once put them on, and leaving her husband and child, flew up to join her celestial family.

Magbolotó, on missing his wife, began calling loudly for her. As he could not find her, he looked for the wings, and seeing that they were gone, knew at once what had happened. He began to weep bitterly, especially as he did not know how to take care of the child. So leaving it in the care of a relative, he set out to find the way to heaven. He had walked a great distance when he met North Wind. "Magbolotó, Magbolotó, why are you weeping?" asked North Wind.

"Ask me nothing if you cannot help me in any way," answered Magbolotó.

"Tell me your trouble and I will help you," said North Wind.

"Well," replied Magbolotó, "I have a wife who came from heaven. But now she has flown away, leaving a little child for me to take care of, and I am in great sorrow. Please show me the way that leads to her home."

"Magbolotó," said North Wind, "I do not know the way, but my brother, East Wind, can tell you. Goodbye."

Magbolotó went on his way, and after a while he met East Wind. "Magbolotó, Magbolotó, why are you weeping?" asked East Wind.

"Ask me nothing if you cannot help me in any way," said Magbolotó.

"Tell me all your trouble and I will help you," answered East Wind.

Then Magbolotó related all his sorrow, just as he had done to North Wind.

"Well," said East Wind, "I do not know the way, but my brother, South Wind, may be able to show it to you. Goodbye."

Magbolotó went on, and at last met South Wind.

"Magbolotó, Magbolotó, why are you weeping?" asked South Wind.

"Ask me nothing if you cannot help me in any way," said Magbolotó.

"Tell me your trouble and I will help you," answered South Wind.

Then Magbolotó told him his story, just as he had done to North Wind and East Wind.

"Well," said South Wind, "I do not know the way to heaven, but my brother, West Wind, can tell you the course to be taken to get there. Goodbye."

Magbolotó went on and on, and at last met West Wind.

"Magbolotó, Magbolotó, why are you weeping?" asked West Wind.

"Ask me nothing if you cannot help me in any way," answered Magbolotó.

"Tell me your trouble and I will help you," answered West Wind, and Magbolotó did as he was bidden.

"Magbolotó," said West Wind, "I don't know the way to heaven, but my friend, Mr. Eagle, does. Goodbye."

Magbolotó went on until he met Mr. Eagle.

"Magbolotó, Magbolotó, why are you weeping?" asked Mr. Eagle.

"Ask me nothing if you cannot help me in any way," answered Magbolotó.

"Tell me your trouble and I will help you," replied Mr. Eagle. Then Magbolotó told Mr. Eagle his trouble.

"Magbolotó," said Mr. Eagle, "get upon my back and I will carry you to your wife's home."

Magbolotó climbed upon Mr. Eagle's back and they flew up until they reached Macaya's house. Then Magbolotó requested Macaya's grandmother, with whom she lived, to let her granddaughter return to earth with him.

"By no means," said the grandmother, "unless you will spread ten jars of luñga (a certain very small grain) out to dry and gather them again in the evening."

So Magbolotó spread the jars of luñga on the sand, and at noon began to gather them up; but sunset had come before he had gathered more than five handfuls, so he sat down and began to cry like a little boy.

The king of the ants heard him, and wishing to help him, asked, "Magbolotó, Magbolotó, why are you weeping?"

"Ask me nothing if you cannot help me."

"Tell me about it and I will help you."

So Magbolotó told the king of the ants all his history, and the condition imposed by the grandmother before he could have his wife, and how impossible it was to fulfil it.

"Well, Magbolotó, you shall be helped," said the king of the ants. Then he blew his horn, and in a little while all his subjects came, and began picking up the grain and putting it into the jars. In a few moments all the grain was in the jars.

The next morning Magbolotó went to get his wife, but the grandmother stopped him, saying:

"You shall not take my granddaughter away until you have first hulled a hundred bushels of rice."

Magbolotó was in despair, for he knew that to hull one hundred bushels of rice would take him not less than one hundred days, and the grandmother required him to do it in one day; so he cried like a child at his misfortune. The king of the rats heard him crying, and at once came to help him.

"Magbolotó, Magbolotó, why are you weeping?" asked King Rat.

"Ask me nothing if you cannot help me."

"Relate the matter, and I will."

Magbolotó told him his trouble. Then the king of the rats called his subjects together and ordered them to gnaw the hulls from the rice. In an instant the rice was all hulled.

The next morning Magbolotó made ready to depart with his wife, but the grandmother stopped him again, saying:

"You may not go until you have chopped down all the trees you see on that mountain over there."

There were more than a million trees, so Magbolotó was in great trouble, and as usual he began to weep.

The king of the wild boars heard him and came up, saying:

"Magbolotó, Magbolotó, why are you weeping?"

"Ask me nothing if you cannot help me."

"Relate the matter, and I will."

Magbolotó related all that had happened to him. Then the king of the wild boars called all his subjects together and set them to work cutting down the trees with their tusks. In a few minutes the trees were all down.

When the grandmother saw that Magbolotó accomplished every task she gave him to do she became tired of trying to think of things for him to do; so she allowed him to depart with Macaya, and leaving the celestial abode they descended to their home on the earth, where they lived happily together for many years.

Masoy and the Ape

MASOY WAS A POOR MAN who lived on a farm some miles from the town. His clothing was very poor, and his little garden furnished him scarcely enough to live on. Every weekday he went to town to sell his fruits and vegetables and to buy rice. Upon his return he noticed each day that someone had entered the garden in his absence and stolen some of the fruit. He tried to protect the garden by making the fence very strong and locking the gate; but, in spite of all he could do, he continued to miss his fruit.

At length Masoy conceived the happy idea of taking some pitch and moulding it into the shape of a man. He put a bamboo hat on it and stood it up in one corner of the garden. Then he went away.

As soon as he was gone, the robber, who was none other than a huge ape, climbed the fence and got in.

"Oh!" he said to himself, "I made a mistake! There is Masoy watching. He did not go away as I thought. He is here with a big bamboo hat, but he could not catch me if he tried. I am going to greet him, for fear he may consider me impolite."

"Good morning, Masoy," he said. "Why do you not answer me? What is the matter with you? Oh! you are joking, are you, by keeping so silent? But you will not do it again." On saying this, the ape slapped the man of pitch with his right hand, and of course it stuck, and he could not get it loose.

"For heaven's sake," cried the ape, "let me go. If you do not, I will slap you with my other hand." Then he struck him with the other hand, which, of course, stuck fast also.

"Well, Masoy," cried the ape, "you have entirely exhausted my patience! If you don't let go of me at once, I shall kick you." No sooner said than done, with a result which may easily be imagined.

"Masoy," cried the now enraged ape, "if you have any regard for your own welfare, let me go, for if you don't, I still have one leg left to kill you with." So saying, he kicked him with the remaining foot, getting so tangled up that he and the tar man fell to the ground, rolling over and over.

Then Masoy came, and, when he saw the ape, he said, "So you are the robber who has stolen my fruit! Now you will pay for it with your life."

But the ape cried, "Oh, spare my life, and I will be your slave forever!"

"Do you promise not to steal my fruit again?"

"I do, and I will serve you faithfully all my life."

Masoy agreed to spare him.

From that time on the ape worked very hard for his master. He sold the fruit and bought the rice and was honest and industrious. One day, on his way to market, he happened to find a small piece of gold and another of silver. At that time this country was not ruled by any foreign power, but each tribe was governed by its own datto or chief. The chief was naturally the bravest and richest of the tribe.

The chief of Masoy's tribe had a very beautiful daughter. The ape schemed to have her marry his master. Now he hit upon a plan. He went to the chief's house and asked for a ganta, which is a measure holding about three quarts and used for measuring rice.

"My master," he said, "begs you to lend him a ganta to measure his gold with."

The chief was astonished at such an extraordinary request, and asked:

"Who is your master?"

"Masoy, who owns many gantas of gold and silver, acres upon acres of land; and uncountable heads of cattle," was the reply.

The ape carried the ganta home, and there he stuck the piece of gold he had found on the inside of the bottom of the measure, and then returned it to the chief.

"Oh, ape!" said the datto, "your master has forgotten to take out one piece of gold. Take it and give it back to him."

"Never mind, sir," answered the ape, "he has so much gold that that small piece is nothing to him. You may keep it."

Some weeks afterwards, the ape went again to borrow the chief's ganta.

"What do you want it for now?" asked the chief.

"To measure my master's silver with," was the answer. So he carried it home, stuck inside the piece of silver he had found, and returned it. The chief found the piece of silver and offered to return it, but was answered as before, that it did not matter.

The chief believed all that the ape said, but was puzzled to know how such a rich man could be living in his territory without his having heard of him.

After a few days the ape, considering the way well prepared for his plans, called upon the datto and said, "My master requests you to give him your daughter in marriage. I am authorized to make all the arrangements with you for the wedding, if you consent to it."

"Very well," answered the chief, "but before we arrange matters I wish to see my future son-in-law. Ask him to come to see me, and I will receive him in a manner befitting his rank."

The ape returned home and said to Masoy, who knew nothing at all of the negotiations with the chief, "I have good news for you. The chief wants to see you, for he intends to give you his daughter in marriage."

"What are you chattering about?" answered Masoy. "Have you lost your senses? Don't you know that I am too poor to marry the chief's daughter? I have not even decent clothes to wear and no means of getting any."

"Do not worry about the clothes. I will get them for you somewhere," replied the ape.

"And how shall I talk? You know that I am ignorant of city ways."

"Oh, Masoy, don't trouble about that! Just answer 'Yes' to the questions they ask you and you will be all right."

Finally Masoy consented to go, and went down to the river to wash off the dirt and grime. A rich merchant was bathing some distance up the river, and the ape slipped along the bank, stole the merchant's clothes, hat and shoes, and running back swiftly to his master, bade him put them on. Masoy did so, and found himself, for the first time in his life, so well dressed that he no longer hesitated about going to the chief's house. When they arrived there they found that the chief was expecting them and had made a big feast and reception in honour of his future son-in-law. The chief began to talk about the wedding and said:

"Shall we have the wedding in your palace, Masoy?"

"Yes," answered Masoy.

"You have a large palace, I suppose, haven't you, sir?"

"Yes," was the reply.

"Don't you think it would be well for us to go there this afternoon?"

"Yes," was again the reply.

Meanwhile the ape had disappeared. He went along the road towards home and said to all the people he met, "The datto will be along this way pretty soon and when he asks you to whom all these farms and cattle belong, you must say that they are Masoy's, for otherwise he will kill you."

The ape knew that in a certain spot stood an enchanted palace invisible to men. He went to the place, and just where the front of a house appeared whenever it was visible, he began to dig a ditch. The witch who lived in the house appeared and asked, "What are you ditching there for, Mr. Ape?"

"Oh, madam," was his answer, "haven't you heard the news? The chief is coming this way soon, and is going to have all witches and the low animals like myself put to death. For this reason I am digging a pit to hide myself in."

"Oh, Mr. Ape!" said the witch, "let me hide myself first, for I am not able to dig for myself, and you are. Do me this favour, please."

"I should be very impolite, if I refused to do a favour for a lady," said the ape. "Come down, but hurry, or you will be too late."

The witch hurried as fast as she could and got down into the pit. Then the ape threw stones down on her until she was dead. The house then became free from enchantment and always visible.

The ape then returned to the chief's house and reported that all was ready for the wedding. So the chief, Masoy and the bride, escorted by a large number of people, set out for Masoy's palace. On the way they saw many rich farms and great herds of cattle. The chief asked the people who the owner of these farms and cattle was. The answer always was that they belonged to Masoy. Consequently the chief was greatly impressed by Masoy's great wealth.

The chief greatly admired the palace and considered himself fortunate to have such a son-in-law. That night the wedding took place, and Masoy lived many years in the palace with his wife, having the ape and a great number of slaves to serve him.

The Mysterious Book

ONCE UPON A TIME there lived a poor father and a poor son. The father was very old, and was named Pedro. The son's name was Juan. Although they were very poor, Juan was afraid of work.

One day the two did not have a single grain of rice in the house to eat. Juan now realized that he would have to find some work, or he and his father would starve. So he went to a neighbouring town to seek a master. He at last found one in the person of Don Luzano, a fine gentleman of fortune.

Don Luzano treated Juan like a son. As time went on, Don Luzano became so confident in Juan's honesty that he began to entrust him with the most precious valuables in the house. One morning Don Luzano went out hunting. He left Juan alone in the house, as usual. While Juan was sweeping and cleaning his master's room, he caught sight of a highly polished box lying behind the post in the corner. Curious to find out what was inside, he opened the box. There appeared another box. He opened this box, and another box still was disclosed. One box appeared after another until Juan came to the seventh. This last one contained a small triangular-shaped book bound in gold and decorated with diamonds and other precious gems. Disregarding the consequences that might follow, Juan picked up the book and opened it. Lo! at once Juan was carried by the book up into the air. And when he looked back, whom did he see? No other than Don Luzano pursuing him, with eyes full of rage. He had an enormous deadly-looking bolo in his hand.

As Don Luzano was a big man, he could fly faster than little Juan. Soon the boy was but a few yards in front of his antagonist. It should also be known that the book had the wonderful power of changing anybody who had laid his hands on it, or who had learned by heart one of its chapters, into whatever form that person wished to assume. Juan soon found this fact out. In an instant Juan had disappeared, and in his place was a little steed galloping as fast as he could down the street. Again, there was Don Luzano after him in the form of a big fast mule, with bubbling and foaming mouth, and eyes flashing with hate. The mule ran so fast that every minute seemed to be bringing Juan nearer his grave.

Seeing his danger, Juan changed himself into a bird, a pretty little bird. No sooner had he done so than he saw Don Luzano in the form of a big hawk about to swoop down on him. Then Juan suddenly leaped into a well he was flying over, and there became a little fish. Don Luzano assumed the form of a big fish, and kept up the chase; but the little fish entered a small crack in the wall of the well, where the big fish could not pursue him farther. So Don Luzano had to give up and go home in great disappointment.

The well in which Juan found himself belonged to three beautiful princesses. One morning, while they were looking into the water, they saw the little fish with its seven-coloured scales, moving gracefully through the water. The eldest of the maidens lowered her bait, but the fish would not see it. The second sister tried her skill. The fish bit the bait; but, just as it was being drawn out of the water, it suddenly released its hold. Now the youngest sister's turn came. The fish allowed itself to be caught and held in the tender hands of this beautiful girl. She placed the little fish in a golden basin of water and took it to her room, where she cared for it very tenderly.

Several months later the king issued a proclamation throughout his realm and other neighbouring kingdoms, saying that the youngest princess was sick. "To anyone who can cure her," he said, "I promise to give one-half of my kingdom." The most skilful doctors had already done the best they could, but all their efforts were in vain. The princess seemed to grow worse and worse every day. "Ay, what foolishness!" exclaimed Don Luzano when he heard the news of the sick princess. "The sickness! Pshaw! That's no sickness, never in the wide world!"

The following morning there was Don Luzano speaking with the king. "I promise to cure her," said Don Luzano. "I have already cured many similar cases."

"And your remedy will do her no harm?" asked the king after some hesitation.

"No harm, sir, no harm. Rely on my honour."

"Very well. And you shall have half of my kingdom if you are successful."

"No, I thank you, your Majesty. I, being a faithful subject, need no payment whatever for any of my poor services. As a token from you, however, I should like to have the fish that the princess keeps in her room."

"O my faithful subject!" exclaimed the king in joy. "How good you are! Will you have nothing except a poor worthless fish?"

"No more. That's enough."

"Well, then," returned the king, "prepare your remedy, and on the third day we shall apply it to the princess. You can go home now, and you may be sure that you shall have the fish."

Don Luzano took his leave of the king, and then went home. On the third day this daring magician came back to the palace to apply his remedy to the princess. Before he began any part of the treatment, however, he requested that the fish be given to him. The king consented to his request: but as he was about to dip his hand into the basin, the princess boldly stopped him. She pretended to be angry on the ground that Don Luzano would soil with his hands the golden basin of the monarch. She told him to hold out his hands, and she would pour the fish into them. Don Luzano did as he was told: but, before the fish could reach his hands, the pretty creature jumped out. No fish now could be seen, but in its stead was a beautiful gold ring adorning the finger of the princess. Don Luzano tried to snatch the ring, but, as the princess jerked her hand back, the ring fell to the floor, and in its place were countless little *mungo* seeds scattered about the room. Don Luzano instantly took the form of a greedy crow, devouring the seeds with extraordinary speed. Juan, who was contained in one of the seeds that had rolled beneath the feet of the princess, suddenly became a cat, and, rushing out, attacked the bird. As soon as you could wink your eyes or snap your fingers, the crow was dead, miserably torn to pieces. In place of the cat stood Juan in an embroidered suit, looking like a gay young prince.

"This is my beloved," confessed the princess to her father as she pointed to Juan. The king forgave his daughter for concealing from him the real condition of her life, and he gladly welcomed his new son-in-law. Prince Juan, as we shall now call our friend, was destined to a life of peace and joy. He was rid of his formidable antagonist; he had a beautiful princess (who was no longer sick) for a wife; and he had an excellent chance of inheriting the throne. There is no more.

The Story of Carancal

ONCE UPON A TIME there lived a couple who had long been married, but had no child. Every Sunday they went to church and begged God to give them a son. They even asked the witches in their town why God would not give them a child. The witches told them that they would have one after a year, but that when born he would be no longer than a span. Nevertheless the couple gave thanks.

After a year a son was born to them. He was very small, as the witches had foretold, but he was stronger than anyone would expect such a small child to be. "It is strange," said a neighbour. "Why, he eats more food than his stomach can hold." The boy grew larger and larger, and the amount of food he ate became greater and greater. When he became four feet tall, his daily requirements were a *cavan* of rice and twenty-five pounds of meat and fish. "I can't imagine how so small a person can eat so much food," said his mother to her husband. "He is like a grasshopper: he eats all the time."

Carancal, as the boy was called, was very strong and very kind-hearted. He was the leader of the other boys of the town, for he could beat all of them in wrestling.

After a few years the family's property had all been sold to buy food for the boy. Day after day they became poorer and poorer, for Carancal's father had no other business but fishing. So one day when Carancal was away playing, the wife said to her husband, "What shall we do with Carancal? He will make us as poor as rats. It is better for us to tell him to go earn his living, for he is old enough to work."

"No, it is a shame to send him off," said the father, "for we asked God for him. I will take him to the forest and there kill him; and if the neighbours ask how he died, we will say that an accident befell him while cutting trees."

Early the next morning his father led Carancal to the forest, and they began to cut down a very big tree. When the tree was about to fall, Carancal's father ordered the son to stand where the tree inclined; so that when it fell, Carancal was entirely buried. The father immediately went home, thinking that his son had surely been killed; but when he and his wife were talking, Carancal came home with the big tree on his shoulders.

"Father, Father, why did you leave me alone in the forest?" said the obedient boy.

The father could not move or speak, for shame of himself. He only helped his son unload the heavy burden. The mother could not speak either, for fear Carancal might suspect their bad intentions towards him. Accordingly she and her husband planned another scheme.

The next day Carancal was invited by his father to go fishing. They rowed and rowed until they were far out into the blue sea. Then they put their net into the water. "Carancal, dive down and see that our net is sound," said the father. Carancal obeyed. In about a minute the water became red and began to foam. This made the old man think that his son had been devoured by a big fish, so he rowed homeward. When he reached home, his wife anxiously asked if Carancal was dead; and the husband said, "Yes." They then cooked their meal and began to eat. But their supper was not half finished when Carancal came in, carrying a big alligator. He again asked his father why he had left him alone to bring such a big load. The father said, "I thought you had been killed by a large fish." Carancal then asked his mother to cook him a *cavan* of rice, for he was tired from swimming such a long distance.

The couple were now discouraged; they could not think of any way by which to get rid of Carancal. At last the impatient woman said, "Carancal, you had better go out into the world to see what you can do towards earning your own living. You know that we are becoming poorer and poorer."

"Mother," interrupted the boy, "I really did not wish to go away from you; but, now that you drive me as if I were not your son, I cannot stay." He paused for a moment to wipe the tears from his cheeks. "You know that I love you; but you, in turn, hate me. What shall I do? I am your son, and so I must not disobey you. But before I depart, Father and Mother, please give me a bolo, a big bolo, to protect myself in case of danger."

The parents willingly promised that he should have one, and after two days an enormous bolo five yards long was finished. Carancal took it, kissed the hands of his parents, and then went away with a heavy heart.

When he had left his little village behind, he did not know which way to go. He was like a ship without a rudder. He walked and walked until he came to a forest, where he met Bugtongpalasan. Carancal asked him where he was going; and Bugtongpalasan said, "I am wandering, but I do not know where to go. I have lost my parents, and they have left me nothing to inherit."

"Do you want to go with me?" said Carancal.

"Yes," said Bugtongpalasan.

"Let us wrestle first, and the loser will carry my bolo," said Carancal as a challenge. They wrestled; and Bugtongpalasan was defeated, so he had to carry the big bolo.

Then they continued their journey until they met Tunkodbola, whom Carancal also challenged to a wrestling match. Tunkodbola laughed at Carancal, and said, "Look at this!" He twisted up a tree near by, and hurled it out of sight.

"That is all right. Let us wrestle, and we will see if you can twist me," said Carancal scornfully. So they wrestled. The earth trembled, trees were uprooted, large stones rolled about; but Tunkodbola was defeated.

"Here, take this bolo and carry it!" said Carancal triumphantly; and they continued their journey.

When they reached the top of a mountain, they saw a big man. This was Macabuhalbundok. Carancal challenged him; but Macabuhalbundok only laughed, and pushed up a hill. As the hill fell, he said, "Look at this hill! I gave it only a little push, and it was overthrown."

"Well, I am not a hill," said Carancal. "I can balance myself." They wrestled together, and Carancal was once more the winner.

The four companions now walked on together. They were all wandering about, not knowing where to go. When they were in the midst of a thick wood, they became hungry; so Carancal, their captain, ordered one of them to climb a tall tree and see if any house was nigh. Bugtongpalasan did so, and he saw a big house near the edge of the forest. They all went to the house to see if they might not beg some food.

It was a very large house; but all the windows were closed, and it seemed to be uninhabited. They knocked at the door, but no one answered. Then they went in, and found a table covered with delicious food; and as they were almost famished, they lost no time in devouring what seemed to have been prepared for them. After all had eaten, three of them went hunting, leaving Bugtongpalasan behind to cook more food for them against their return.

While Bugtongpalasan was cooking, he felt the earth tremble, and in a short time he saw a big giant ascending the stairs of the house, saying, "*Ho, bajo tao cainco*," which means "I smell a man whom I will eat." Bugtongpalasan faced him, but what could a man do to a big giant? The monster pulled a hair out of his head and tied Bugtongpalasan to a post. Then he cooked his own meal. After eating, he went away, leaving his prisoner in the house.

When the three arrived, they were very angry with Bugtongpalasan because no food had been prepared for them; but they untied him, and made him get the meal. Tunkodbola was the next one left behind as cook while the others went hunting, but he had the same experience as Bugtongpalasan. Then Macabuhalbundok; but the same thing happened to him too.

It was now the turn of Carancal to try his wit, strength and luck. Before the three left, he had them shave his head. When the giant came and saw that Carancal's head was white, he laughed. "It is a very fine thing to have a white head," said the giant. "Make my head white too."

"Your head must be shaved to be white," said Carancal, "and it is a very difficult thing to shave a head."

"Never mind that! I want to have my head shaved," said the giant impatiently.

Carancal then got some ropes and wax. He tied the giant tightly to a post, and then smeared his body with wax. He next took a match and set the giant's body on fire. Thus the giant was destroyed, and the four lived in the house as if it were their own.

Not long afterwards a rumour reached their ears. It was to this effect: that in a certain kingdom on the other side of the sea lived a king who wanted to have a huge stone removed from its place. This stone was so big that it covered much ground. The prize that would be given to the one who could remove it was the hand of the king's prettiest daughter.

The four set out to try their strength. At that time there were no boats for them to sail on, so they had to swim. After three weeks' swimming, they landed on an island-like place in the sea, to rest. It was smooth and slippery, which made them wonder what it could be. Carancal, accordingly, drew his bolo and thrust it into the island. How fast the island moved after the stroke! It was not really an island, but a very big fish. Fortunately the fish carried the travellers near the shores of the kingdom they were seeking.

When the four arrived, they immediately presented themselves to the king, and told him that they would try to move the stone. The king ordered one of his soldiers to show them the stone. There a big crowd of people collected to watch the four strong men.

The first to try was Bugtongpalasan. He could hardly budge it. Then Tunkodbola tried, but moved it only a few yards. When Macabuhalbundok's turn came, he moved the great stone half a mile; but the king said that it was not satisfactory. Carancal then took hold of the rope tied to the stone, and gave a swing. In a minute the great stone was out of sight.

The king was very much pleased, and asked Carancal to choose a princess for his wife. "I am not old enough to marry, my lord," said Carancal sadly. "I will marry one of my companions to your daughter, however, if you are willing." The king agreed, and Bugtongpalasan was made a prince.

The three unmarried men lived with Bugtongpalasan. By this time they were known not only throughout the whole kingdom where they were, but also in other countries. They had not enjoyed a year's hospitality in Bugtongpalasan's home when a letter addressed to the four men came. It was as follows:

> *I have heard that you have superhuman strength, which I now greatly need. About a week ago a monster fish floated up to the shore of my town. It is decaying, and has a most offensive odour. My men in vain have tried to drag the fish out into the middle of the sea. I write to inform you that if you can rid us of it, I will let one of you marry my prettiest daughter.*
>
> *King Walangtacut.*

After Carancal had read the letter, he instantly remembered the fish that had helped them in travelling. The three companions made themselves ready, bade Bugtongpalasan goodbye, and set out for Walangtacut's kingdom. They travelled on foot, for the place was not very far away.

In every town they passed through, the people cried, "Hurrah for the strong men!" The king received them with a banquet, and all the houses of the town were decorated with flags. In a word, everyone welcomed them.

After the banquet was over, the three men marched with the king and all his counsellors, knights, dukes and the common people to where the decaying fish lay. In this test, too, Carancal was the only successful one. Again he refused to marry; but as the princess was very anxious to have a strong man for her husband, Tunkodbola was chosen by Carancal, and he became her husband.

The fame of the strong men was now nearly universal. All the surrounding kings sent congratulations. The heroes received offers of marriage from many beautiful ladies of the neighbouring kingdoms.

One day when Carancal and Macabuhalbundok were talking together, one of them suggested that they go on another journey. The other agreed, and both of them made preparations. But when they were about to start, a letter from another king came, addressed to Carancal. The king said in his letter that a great stone had fallen in his park. "It is so big that I thought it was the sky that fell," he wrote. "I am willing to marry you to my youngest daughter if you can remove it from its present place," said the king.

The two friends accepted the invitation, and immediately began their journey. They travelled by land and sea for many a day. At last they reached the place. There they found the same stone which they had removed before. As he knew that he could not move it far enough, Macabuhalbundok did not make any attempt: Carancal was again the one who did the work.

Once more Carancal refused to marry. "I am too young yet to marry," he said to the king. "In my place I will put my companion." So Macabuhalbundok was married.

Carancal remained a bachelor, for he did not wish to have a wife. The three princes considered him as their father, though he was younger than any of them. For a long time Carancal lived with each of them a year in rotation. Not long after the marriage of Macabuhalbundok, the father-in-law of Bugtongpalasan died, and so Bugtongpalasan became the king. Then the following year Tunkodbola's father-in-law died, and Tunkodbola became also a king. After many years the father-in-law of Macabuhalbundok died, and Macabuhalbundok succeeded to the throne. Thus Carancal was the benefactor of three kings.

One day Carancal thought of visiting his cruel parents and of living with them. So he set out, carrying with him plenty of money, which the three kings had given him. This time his parents did not drive him away, for he had much wealth. Carancal lived once more with his parents, and had three kings under him.

The Story of Juan del Mundo de Austria and the Princess Maria

THERE WAS ONCE a king who had three very beautiful daughters, Princess Clara, Princess Catalina and Princess Maria.

This king was sick for a long time with a dreadful disease, and although he spent much money on medicines and doctors he was only worse instead of better.

At last he sent word to all his people proclaiming that whoever would cure him might have one of the princesses to marry.

After several days one of the heralds returned, saying he had met a snake who enquired if the king would give his daughter to a snake to wife if he were cured. The king called his daughters and asked if they would be willing to marry a snake.

Said Princess Clara, "I will be stung by a snake till I am dead before I give my virginity to a snake." Said Princess Catalina, "I may be beaten to death with sticks, but I will not give my virginity to a snake." Said Princess Maria, "Father, so you be but well, I care not what becomes of me. If a snake can cure you, I am willing to marry him."

So the king's message was carried to the snake, and the king was made well. The snake and the princess were married, and set off through the forest together. After a long journey they came to a house in the forest, and there the snake and the beautiful Maria lived together many days. But the snake, being very wise, saw that the princess ate little and cried very much, and asked her why it was so. She told him that it was hard for her to live with a snake. "Very well," said the snake, and went into a house near by; after a little there came out a handsome man with silken clothes, and rings on his fingers, who told her that he was her husband, that he was known among men as Don Juan del Mundo de Austria, and that he was king of all the beasts, being able to take the form of any of them at will.

They passed many happy days together till the time came for the great feast at the court of Princess Maria's father. Don Juan told her that she might go, but that she must on no account tell his name or rank, otherwise when she came to their trysting place by the seashore she would not find him. He gave her a magic ring by means of which she might obtain anything she wanted, and left her close to her own city.

When she arrived at home her sisters were greatly surprised to see her looking well, happy, and much more finely dressed than when she went away, but her father was very glad to see her. The elder sisters often asked her the secret of her husband's identity, but her answer was always the same, "Did you not both see that I married a snake? Who else could it be?" The wicked women then determined to make her tell, whether she wished or not, and so they asked her to walk with them in a secluded garden.

Then they took sticks and set upon her, beating her and telling her that she must tell who her husband was. The poor little princess defended herself a long time, saying that if she told she would never see him again, but finally, when she was nearly dead from beating, she told them that her husband was Don Juan de Austria. Then she was beaten for not telling the truth, but her tormentors finally desisted and she went to her father and told him all.

He did not wish her to return to the forest and begged her to remain with him, but she insisted.

When she arrived at the trysting place, Don Juan was not there, but she set out bravely, asking of her ring whatever she needed for food, drink and clothing. Wherever she went she enquired of the beasts and birds the whereabouts of her husband, Don Juan de Austria, and, when they knew who she was, they worshipped her and did all that was required.

After many days of wandering she came to a place where there was a giant, who was about to eat her, but when he knew her for Don Juan's wife he worshipped her and sent her on her way. Soon she was found by a young giantess who, too, was about to eat her, but when she learned that Maria was the wife of Don Juan she carried her to her own house and hid her, saying that she must be cared for a while until her parents should return, for they might eat her without asking who she was. When the old giant and his wife came back, they told her that she must stay with them for a while, until they could find out about the whereabouts of Don Juan, when they would help her further.

They were very good to her, for, said they, "Don Juan is not only king of the animals but of the giants and monsters of every kind."

Then the giants took her to Don Juan's city and found her a place in the house of an old childless couple, and there she made her home. But Don Juan had taken another wife, the Lady Loriana, and the new wife saw the old and desired her for a servant. So the Princess Maria became a servant of her rival, and often sat in old rags under the stairs at her work, while her faithless husband passed her without seeing her.

The poor girl was torn with jealousy and spent much time thinking about how she might win her husband again. So she asked the ring for a toy in the form of a beautiful little chick, just from the egg.

The Lady Loriana saw the pretty toy and begged for it. "No," said Maria, "unless you grant me a little favour, that I may sleep on the floor tonight in your room." So Loriana, suspecting no deceit, agreed.

That night Maria wished on her ring that Loriana might be overcome with sleep, and again that her own rags might be transformed into royal raiment and that her tiara should glitter on her forehead. Then she went to the head of the bed and called Don Juan. At first he would not answer, then, without turning to look at the speaker, he bade her go away, as his wife would be angry. "But that is not your wife, Don Juan," said Maria; "I am your true wife, Maria. Look at my dress and the jewels on my forehead – my face, the ring on my finger." And Don Juan saw that she was indeed the deserted wife, and after he had heard the sad story of her wanderings he loved her afresh. The next day at noontime Maria was not to be found, although Dona

Loriana looked everywhere. At last she looked into Don Juan's room, and there, locked in each other's arms fast asleep, were Don Juan and Princess Maria.

Loriana aroused them, angrily saying to Maria, "Why do you wish to steal my husband? You must leave this house at once." But Maria resisted saying, "No, he is not your husband but mine, and I will not give him up." And so they quarrelled long and bitterly, but at last agreed to be judged by the council.

There each told her story, and Maria showed Don Juan's enchanted ring, which worked its wonders for her but would not obey the Lady Loriana.

When the matter was decided, it was the judgement of all, including the Archbishop, that Maria was the lawful wife, but that she and Don Juan must go away and never return.

So Don Juan and the Princess Maria went away and lived long and happily.

Suac and His Adventures

ONCE UPON A TIME, in a certain town in Pampanga, there lived a boy named Suac. In order to try his fortune, one day he went a-hunting with Sunga and Sacu in Mount Telapayong. When they reached the mountain, they spread their nets, and made their dogs ready for the chase, to see if any wild animals would come to that place. Not long afterwards they captured a large hog. They took it under a large tree and killed it. Then Sunga and Suac went out into the forest again.

Sacu was left to prepare their food. While he was busy cooking, he heard a voice saying, "Ha, ha! what a nice meal you are preparing! Hurry up! I am hungry." On looking up, Sacu saw on the top of the tree a horrible creature – a very large black man with a long beard. This was Pugut.

Sacu said to him, "*Aba*! I am not cooking this food for you. My companions and I are hungry."

"Well, let us see who shall have it, then," said Pugut as he came down the tree. At first Sacu did not want to give him the food; but Pugut knocked the hunter down, and before he had time to recover had eaten up all the food. Then he climbed the tree again. When Sunga and Suac came back, Sunga said to Sacu, "Is the food ready? Here is a deer that we have caught."

Sacu answered, "When the food was ready, Pugut came and ate it all. I tried to prevent him, but in vain: I could not resist him."

"Well," said Sunga, "let me be the cook while you and Suac are the hunters." Then Sacu and Suac went out, and Sunga was left to cook. The food was no sooner ready than Pugut came again, and ate it all as before. So when the hunters returned, bringing a hog with them, they still had nothing to eat.

Accordingly Suac was left to cook, and his companions went away to hunt again. Suac roasted the hog. Pugut smelled it. He looked down, and said, "Ha, ha! I have another cook; hurry up! boy, I am hungry."

"I pray you, please do not deprive us of this food too," said Suac.

"I must have it, for I am hungry," said Pugut. "Otherwise I shall eat you up." When the hog was roasted a nice brown, Pugut came down the tree. But Suac placed the food near the fire and stood by it; and when Pugut tried to seize it, the boy pushed him into the fire. Pugut's beard was burnt, and it became kinky. The boy then ran to a deep pit. He covered it on the top with grass. Pugut did not stay to eat the food, but followed Suac. Suac was very cunning. He stood on the opposite side of the pit, and said, "I pray you, do not step on my grass!"

"I am going to eat you up," said Pugut angrily, as he stepped on the grass and fell into the pit. The boy covered the pit with stones and earth, thinking that Pugut would perish there; but he was mistaken. Suac had not gone far when he saw Pugut following him; but just then he saw, too, a crocodile. He stopped and resolutely waited for Pugut, whom he gave a blow and pushed into the mouth of the crocodile. Thus Pugut was destroyed.

Suac then took his victim's club, and returned under the tree. After a while his companions came back. He related to them how he had overcome Pugut, and then they ate. The next day they returned to town.

Suac, on hearing that there was a giant who came every night into the neighbourhood to devour people, went one night to encounter the giant.

When the giant came, he said, "You are just the thing for me to eat." But Suac gave him a deadly blow with Pugut's club, and the giant tumbled down dead.

Later Suac rid the islands of all the wild monsters, and became the ruler over his people.

The Three Brothers

ONCE UPON A TIME, when wishing was having, there dwelt in the joyous village of Delight a poor farmer, Tetong, with his loving wife Maria. His earning for a day's toil was just enough to sustain them; yet they were peaceful and happy. Nevertheless they thought that their happiness could not be complete unless they had at least one child. So morning and night they would kneel before their rustic altar and pray God to grant them their desire. As they were faithful in their purpose, their wish was fulfilled. A son was born to them, and joy filled their hearts. The couple's love for their child grew so intense that they craved for another, and then for still another. The Lord was mindful of their prayers; and so, as time went on, two more sons were born to them. The second son they named Felipe; and the youngest, Juan. The name of the oldest was Pedro. All three boys were lovely and handsome, and they greatly delighted their parents.

In the course of time, however, when they were about eight, seven and six years old, Pedro, Felipe and Juan became monstrously great eaters. Each would eat at a single meal six or seven *chupas* of rice: consequently their father was obliged to work very hard, for he had five mouths to feed. In this state of affairs, Tetong felt that, although these children had been born to him and his wife as an increase of their happiness, they would finally exhaust what little he had. Nor was Maria any the less aware of the gluttony of her sons. By degrees their love for their sons ripened into hatred, and at last Tetong resolved to do away with his children.

One night, while he and his wife were sitting before their dim light and their three sons were asleep, Tetong said to his wife, "Do you not think it would be better to get rid of our sons? As you see, we are daily becoming poorer and poorer because of them. I have decided to cast them away into some distant wild forest, where they may feed themselves on fruits or roots."

On hearing these words of her husband, Maria turned pale: her blood ran cold in her veins. But what could she do? She felt the same distress as her husband. After a few moments of silence, she replied in a faltering voice, "My husband, you may do as you wish." Accordingly Tetong made ready the necessary provisions for the journey, which consisted of a sack of rice and some preserved fish.

The next morning, on the pretext of planting camotes and corn on the hill some thirty miles away from the village, he ordered his sons to accompany him. When they came to a forest, their father led them through a circuitous path, and at last took them to the hill. As soon as they arrived there, each set to work: one cut down trees, another built a shed, and the others cleared a piece of land in which to plant the camotes and corn.

After two weeks their provisions were almost used up. Tetong then called his sons together, and said to them, "My sons, we have very little to eat now. I am going to leave you for some days: I am going back to our village to get rice and fish. Be very good to one another, and continue working, for our camotes will soon have roots, and our corn ears." Having said these words, he blessed them and left.

Days, weeks and months elapsed, but Tetong did not reappear. The corn bore ears, and the camotes produced big sound roots; but these were not sufficient to support the three brothers. Nor did they know the way back to their home. At last, realizing that their father and mother did not care for them anymore, they agreed to wander about and look for food. They roved through woods, thickets and jungles. At last, fatigued and with bodies tired and bruised, they came to a wide river, on the bank of which they stopped to rest. While they were bewailing their unhappy lot, they caught sight, on the other side of the river, of banana trees with bunches of ripe fruit. They determined to get those fruits; but, as they knew nothing about swimming, they had to cut down bamboos and join them together to bridge the stream. So great was their hunger that each ate three bunches of the ripe bananas. After they had satisfied their hunger, they continued on their way refreshed.

Soon they came upon a dark abyss. Curious to know what it might contain, the three brothers looked down into it, but they could not see the bottom. Not contented, however, with only seeing into the well, they decided to go to the very bottom: so they gathered vines and connected them into a rope.

Pedro was the first to make the attempt, but he could not stand the darkness. Then Felipe tried; but he too became frightened, and could not stay long in the dark. At last Juan's turn came. He went down to the very bottom of the abyss, where he found a vast plain covered with trees and bushes and shrubs. On one side he saw at a short distance a green house. He approached the house, and saw a most beautiful lady sitting at the door. When she saw him, she said to him in friendly tones, "Hail, Juan! I wonder at your coming, for no earthly creature has ever before been here. However, you are welcome to my house." With words of compliment Juan accepted her invitation, and entered the house. He was kindly received by that lady, Maria. They fell in love with each other, and she agreed to go with Juan to his home.

They had talked together but a short while, when Maria suddenly told Juan to hide, for her guardian, the giant, was coming. Soon the monster appeared, and said to Maria in a terrible voice, "You are concealing someone. I smell human flesh." She denied that she was, but the giant searched all corners of the house. At last Juan was found, and he boldly fought with the monster. He received many wounds, but they were easily healed by Maria's magic medicine. After a terrific struggle, the giant was killed. Maria applauded Juan's valour. She gave him food, and related stories to him while he was eating. She also told him of her neighbour Isabella, none the less beautiful than she. Juan, in turn, told her of many things in his own home that were not found in that subterranean plain.

When he had finished eating and had recovered his strength, Juan said that they had better take Isabella along with them too. Maria agreed to this. Accordingly Juan set out to get Isabella. When he came to her house, she was looking out the window. As soon as she saw him, she exclaimed in a friendly manner, "O Juan! what have you come here for? Since my birth I have never seen an earthly creature like you!"

"Madam," returned Juan in a low voice, "my appearance before you is due to some Invisible Being I cannot describe to you." The moment Isabella heard these words, she blushed. "Juan," she said, "come up!"

Juan entered, and related to her his unfortunate lot, and how he had found the abyss. Finally, struck with Isabella's fascinating beauty, Juan expressed his love for her. They had not been talking long together when footsteps were heard approaching nearer and nearer. It was her guardian, the seven-headed monster. "Isabella," it growled, with an angry look about, "some human creature must be somewhere in the house."

"There is nobody in the house but me," she exclaimed. The monster, however, insisted. Seeking all about the house, it at last discovered Juan, who at once attacked with his sword. In this encounter he was also successful, cutting off all the seven heads of the monster.

With great joy Juan and Isabella returned to Maria's house. Then the three went to the foot of the well. There Juan found the vine still suspended. He tied one end of it around Isabella's waist, and then she was pulled up by the two brothers waiting above. When they saw her, Pedro and Felipe each claimed her, saying almost at the same time, "What a beauty! She is mine." Isabella assured them that there were other ladies below prettier than she. When he heard these words, Felipe dropped one end of the vine again. When Maria reached the top of the well, Felipe felt glad, and claimed her for himself. As the two brothers each had a maiden now, they would not drop the vine a third time; but finally Maria persuaded them to do so. On seeing only their brother's figure, however, the two unfeeling brothers let go of the vine, and Juan plunged back into the darkness. "O my friends!" said Maria, weeping, "this is not the way to treat a brother. Had it not been for him, we should not be here now." Then she took her magic comb, saying to it, "Comb, if you find Juan dead, revive him; if his legs and arms are broken, restore them." Then she dropped it down the well.

By means of this magic comb, Juan was brought back to life. The moment he was able to move his limbs, he groped his way in the dark, and finally he found himself in the same subterranean plain again. As he knew of no way to get back to earth, he made up his mind to accept his fate.

As he was lazily strolling about, he came to a leafy tree with spreading branches. He climbed up to take a siesta among its fresh branches. Just as he closed his eyes, he heard a voice calling, "Juan, Juan! Wake up! Go to the Land of the Pilgrims, for there your lot awaits you." He opened his eyes and looked about him, but he saw nothing. "It is only a bird," he said, "that is disturbing my sleep." So he shut his eyes again. After some moments the same voice was heard again from the top of the tree. He looked up, but he could not see anyone. However, the voice continued calling to him so loudly that he could not sleep. So he descended from the tree to find that land.

In his wanderings he met an old man wearing very ragged, worn-out clothes. Juan asked him about the Land of the Pilgrims. The old man said to him, "Here, take this piece of cloth, which, as you see, I have torn off my garment, and show it to a hermit you will find living at a little distance from here. Then tell him your wish." Juan took the cloth and went to the hermit. When the hermit saw Juan entering his courtyard without permission, he was very angry. "Hermit," said Juan, "I have come here on a very important mission. While I was sleeping among the branches of a tree, a bird sang to me repeatedly that I must go to the Land of the Pilgrims, where my lot awaits me. I resolved to look for this land. On my way I met an old man, who gave me this piece of cloth and told me to show it to you and ask you about this place I have mentioned." When the hermit saw the cloth, his anger was turned into sorrow and kindness. "Juan," he said, "I have been here a long time, but I have never seen that old man."

Now, this hermit had in his care all species of animals. He summoned them all into his courtyard, and asked each about the Land of the Pilgrims; but none could give any information. When he had asked them all in vain, the hermit told Juan to go to another hermit living some distance away.

Accordingly Juan left to find this hermit. At first, like the other, this hermit was angry on seeing Juan; but when he saw the piece of cloth, his anger was turned into pity and sorrow. Juan told him what he was looking for, and the hermit sounded a loud trumpet. In a moment there was an instantaneous rushing of birds of every description. He asked everyone about the Land of the Pilgrims, but not one knew of the place. But just as Juan was about to leave, suddenly there came an eagle swooping down into the courtyard. When asked if it knew of the Land of the Pilgrims, it nodded its head. The hermit then ordered it to bear Juan to the Land of the Pilgrims. It willingly obeyed, and flew across seas and over mountains with Juan on its back. After Juan had been carried to the wished-for land, the eagle returned to its master.

Here Juan lived with a poor couple, who cared for him as if he were their own child, and he served them in turn. He asked them about the land they were living in. They told him that it was governed by a tyrannical king who had a beautiful daughter. They said that many princes who courted her had been put to death because they had failed to fulfil the tasks required of them. When Juan heard of this beautiful princess, he said to himself, "This is the lot that awaits me. She is to be my wife." So, in spite of the dangers he ran the risk of, he resolved to woo her.

One day, when her tutors were away, he made a kite, to which he fastened a letter addressed to the princess, and flew it. While she was strolling about in her garden, the kite suddenly swooped down before her. She was surprised, and wondered. "What impudent knave," she said, "ventures to let fall his kite in my garden?" She stepped towards the kite, looked at it, and saw the letter written in a bold hand. She read it. After a few moments' hesitation, she replaced it with a letter of her own in which she told him to come under the window of her tower.

When he came there, the princess spoke to him in this manner: "Juan, if you really love me, you must undergo hardships. Show yourself to my father tomorrow, and agree to do all that he commands you to do. Then come back to me." Juan willingly promised to undertake any difficulties for her sake.

The next morning Juan waited at the stairway of the king's palace. The king said to him, "Who are you, and what do you come here for?"

"O king! I am Juan, and I have come here to marry your daughter."

"Very well, Juan, you can have your wish if you perform the task I set you. Take these grains of wheat and plant them in that hill, and tomorrow morning bring me, out of these same grains, newly baked bread for my breakfast. Then you shall be married immediately to my daughter. But if you fail to accomplish this task, you shall be beheaded."

Juan bowed his head low, and left. Sorrowful he appeared before the princess.

"What's the matter, Juan?" she said.

"O my dear princess! your father has imposed on me a task impossible to perform. He gave me these grains of wheat to be planted in that hill, and tomorrow he expects a newly baked loaf of bread from them."

"Don't worry, Juan. Go home now, and tomorrow show yourself to my father. The bread will be ready when he awakes."

The next morning Juan repaired to the palace, and was glad to find the bread already on the table. When the king woke up, he was astonished to see that Juan had performed the task.

"Now, Juan," said the king, "one more task for you. Under my window I have two big jars – one full of mongo, the other of very fine sand. I will mix them, and you have to assort them so that each kind is in its proper jar again." Juan promised to fulfil this task. He passed by the window of the princess, and told her what the king had said. "Go home and come back here tomorrow," she said to him. "The king will find the mongo and sand in their proper jars."

The next morning Juan went back to the palace. The king, just arisen from bed, looked out of the window, and was astounded to see the mongo and sand perfectly assorted. "Well, Juan," said the king, "you have successfully performed the tasks I required of you. But I have one thing more to ask of you. Yesterday afternoon, while my wife and I were walking along the seashore, my gold ring fell into the water. I want you to find it, and bring it to me tomorrow morning."

"Your desire shall be fulfilled, O king!" replied Juan.

He told the princess of the king's wish. "Come here tomorrow just before dawn," she said, "and bring a big basin and a bolo. We will go together to find the ring."

Just before dawn the next day he went to her tower, where she was waiting for him in the disguise of a village maid. They went to the seashore where the ring was supposed to have been lost. There the princess Maria – that was her name – said to him, "Now take your basin and bolo and cut me to pieces. Pour out the chopped mass into the water in which my father's ring was dropped, but take care not to let a single piece of the flesh fall to the ground!"

On hearing these words, Juan stood dumbfounded, and began to weep. Then in an imploring tone he said, "O my beloved! I would rather have you chop my body than chop yours."

"If you love me," she said, "do as I tell you."

Then Juan reluctantly seized the bolo, and with closed eyes cut her body to pieces and poured the mass into the water where the ring was supposed to be. In five minutes there rose from the water the princess with the ring on her finger. But Juan fell asleep; and before he awoke, the ring fell into the water again.

"Oh, how little you love me!" she exclaimed. "The ring fell because you did not catch it quickly from my finger. Cut up my body as before, and pour the mass of flesh into the water again." Accordingly Juan cut her to pieces a second time, and again poured the mass into the water. Then in a short time Maria rose from the water with the ring on her finger; but Juan fell asleep again, and again the ring fell back into the water.

Now Maria was angry: so she cut a gash on his finger, and told him to cut her body to pieces and pour the mass out as before. At last the ring was found again. This time Juan was awake, and he quickly caught the ring as she rose from the water.

That morning Juan went before the king and presented the ring to him. When the monarch saw it, he was greatly astonished, and said to himself, "How does he accomplish all the tasks I have given him? Surely he must be a man of supernatural powers." Raising his head, he said to Juan, "Juan, you are indeed the man who deserves the hand of my daughter; but I want you to do me one more service. This will be the last. Fetch me my horse, for I want to go out hunting today." Now, this horse could run just as fast as the wind. It was a very wild horse too, and no one could catch it except the king himself and the princess.

Juan promised, however, and repaired to Maria's tower. When she learned her father's wish, she went with Juan and helped him catch the horse. After they had caught it, she caught hers too. Then they returned to the palace. Juan and Maria now agreed to run away. So after Juan had tied the king's horse near the stairway, they mounted Maria's horse and rode off rapidly.

When the king could not find his daughter, he got on his horse and started in pursuit of Juan and Maria, who were now some miles ahead. But the king's horse ran so fast that in a few minutes he had almost overtaken the fugitives. Maria, seeing her father behind them, dropped her comb, and in the wink of an eye a thick grove of bamboos blocked the king's way. By his order, a road was made through the bamboo in a very short time. Then he continued his chase; but just as he was about to overtake them a second time, Maria flung down her ring, and there rose up seven high hills behind them. The king was thus delayed again; but his horse shot over these hills as fast as the wind, so that in a few minutes he was once more in sight of the fugitives. This time Maria turned around and spat. Immediately a wide sea appeared behind them. The king gave up his pursuit, and only uttered these words: "O ungrateful daughter!" Then he turned back to his palace.

The young lovers continued their journey until they came to a small village. Here they decided to be married, so they at once went to the village priest. He married them that very day. Juan and Maria now determined to live in that place the rest of their lives, so they bought a house and a piece of land. As time went by, Juan thought of his parents.

One day he asked permission from his wife to visit his father and mother. "You may go," she said; "but remember not to let a single drop of your father's or mother's tears fall on your cheeks, for you will forget me if you do." Promising to remember her words, Juan set out.

When his parents saw him, they were so glad that they embraced him and almost bathed him with tears of joy. Juan forgot Maria. It happened that on the day Juan reached home, Felipe, his brother, was married to Maria, the subterranean lady, and a feast was being held in the family circle. The moment Maria recognized Juan, whom she loved most, she annulled her marriage with Felipe, and wanted to marry Juan. Accordingly the village was called to settle the question, and Maria and Juan were married that same day. The merrymaking and dancing continued.

In the meantime there came, to the surprise of everyone, a beautiful princess riding in a golden carriage drawn by fine horses. She was invited to the dance. While the people were enjoying themselves dancing and singing, they were suddenly drawn together around this princess to see what she was doing. She was sitting in the middle of the hall. Before her she had a dog chained. Then she began to ask the dog these questions:

"Did you not serve a certain king for his daughter?"

"No!" answered the dog.

"Did he not give you grains of wheat to be planted in a hill, and the morning following you were to give him newly baked bread made from the wheat?"

"No!"

"Did he not mix together two jars of mongo and sand, then order you to assort them so that the mongo was in one jar and the sand in the other?"

"No!"

"Do you not remember when you and a princess went together to the seashore to find the ring of her father, and when you cut her body to pieces and poured the chopped mass into the water?"

When Juan, who was watching, heard this last question, he rushed from the ring of people that surrounded her and knelt before her, saying, "O my most precious wife! I implore your forgiveness!" Then the newcomer, who was none other than Maria, Juan's true wife, embraced him, and their former love was restored. So the feast went on. To the great joy of Felipe, Maria, the subterranean lady, was given back to him; and the two couples lived happily the rest of their lives.

The Tuglay and the Bia

LONG AGO, IN THE DAYS of the Mona, the Tuglay lived on a high mountain. He lived very well, for his coconut trees grew on both sides of the mountain. But he had no hemp plants, and so he had to make his clothes of the soft dry sheath that covers the trunk of the coconut palm (bunut). This stuff caught fire easily, and many a time his clothes ignited from the flame where his dinner was cooking, and then he would have to make fresh garments from bunut.

One day he looked from his house over the neighbouring mountains, and saw the village of Koblun. He thought it looked pretty in the distance. Then he looked in another direction, and saw the town of the Malaki Tuangun, and said, "Ah! that is just as nice looking as the Koblun town. I will go and see the town of the Malaki Tuangun."

Immediately he got ready for the journey. He took his spear (that was only half a spear, because the fire had burned off a part of the handle) and his shield, that was likewise only half a shield. He started out, and walked on and on until he reached the mountains called "Pabungan Mangumbiten."

Now, on another mountain there lived a young man named the Malaki Itanawa, with his little sister. They lived alone together, for they were orphans. The young girl said to her brother, "Let us travel over the mountains today."

And the boy answered, "Yes, my sister, we will go."

And the two climbed over the hills, and they reached the Pabungan Mangumbiten soon after the Tuglay. And they were astonished to see the great Tuglay. But when the Tuglay saw the young girl, who was named Bia Itanawa Inelu, he was so bewildered and startled that he turned away his eyes, and could not look at the sister and brother.

Then the girl prepared a betel nut and offered it to the Tuglay, but he did not like to accept it. But when she had pressed it upon him many times, he took the betel and chewed it.

Then the girl said, "Come with my brother and me to my house, for we have no companion."

But when the girl saw the Tuglay hesitate, she asked him, "Where were you going when we met you?"

The Tuglay answered, "I want to go to the town of the Malaki Tuangun, for to my home has come the word that the Malaki is a mighty man, and his sister a great lady."

Then the girl looked at the Tuglay, and said, "If you want to make ready to go to the Malaki Tuangun's town, you ought to put on your good trousers and a nice jacket."

At that, the Tuglay looked mournful; for he was a poor man, and had no fine clothes. Then, when the girl saw how the case stood, she called for beautiful things, such as a malaki wears – fine hemp trousers, beaded jacket, good war shield and brass-bound spear, earplugs of pure ivory, and eight necklaces of beads and gold. Straightway at the summons of the Bia, all the fine things appeared; and the Tuglay got ready to go away. He was no longer the poor Tuglay. His name was now the Malaki Dugdag Lobis Maginsulu. Like two big moons, his ivory earplugs shone; when he moved his shield, flames of living fire shot from it; and when he held up his spear, the day would grow dark, because he was a brave man. His new clothes he sent upon the swift wind to the Malaki Tuangun's town.

When the Tuglay started, the Bia gave him her own brass betel box (katakia) to take with him. It was a katakia that made sounds, and was called a "screaming katakia".

"May I eat the betel nut from your box?" asked the man; and she replied, "Yes, but do not throw away the other things in the box."

The Malaki Dugdag Lobis Maginsulu walked on until he reached the town of the Malaki Tuangun, and sat down on the ground before the house. The Malaki Tuangun was a great brass-smith: he made katakia and other objects of brass, and hence was called the Malaki Tuangun Katakia. As soon as he heard the other malaki call from outside, "May I come up into your house?" he sent down eight of his slaves to look and see who wanted to visit him.

And the eight slaves brought word to their master that the Malaki Dugdag Lobis Maginsulu waited to enter.

Then the Malaki Tuangun Katakia called to his visitor, "Come up, if you can keep from bringing on a fight, because there are many showers in my town."

Then the other malaki went up the steps into the house, and the Malaki Tuangun said to him, "You shall have a good place to sit in my house, a place where nobody ever sat before."

Then the Malaki Tuangun prepared a betel nut for his guest. But the Malaki Dugdag Lobis Maginsulu would not take the betel nut from him. So the Malaki Tuangun called his sister, who was called Bia Tuangun Katakia, and said to her, "You go outside and prepare a betel nut for the Malaki."

As soon as the Bia had finished preparing the betel, she took the (screaming?) katakia from the Malaki, and set it on the floor. Then the Malaki Dugdag Lobis Maginsulu took the betel nut from the lady. When he had finished chewing it, he stood up and went to the place where the Bia Tuangun Katakia was sitting, and he lay down beside her, and said, "Come, put away your work, and comb my hair."

"No, I don't like to comb your hair," she replied.

The Malaki was displeased at this retort, so at last the woman agreed to comb his hair, for she did not want to see the Malaki angry. By and by the Malaki felt sleepy while his hair was being combed; and he said to the Bia, "Do not wake me up."

He fell asleep, and did not waken until the next day. Then he married the Bia Tuangun Katakia.

After they had been married for three months, the Bia said to the Malaki, "The best man I know is the Manigthum. He was my first husband."

But the Manigthum had left home, and had gone off to do some big fighting. He killed the Malaki Taglapida Pabungan, and he killed the Malaki Lindig Ramut ka Langit.

After the Manigthum had slain these great men, he came back to the home of his wife. When he came near the house he saw, lying down on the ground under the kinarum tree, the things that he had given his wife before he went away – pendants of pearl, bracelets and leglets of brass, gold necklaces (kamagi), hair ornaments of dyed goats' hair and birds' down, finger rings, and leg-bands of twisted wire hung with bells. As he looked at the beautiful ornaments all thrown on the ground, he heard the voice of the Malaki Dugdag Lobis Manginsulu calling to him, "Do not come up, because your wife is mine."

Then the two malaki went to fighting with sword and spear. After a sharp fight, the Manigthum was killed, and the Malaki Dugdag Lobis Maginsulu had the Bia for his wife.

The Woman and the Squirrel

ONE DAY A WOMAN went out to find water. She had no water to drink, because all the streams were dried up. As she went along, she saw some water in a leaf. She drank it, and washed her body. As soon as she had drunk the water, her head began to hurt. Then she went home, spread out a mat, lay down on it, and

went to sleep. She slept for nine days. When she woke up, she took a comb and combed her hair. As she combed it, a squirrel-baby came out from her hair. After the baby had been in the house one week, it began to grow and jump about. It stayed up under the roof of the house.

One day the Squirrel said to his mother, "O mother! I want you to go to the house of the Datu who is called 'sultan', and take these nine kamagi and these nine finger rings to pay for the sultan's daughter, because I want to marry her."

Then the mother went to the sultan's house and remained there an hour. The sultan said, "What do you want?"

The woman answered, "Nothing. I came for betel nuts." Then the woman went back home.

The Squirrel met her, and said, "Where are my nine necklaces?"

"Here they are," said the woman.

But the Squirrel was angry at his mother, and bit her with his little teeth.

Again he said to his mother, "You go there and take the nine necklaces."

So the woman started off again. When she reached the sultan's house, she said to him, "I have come with these nine necklaces and these nine finger rings that my son sends to you."

"Yes," said the sultan; "but I want my house to become gold, and I want all my plants to become gold, and everything I have to turn into gold."

But the woman left the presents to pay for the sultan's daughter. The sultan told her that he wanted his house to be turned into gold that very night. Then the woman went back and told all this to her son. The Squirrel said, "That is good, my mother."

Now, when night came, the Squirrel went to the sultan's house, and stood in the middle of the path, and called to his brother, the Mouse, "My brother, come out! I want to see you."

Then the great Mouse came out. All the hairs of his coat were of gold, and his eyes were of glass.

The Mouse said, "What do you want of me, my brother Squirrel?"

"I called you," answered the Squirrel, "for your gold coat. I want some of that to turn the sultan's house into gold."

Then the Squirrel bit the skin of the Mouse, and took off some of the gold, and left him. Then he began to turn the sultan's things into gold. First of all, he rubbed the gold on the betel nut trees of the sultan; next, he rubbed all the other trees and all the plants; third, he rubbed the house and all the things in it. Then the sultan's town you could see as in a bright day. You would think there was no night there – always day.

All this time, the sultan was asleep. When he woke up, he was so frightened to see all his things, and his house, of gold, that he died in about two hours.

Then the Squirrel and the daughter of the sultan were married. The Squirrel stayed in her father's home for one month, and then they went to live in the house of the Squirrel's mother. And they took from the sultan's place, a deer, a fish and all kinds of food. After the sultan's daughter had lived with the Squirrel for one year, he took off his coat and became a Malaki T'oluk Waig.

Tales of Cunning, Deceit & Folly

MANY OF THE TRICKSTER tales found in the Philippines usually have a Juan at the centre: Juan Tamad for the Tagalogs, Juan Usong or Osong for the Bicolanos or Juan Pusong for the Visayas. These characters are normally boys or young men who are either lazy (*tamad*) or mischievous; they are usually able to get away with their actions, either by tricking others or exposing the unfairness or injustice of the authorities. However, some stories of cunning focus on a young woman who upends or showcases her cleverness as part of her virtuous traits.

Many of the trickster stories have also been adapted from precolonial influences, such as localized versions of *The Arabian Nights*. Some trickster tales are also conflated with numbskull tales or 'tales of the fool', which are usually retold for comedic purposes. The Kapampangan tale 'Juan Wearing a Monkey's Skin' combines a trickster tale with a quest narrative. In the story, the monkey-son Juan is able to use his wiles to make his way across the world and win the hand of a beautiful princess, whereupon he is able to shed his monkey's skin and become a human. On the opposite end of the spectrum is the tale of 'Sagacious Marcela'. Here the young heroine is able to outsmart the king and his absurd requests, showing her intelligence to the kingdom and earning her place as the prince's wife.

The Adventures of Juan

JUAN WAS LAZY, Juan was a fool, and his mother never tired of scolding him and emphasizing her words with a beating. When Juan went to school he made more noise at his study than anybody else, but his reading was only gibberish.

His mother sent him to town to buy meat to eat with the boiled rice, and he bought a live crab which he set down in the road and told to go to his mother and be cooked for dinner. The crab promised, but as soon as Juan's back was turned ran in the other direction.

Juan went home after a while and asked for the crab, but there was none, and they ate their rice without ulam. His mother then went herself and left Juan to care for the baby. The baby cried and Juan examined it to find the cause, and found the soft spot on its head. "Aha! It has a boil. No wonder it cries!" And he stuck a knife into the soft spot, and the baby stopped crying. When his mother came back, Juan told her about the boil and that the baby was now asleep, but the mother said it was dead, and she beat Juan again.

Then she told Juan that if he could do nothing else he could at least cut firewood, so she gave him a bolo and sent him to the woods.

He found what looked to him like a good tree and prepared to cut it, but the tree was a magic tree and said to Juan, "Do not cut me and I will give you a goat that shakes silver money from its whiskers." Juan agreed, and the bark of the tree opened and the goat came out, and when Juan told him to shake his whiskers, money dropped out. Juan was very glad, for at last he had something he would not be beaten for. On his way home he met a friend, and told him of his good fortune. The man made him dead drunk and substituted another goat which had not the ability to shake money from its whiskers, and when the new goat was tried at home poor Juan was beaten and scolded.

Back he went to the tree, which he threatened to cut down for lying to him, but the tree said, "No, do not kill me and I will give you a magic net which you may cast even on dry ground or into a treetop and it will return full of fish," and the tree did even so.

Again he met the friend, again he drank tuba until he was dead drunk, and again a worthless thing was substituted, and on reaching home he was beaten and scolded.

Once more Juan went to the magic tree, and this time he received a magic pot, always full of rice; and spoons always full of whatever ulam might be wished, and these went the way of the other gifts, to the false friend.

The fourth time he asked of the tree he was given a magic stick that would without hands beat and kill anything that the owner wished. "Only say to it 'Boombye, boomba', and it will obey your word," said the tree.

When Juan met the false friend again, the false friend asked him what gift he had this time. "It is only a stick that if I say, 'Boombye, boomba', will beat you to death," said Juan, and with that the stick leaped from his hand and began to belabour the wicked man. "Lintic na cahoy ito ay! Stop it and I will give you everything I stole from you." Juan ordered the stick to stop, but made the man, bruised and sore, carry the net, the pot and the spoons, and lead the goat to Juan's home. There the goat shook silver from his beard till Juan's three brothers and his mother had all they could carry, and they dined from the pot and the magic spoons until they were full to their mouths.

"Now," said Juan, "you have beaten me and called me a fool all my life, but you are not ashamed to take good things when I get them. I will show you something else. Boombye, boomba!" and the stick began to beat them all. Quickly they agreed that Juan was head of the house, and he ordered the beating to stop.

Juan now became rich and respected, but he never trusted himself far from his stick day or night. One night a hundred robbers came to break into the house, to take all his goods, and kill him, but he said to the stick, "Boombye, boomba!" and with the swiftness of lightning the stick flew around, and all those struck fell dead till there was not one left. Juan was never troubled again by robbers, and in the end married a princess and lived happily ever after.

The Buso and the Cat

THE CAT IS THE BEST ANIMAL. She keeps us from the Buso. One night the Buso came into the house, and said to the cat, "I should like to eat your mistress."

"I will let you do it," replied the cat; "but first you must count all the hairs of my coat."

So the Buso began to count. But while he was counting, the cat kept wriggling her tail, and sticking up her back. That made her fur stand up on end, so that the Buso kept losing count, and never knew where he left off. And while the Buso was still trying to count the cat's hairs, daylight came.

This is one reason why we must not kill the cat. If a Bagobo should kill a cat, it would make him very sick. He would get skinny, and die. Some Bagobo have been known to kill the cat; but they always got sick afterwards

The Artificial Earthquake

THERE WAS ONCE in another town a man who had three daughters, all very beautiful. But one of them had an admirer, who by some means excited the old man's wrath, and the daughter was sent to a distant place.

This in turn made the young man angry, and he determined to have revenge. He took a strong rope and attached it to one of the corner upright posts of the house, and waiting till it was dark and still inside, he hid behind a tree and began to pull the rope, alternately hauling and slacking.

"Oh!" said one of the girls, "there is an earthquake."

The old man jumped up and, seizing his crucifix, began to recite the prayers against earthquakes. But the trembling kept up. For more than an hour the old man prayed to all the saints in the calendar, but the earthquake still shook the house.

Then the earthquake stopped a moment, and a voice called him to come outside. His daughters begged him not to go, for said they, "You never can stand such a terrible earthquake." Taking his saw, his axe and his long bolo, the old man went down, only to find everything quiet outside. He began to explore the surroundings of the house to see if he could find the cause of the disturbance, and fell over the rope. With that he began to curse and swear, saying, "May lightning blast the one of ill-omened ancestry who has shaken my house, frightened my family, and broken my bones," and many other harsh things, but he got no answer but a laugh, and the young man had his revenge.

The Charcoal-Maker Who Became King

ONCE UPON A TIME there lived a king who had one beautiful daughter. When she was old enough to be married, her father, as was the custom in ancient times, made a proclamation throughout his kingdom thus: "Whosoever shall be able to bring me ten carloads of money for ten successive days shall have the hand of my beautiful daughter and also my crown. If, however, anyone undertakes and fails, he shall be put to death."

A boy, the only son of a poor charcoal-maker, heard this announcement in his little town. He hurried home to his mother, and said that he wanted to marry the beautiful princess and to be king of their country. The mother, however, paid no attention to what her foolish son had said, for she well knew that they had very little money.

The next day the boy, as usual, took his hatchet and went to the forest to cut wood. He started to cut down a very huge tree, which would take him several days to finish. While he was busy with his hatchet, he seemed to hear a voice saying, "Cut this tree no more. Dip your hand into the hole of the trunk, and you will find a purse which will give you all the money you wish." At first he did not pay any attention to the voice, but finally he obeyed it. To his surprise, he got the purse, but found it empty. Disappointed, he angrily threw it away; but as the purse hit the ground, silver money rolled merrily out of it. The youth quickly gathered up the coins; then, picking up the purse, he started for home, filled with happiness.

When he reached the house, he spread *petates* over the floor of their little hut, called his mother, and began shaking the purse. The old woman was amazed and delighted when she saw dollars coming out in what seemed to be an inexhaustible stream. She did not ask her son where he had found the purse, but was now thoroughly convinced that he could marry the beautiful princess and be king afterwards.

The next morning she ordered her son to go to the palace to inform his Majesty that he would bring him the money he demanded in exchange for his daughter and his crown. The guard of the palace, however, thought that the youth was crazy; for he was poorly dressed and had rude manners. Therefore he refused to let him in. But their talk was overheard by the king, who ordered the guard to present the youth before him. The king read the announcement, emphasizing the part which said that in case of failure the contestant would be put to death. To this condition the charcoal-maker agreed. Then he asked the king to let him have a talk with his daughter. The meeting was granted, and the youth was extremely pleased with the beauty and vivacity of the princess.

After he had bidden her goodbye, he told the king to send the cars with him to get the first ten carloads of money. The cars were sent with guards. The drivers and the guards of the convoy were astonished when they saw the poor charcoal-maker fill the ten cars with bright new silver dollars. The princess, too, at first was very much pleased with such a large sum of money.

Five days went by, and the youth had not failed to send the amount of money required. "Five days more, and I shall surely be married!" said the princess to herself. "Married? Yes, married life is like music without words. But will it be in my case? My future husband is ugly, unrefined, and of low descent. But he is rich. Yes, rich; but what are riches if I am going to be wretched? No, I will not marry him for all the world. I will play a trick on him."

The next day the guard informed her that the riches of the young man were inexhaustible, for the purse from which he got his money seemed to be magical. When she heard this, she commanded the guard to tell the young man that she wished to see him alone. Filled with joy because of this sign of her favour, the youth hastened to the palace, conducted by the guard. The princess entertained him regally, and tried all sorts of tricks to get possession of the magical purse. At last she succeeded in inducing him to go to sleep. While he was unconscious, the deceitful princess stole the purse and left him alone in the chamber.

When he awoke, he saw that the princess had deserted him and that his purse was gone. "Surely I am doomed to die if I don't leave this kingdom at once," said he to himself. "My purse is gone, and I cannot now fulfil my contract." He at once hurried home, told his parents to abandon their home and town, and he himself started on a journey for another kingdom. After much travelling, he reached mountainous places, and had eaten but little for many a day.

By good luck he came across a tree heavily laden with fruits. The tree was strange to him; but the delicious appearance of its fruit, and his hunger, tempted him to try some. While he was eating, he was terrified to find that two horns had appeared on his forehead. He tried his best to pull them off, but in vain. The next day he saw another tree, whose fruit appeared even more tempting. He climbed it, picked some fruits, and ate them. To his surprise, his horns immediately fell off. He wrapped some of this fruit up in his handkerchief, and then went back to find the tree whose fruit he had eaten the day before. He again ate some of its fruit, and again two horns grew out of his head. Then he ate some of the other kind, and the horns fell off. Confident now that he had a means of recovering his purse, he gathered some of the horn-producing fruits, wrapped them in his shirt, and started home. By this time he had been travelling for nearly two years, and his face had so changed that he could not be recognized by his own parents, or by his townmates who had been hired by the king to search for him for execution.

When he reached his town, he decided to place himself in the king's palace as a helper of the royal cook. As he was willing to work without pay, he easily came to terms with the cook. One of the conditions of their agreement was that the cook would tell him whatever the king or the king's family were talking about. After a few months the charcoal-maker proved himself to be an excellent cook. In fact, he was now doing all the cooking in the palace; for the chief cook spent most of his time somewhere else, coming home only at meal times.

Now comes the fun of the story. One day while the cook was gone, the youth ground up the two kinds of fruit. He mixed the kind that produced horns with the king's food: the other kind, which caused the horns to fall off, he mixed with water and put into a jar. The cook arrived, and everything was ready. The table was prepared, and the king and his family were called to eat. The queen and the king and the beautiful princess, who were used to wearing golden crowns set with diamonds and other precious stones, were then to be seen with sharp ugly horns on their heads. When the king discovered that they all had horns, he summoned the cook at once, and asked, "What kind of food did you give us?"

"The same food that your Highness ate a week ago," replied the cook, who was terrified to see the royal family with horns.

"Cook, go and find a doctor. Don't tell him or anyone else that we have horns. Tell the doctor that the king wants him to perform an operation," ordered the king.

The cook set out immediately to find a doctor; but he was intercepted by the charcoal-maker, who was eager to hear the king's order. "Where are you going? Say, cook, why are you in such a hurry? What is the matter?"

"Don't bother me!" said the cook. "I am going to find a doctor. The king and his family have horns on their heads, and I am ordered to find a doctor who can take them off."

"I can make those horns fall off. You needn't bother to find a doctor. Here, try some of this food, cook!" said the helper, giving him some of the same food he had prepared for the king. The cook tried it, and it was good; but, to his alarm, he felt two horns on his head. To prevent rumours from reaching the ears of the king, the youth then gave the cook a glass of the water he had prepared, and the horns fell off. While the charcoal-maker was playing this trick on the cook, he related the story of his magical purse, and how he had lost it.

"Change your clothes, then, and get ready, and I will present you to the king as the doctor," said the cook.

The helper then dressed himself just like a doctor of surgery, and was conducted by the cook into the king's presence.

"Doctor, I want you to do all you can, and use the best of your wisdom, to take off these horns from our heads. But before doing it, promise me first that you will not unfold the matter to the people; for my queen, my daughter and I would rather die than be known to have lived with horns. If you succeed in taking them off, you shall inherit one-half of my kingdom and have the hand of my fair daughter," said the king.

"I do promise. But listen, O king! In order to get rid of those horns, you must undergo the severest treatment, which may cause your death," replied the doctor.

"It is no matter. If we should die, we would rather die hornless than live with horns," said the king.

After the agreement was written out, the doctor ordered the treatment. The king and the queen were to be whipped until they bled, while the princess was to dance with the doctor until she became exhausted. These were the remedies given by the doctor.

While the king and queen were being whipped, the doctor who, we must remember, was the cook's helper, went to the kitchen to get the jar of water which he had prepared. The cruel servants who were scourging the king and the queen took much delight in their task, and did not quit until the king and queen were almost lifeless. The doctor forgot the royal couple while he was dancing with the princess, and found them just about to die. He succeeded, however, in giving them some of the fruit water he had made ready, and the horns fell off. The princess, exhausted, also asked for a drink when she stopped dancing, and the horns fell off her head too.

A few days afterwards the king and the queen died, and the doctor succeeded to the throne, with the beautiful princess as his wife. Then the doctor told her that he was the poor charcoal-maker who had owned the magic purse that she had stolen from him. As soon as he was seated on the throne, he made his friend the cook one of his courtiers. Although the new king was uneducated and unrefined, he welcomed all wise men to his palace as his counsellors, and his kingdom prospered as it had never done under its previous rulers.

The Clever Husband and Wife

PEDRO HAD BEEN LIVING as a servant in a doctor's house for more than nine years. He wanted very much to have a wife, but he had no business of any kind with which to support one.

One day he felt very sad. His look of dejection did not escape the notice of his master, who said, "What is the matter, my boy? Why do you look so sad? Is there anything I can do to comfort you?"

"Oh, yes!" said Pedro.

"What do you want me to do?" asked the doctor.

"Master," the man replied, "I want a wife, but I have no money to support one."

"Oh, don't worry about money!" replied his master. "Be ready tomorrow, and I will let you marry the woman you love."

The next day the wedding was held. The doctor let the couple live in a cottage not far from his hacienda, and he gave them two hundred pieces of gold. When they received the money, they hardly knew what to do with it, as Pedro had never had any business of any sort. "What shall we do after we have spent all our money?" asked the wife. "Oh, we can ask the doctor for more," answered Pedro.

Years passed by, and one day the couple had not even a cent with which to buy food. So Pedro went to the doctor and asked him for some money. The doctor, who had always been kind to them, gave him twenty pieces of gold; but these did not last very long, and it was not many days before the money was all spent. The husband and wife now thought of another way by which they could get money from the doctor.

Early one day Pedro went to the doctor's house weeping. He said that his wife had died, and that he had nothing with which to pay for her burial. (He had rubbed onion juice on his eyes, so that he looked as if he were really crying.) When the doctor heard Pedro's story, he pitied the man, and said to him, "What was the matter with your wife? How long was she sick?"

"For two days," answered Pedro.

"Two days!" exclaimed the doctor, "why did you not call me, then? We should have been able to save her. Well, take this money and see that she gets a decent burial."

Pedro returned home in good spirits. He found his wife Marta waiting for him at the door, and they were happy once more; but in a month the money was all used up, and they were on the point of starving again.

Now, the doctor had a married sister whom Pedro and his wife had worked for off and on after their marriage. Pedro told his wife to go to the doctor's sister, and tell her that he was dead and that she had no money to pay for the burial. Marta set out, as she was told; and when she arrived at the sister's house, the woman said to her, "Marta, why are you crying?"

"My husband is dead, and I have no money to pay for his burial," said Marta, weeping.

"You have served us well, so take this money and see that masses are said for your husband's soul," said the kind-hearted mistress.

That evening the doctor visited his sister to see her son who was sick. The sister told him that Marta's husband had died. "No," answered the doctor, "it was Marta who died." They argued and argued, but could not agree; so they finally decided to send one of the doctor's servants to see which one was dead. When Pedro saw the servant coming, he told his wife to lie flat and stiff in the bed as if she were dead; and when the servant entered, Pedro showed him his dead wife.

The servant returned, and told the doctor and his sister that it was Marta who was dead; but the sister would not believe him, for she said that perhaps he was joking. So they sent another servant. This time Marta made Pedro lie down stiff and flat in the bed; and when the servant entered the house, he saw the man lying as if dead. So he hurried back and told the doctor and his sister what he had seen. Now neither knew what to believe. The next morning, therefore, the doctor and his sister together visited the cottage of Pedro. They found the couple both lying as if dead. After examining them, however, the doctor realized that they were merely feigning death. He was so pleased by the joke, and so glad to find his old servants alive, that he took them home with him and made them stay at his house.

The Enchanted Shell

IN THE OLDEN TIME there lived a man and his wife who had no son. They prayed that they might have a son, even if he were only like a little shell. When their son was born, he was very small, and just like a shell, so he was named Shell.

One day Shell asked permission of his mother to go and get some food. His mother at first would not let him, as she was afraid he would meet some animal which would kill him; but at last she consented, and he set out.

He went to the river, where some women were catching fish and putting them into baskets. One of them laid her basket on the grass near the river and Shell crept into it. In a few minutes the woman picked up her basket and started for home. All at once Shell began to cry, "Rain! Rain!" The woman was so frightened at hearing the fishes talk, as she supposed, that she threw down her basket and ran away. Then Shell took the basket full of fish to his mother.

The next day Shell went out again. He saw an old man walking along the road and carrying the head of a cow, so he followed him. The old man went into the house of a friend, leaving the cow's head hanging on the fence. Shell climbed up the fence and got into the cow's ear, keeping very quiet. When the old man came out of the house he took the head and continued his walk. As he reached a desert place called Cahana-an, the head began to say, "Ay! Ay!" The old man became so frightened that he threw the head away, and Shell carried it home.

Days passed. Shell told his mother that he was in love with a beautiful daughter of the chief and must have her for his wife. The poor mother was amazed and did not want to present his request to the chief. "My dear Shell," she said, "you are beside yourself." But he urged her and urged her, until at last she went. She begged the chief's pardon for her boldness and made known her errand. The chief was astonished, but agreed to ask his daughter if she were willing to take Shell for a husband. Much to his surprise and anger she stated that she was willing to marry him. Her father was so enraged that he exclaimed, "I consider you as being lower than my servants. If you marry this Shell I will drive you out of the village." But Shell and the girl were married, and escaped from the town to a little house in the fields, where they lived in great sorrow for a week. But at the end of that time, one night at midnight, the shell began to turn into a good-looking man, for he had been enchanted at his birth by an evil spirit. When his wife saw how handsome he was, she was very glad, and afterwards the chief received them back into his favour.

The Fifty-One Thieves

THERE WERE ONCE two brothers, Juan and Pedro. Pedro was rich and was the elder, but Juan was very poor and gained his living by cutting wood. Juan became so poor at last that he was forced to ask alms from his brother, or what was only the same thing, a loan. After much pleading, Pedro gave his brother enough rice for a single meal, but repenting of such generosity, went and took it off the fire, as his brother's wife was cooking it, and carried it home again.

Juan then set out for the woods, thinking he might be able to find a few sticks that he could exchange for something to eat, and went much farther than he was accustomed to go. He came to a road he did not know and followed it for some distance to where it led to a great rocky bluff and there came to an end.

Juan did not know exactly what to think of such an abrupt ending to the roadway, and sat down behind a large rock to meditate. As he sat there a voice within the cliff said, "Open the door," and a door in the cliff opened itself. A man richly dressed came out, followed by several others, whom he told that they were going to a town at a considerable distance. He then said, "Shut the door," and the door closed itself again.

Juan was not sure whether anyone else was inside, but he was no coward and besides he thought he might as well be murdered as starved to death, so when the robbers had ridden away to a safe distance without seeing him, he went boldly up to the cliff and said, "Open the door." The door opened as obediently to him as to the robber, and he went in. He found himself inside a great cavern filled with money, jewels and rich stuffs of every kind.

Hastily gathering more than enough gold and jewels to make him rich, he went outside, not forgetting to say, "Close the door," and went back to his house.

Having hidden all but a little of his new wealth, he wished to change one or two of his gold pieces for silver so that he could buy something to eat. He went to his brother's house to ask him for the favour, but Pedro was not at home, and his wife, who was at least as mean as Pedro, would not change the money. After a while Pedro came home, and his wife told him that Juan had some money; and Pedro, hoping in turn to gain some advantage, went to Juan's house and asked many questions about the money. Juan told him that he had sold some wood in town and had been paid in gold, but Pedro did not believe him and hid himself under the house to listen. At night he heard Juan talking to his wife, and found out the place and the password. Immediately taking three horses to carry his spoils, he set out for the robbers' cave.

Once arrived, he went straight to the cliff and said, "Open the door," and the door opened immediately. He went inside and said, "Close the door," and the door closed tight. He gathered together fifteen great bags of money, all he could lift, and carried them to the door ready to put on the horses. He found all the rich food and wine of the robbers in the cave, and could not resist the temptation to make merry at their expense; so he ate their food and drank their fine wines till he was foolishly drunk. When he had reached this state, he began to think of returning home. Beating on the door with both hands, he cried out, "Open, beast. Open, fool. May lightning blast you if you do not open!" and a hundred other foolish things, but never once saying, "Open the door."

While he was thus engaged, the robbers returned, and hearing them coming he hid under a great pile of money with only his nose sticking out.

The robbers saw that someone had visited the cave in their absence and hunted for the intruder till one of them discovered him trembling under a heap of coin. With a shout they hauled him forth and beat him until his flesh hung in ribbons. Then they split him into halves and threw the body into the river, and cut his horses into bits, which they threw after him.

When Pedro did not return, his wife became anxious and told Juan where he had gone. Juan stole quietly to the place by night, and recovered the body, carried it home, and had the pieces sewn together by the tailor.

Now the robbers knew that they had been robbed by someone else, and so, when Pedro's body was taken away, the captain went to town to see who had buried the body, and by enquiring, found that Juan had become suddenly rich, and also that it was his brother who had been buried.

So the captain of the robbers went to Juan's house, where he found a ball going on. Juan knew the captain again and that he was asking many questions, so he made the captain welcome and gave him a great deal to eat and drink. One of the servants came in and pretended to admire the captain's sword till he got it into his own hands; and then he began to give an exhibition of fencing, making the sword whirl hither and thither and ending with a wonderful stroke that made the captain's head roll on the floor.

A day or two later, the lieutenant also came to town, and began to make enquiries concerning the captain. He soon found out that the captain had been killed in Juan's house, but Juan now had soldiers on guard at his door, so that it was necessary to use strategy. He went to Juan and asked if he could start a "tienda," or wine shop, and Juan, who recognized the lieutenant, said, "Yes." Then the lieutenant went away, soon returning with seven great casks, in each of which he had seven men.

These he stored under Juan's house until such time as Juan, being asleep, could be killed with certainty and little danger. When this was done, he went into the house, intending to make Juan drunk and then kill him as Juan had the captain. Juan, however, got the lieutenant drunk first, and soon his head, like the captain's, rolled on the floor.

The soldiers below, like all soldiers, wished to have a drink from the great casks, and so one of them took a borer and bored into one of the casks. As he did so, a voice whispered, "Is Juan asleep yet?" The soldier replied, "Not yet," and went and told Juan. The casks by his order were all put into a boat, loaded with stones and chains, and thrown into the sea. So perished the last of the robbers.

Juan, being no longer in fear of the robbers, often went to their cave, and helped himself to everything that he wanted. He finally became a very great and wealthy man.

A Filipino (Tagalog) Version of Aladdin

ONCE ON A TIME a poor boy and his mother went far from their home city to seek their fortune. They were very poor, for the husband and father had died, leaving them little, and that little was soon spent. The boy went into the marketplace to seek for work, and a travelling merchant, seeing his distress, spoke to him and asked many questions. When he had enquired the name of the boy's father, he embraced him with many kind words, and told him that he was the father's long-lost brother, and that as he had no children of his own the boy should be his heir and for the present live with him as his son. He sent the boy to call his mother, and when she came he kissed her with many words of endearment, and would have it that she was his sister-in-law, though she told him that her husband had no brother. He treated her well and made her many presents, so that she was forced to believe he really was her brother-in-law.

The merchant then invited the boy to go for a visit with him, promising that the mother should soon follow. Mother and son consented, and the merchant set off with his nephew in the afternoon. They went far and came to a mountain which they crossed, and then to a second, which seemed very high to the poor boy so that he begged to rest. The man would not allow this, and when the boy cried, beat him till he agreed to do whatever he was told. They crossed this mountain also, and came to a third, and on the very top they stopped. The merchant drew a ring from his own finger and put it on that of the boy. Then he drew a circle around the boy and told him not to be frightened at what would happen, but to stretch out his arms three times, and that the third time the ground would open, and that then he must descend and get a tabo that he would find, and that with that in their hands they could quickly return. The boy, from fear of the man, did as he was told, and when the ground opened, went down into the cave and got the tabo. As he reached up his hand to be pulled from the cave, the man took the ring from his finger, and told him to hand up the vessel, but the boy, now much frightened, refused unless he were first helped out himself. That the man would not do, and after much talk drew another circle around the cave mouth, bade it close, and left the boy a prisoner in most evil plight.

Alone and helpless for three days in the underground darkness, the boy was prey to awful fear, but at the end of the third day, having by accident rubbed slightly the tabo with his hand, at once a great sinio or multo stood before him, saying that he was the slave of the tabo, and that all things earthly were within his power. At once mindful of his mother, he told the multo to take him home, and in the winking of an eye, still carrying the tabo in his hand, he stood before his mother. He found her very hungry and sorrowful, and recounted all that had happened and again rubbed the tabo lightly. The multo reappeared and the good woman hid her face for terror at the sight, but the lad bade the multo bring him a dinner for them both on a service of silver with everything to match.

After they had dined well for several days on the remnants of the food, the boy went to the market and sold the spoons that the multo had brought for two gold pieces, and on that they lived a long time: and as from time to time their money became exhausted, he sold more, till at last there was nothing left. Then, as he had become a young man, he required the multo to bring him a great chest of money, and soon became known as a very rich and generous person.

Now there was in that city a woman who had a very handsome daughter whom she wished to marry to the young man, and by way of opening the matter, she and her daughter went one day to try to buy some of the rich tableware which he had, or at least so they pretended. The young man was not of a mind for that kind of alliance, and so told the old woman to rub the magic vessel. She did so and the multo at once whisked her inside. The daughter also went in to enquire for her mother, and as she admiringly touched the tabo the multo made her prisoner, and the two became the slaves of the young man and were never heard of again.

How Suan Became Rich

PEDRO AND SUAN were friends. Pedro inherited a great fortune from his parents, who had recently died; but Suan was as poor as the poorest of beggars that ever lived. Early one morning Suan went to his friend, and said, "I wonder if you have a post that you do not need."

"Yes, I have one," said Pedro. "Why? Do you need it?"

"Yes, I need one badly, to build my house."

"Very well, take it," said Pedro. "Do not worry about paying for it."

Suan, who had not thought evil of his friend, took the post and built his house. When it was finished, his house was found to surpass that of his friend. This fact made Pedro so envious of Suan, that at last he went to him and asked Suan for the post back again.

"Why, if I take it from its place, my house will be destroyed. So let me pay you for it, or let me look for another post in the town and get it for you!"

"No," said Pedro, "I must have my own post, for I wish to use it."

Finally Suan became so greatly annoyed by his friend's insistence, that he exclaimed, "I will not give you back your post."

"Take heed, Suan! for I will accuse you before the king."

"All right! do as you please."

"We will then go to the king Monday," said Pedro.

"Very well; I am always ready."

When Monday came, both prepared to go to the palace. Pedro, who cared for his money more than for anything else, took some silver coins along with him for the journey. Suan took cooked rice and fish instead. Noon came while they were still on the road. Suan opened his package of food and began to eat. Pedro was also very hungry at this time, but no food could be bought on the way. So Suan generously invited Pedro to eat with him, and they dined together.

After eating, the two resumed their journey. At last they came to a river. The bridge over it was broken in the middle, and one had to jump in order to get to the other side. Pedro jumped. Suan followed him, but unfortunately fell. It so happened that an old man was bathing in the river below, and Suan accidentally fell right on him. The old man was knocked silly, and as a consequence was drowned. When Isidro, the son, who dearly loved his father, heard of the old man's death, he at once made up his mind to accuse Suan before the king. He therefore joined the two travellers.

After a while the three came to a place where they saw Barbekin having a hard time getting his carabao out of the mire. Suan offered to help. He seized the carabao by the tail, and pulled with great force. The carabao was rescued, but its tail was broken off short by a sudden pull of Suan. Barbekin was filled with rage because of the injury done to his animal: so he, too, resolved to accuse Suan before the king.

When they came to the palace, the king said, "Why have you come here?"

Pedro spoke first. "I have come," he said, "to accuse Suan to you. He has one of my posts, and he won't return it to me."

On being asked if the accusation was true, Suan responded with a nod, and said in addition, "But Pedro ate a part of my rice and fish on the way here."

"My decision, then," said the king, "is that Suan shall give Pedro his post, and that Pedro shall give Suan his rice and fish."

Isidro was the next to speak. "I have come here to accuse Suan. While my father was bathing in the river, Suan jumped on him and killed him."

"Suan, then, must bathe in the river," said the king, "and you may jump on him."

When Barbekin was asked why he had come, he replied, "I wish to accuse Suan. He pulled my carabao by the tail, and it was broken off short."

"Give Suan your carabao, then," said the king. "He shall not return it to you until he has made its tail grow to its full length."

The accused and the accusers now took their leave of the king.

"Give me the carabao now," said Suan to Barbekin when they had gone some distance from the palace.

The carabao was young and strong, and Barbekin hated to give it up. So he said, "Don't take the carabao, and I will give you fifty pesos."

"No; the decision of the king must be fulfilled," said Suan. Barbekin then raised the sum to ninety pesos, and Suan consented to accept the offer. Thus Suan was rewarded for his work in helping Barbekin.

When they came to the bridge, Suan went down into the river, and told Isidro to jump on him. But the bridge was high, and Isidro was afraid to jump. Moreover, he did not know how to swim, and he feared that he would but drown himself if he jumped. So he asked Suan to pardon him.

"No, you must fulfil the decision of the king," answered Suan.

"Let me off from jumping on you, and I will give you five hundred pesos," said Isidro.

The amount appealed to Suan as being a good offer, so he accepted it and let Isidro go.

As soon as Suan reached home, he took Pedro's post from his house, and started for Pedro's house, taking a razor along with him. "Here is your post," he said; "but you must lie down, for I am going to get my rice and fish from you."

In great fright Pedro said, "You need not return the post anymore."

"No," said Suan, "we must fulfil the decision of the king."

"If you do not insist on your demand," said Pedro, "I will give you half of my riches."

"No, I must have my rice and fish." Suan now held Pedro by the shoulder, and began to cut Pedro's abdomen with the razor. He had no sooner done that than Pedro, in great terror, cried out,

"Don't cut me, and you shall have all my riches!"

Thus Suan became the richest man in town by using his tact and knowledge in outwitting his enemies.

How the Moon Tricks the Buso

THE MOON IS A GREAT LIAR. One night long ago, the Buso looked over the earth and could not discover any people, because everybody was asleep. Then Buso went to the Moon, and asked her where all the people were to be found.

"Oh, you will not find a living person on the earth!" replied the Moon. "Everybody in the world is dead."

"Good!" thought Buso. "Tomorrow I shall have a fine meal of them."

Buso never eats living flesh, only dead bodies.

Next morning, Buso started for the graveyard; but on the way he met the Sun, and stopped to speak to him.

"How about the men on earth?" he questioned.

"They're all right," said the Sun. "All the people are working and playing and cooking rice."

The Buso was furious to find himself tricked. That night he went again to the Moon and asked for the men, and, as before, the Moon assured him that everybody was dead. But the next morning the Sun showed him all the people going about their work as usual. Thus the Buso has been fooled over and over again. The Moon tells him every night the same story.

Juan Gathers Guavas, and Other Short Tales

THE GUAVAS WERE RIPE, and Juan's father sent him to gather enough for the family and for the neighbours who came to visit them. Juan went to the guava bushes and ate all that he could hold. Then he began to look around for mischief. He soon found a wasp nest and managed to get it into a tight basket. He gave it to his father as soon as he reached home, and then closed

the door and fastened it. All the neighbours were inside waiting for the feast of guavas, and as soon as the basket was opened they began to fight to get out of the windows. After a while Juan opened the door and when he saw his parents' swollen faces, he cried out, "What rich fine guavas those must have been! They have made you both so very fat."

Juan Hides the Salt

Juan's father came into possession of a sack of salt, which used to be very precious and an expensive commodity. He wished it hidden in a secure place and so told Juan to hide it till they should need it. Juan went out and after hunting for a long time hid it in a carabao wallow, and of course when they went to fetch it again nothing was left but the sack.

Juan Makes Gulay of His Own Child

After Juan was married about a year a baby was born, and he and his wife loved it very much. But Juan was always obedient to his wife, being a fool, and when she told him to make gulay or stew he enquired of her of what he should make it. She replied of anac, meaning anac hang gabi. Then she went away for a while, and when she returned Juan had the gulay ready. She asked for the baby and was horrified to learn that Juan had made a stew of his own child, having taken her words literally.

Juan Pusong

THE VISAYANS TELL many stories which have as their hero Juan Pusong, or Tricky John. As the name implies, he is represented as being deceitful and dishonest, sometimes very cunning, and, in some of the stories told of him, endowed with miraculous power. The stories are very simple and of not

very great excellence. The few which follow will serve as samples of the narratives told of this popular hero.

Juan Pusong was a lazy boy. Neither punishment nor the offer of a reward could induce him to go to school, but in schooltime he was always to be found on the plaza, playing with the other boys.

His mother, however, believed him to be in school, and each day prepared some dainty for him to eat upon his return home. Juan was not satisfied with deceiving his mother in this way, but used to play tricks on her.

"Mother," he said, one day, "I have already learned to be a seer and to discover what is hidden. This afternoon when I come home from school I will foretell what you have prepared for me."

"Will you?" said his mother joyfully, for she believed all he said. "I will try to prepare something new and you will not be able to guess it."

"I shall, mother, I shall, let it be whatever it may," answered Juan. When it was time to go to school, Juan pretended to set out, but instead he climbed a tree which stood near the kitchen, and hiding himself among the leaves, watched through the window all that his mother did.

His mother baked a bibingca, or cake made of rice and sweet potato, and hid it in a jar. "I will bet anything," she said, "that my son will not guess what it is." Juan laughed at his mother's self-conceit. When it was time for school to close he got down, and with a book in his hand, as though he had really come from school, appeared before his mother and said, "Mother, I know what you are keeping for me."

"What is it?" asked his mother.

"The prophecy that I have just learned at school says that there is a bibingca hidden in the olla." The mother became motionless with surprise. "Is it possible?" she asked herself, "my son is indeed a seer. I am going to spread it abroad. My son is a seer."

The news was spread far and wide and many people came to make trial of Pusong's powers. In these he was always successful, thanks to his ability to cheat.

One day a ship was anchored in the harbour. She had come from a distant island. Her captain had heard of Pusong's power and wished to try him. The trial consisted in foretelling how many seeds the oranges with which his vessel was loaded contained. He promised to give Juan a great quantity of money if he could do this.

Pusong asked for a day's time. That night he swam out to the vessel, and, hidden in the water under the ship's stern, listened to the conversation of the crew. Luckily they were talking about this very matter of the oranges, and one of them enquired of the captain what kind of oranges he had.

"My friend," said the captain, "these oranges are different from any in this country, for each contains but one seed."

Pusong had learned all that he needed to know, so he swam back to the shore, and the next morning announced that he was ready for the trial.

Many people had assembled to hear the great seer. Pusong continued to read in his book, as though it was the source of his information. The hour agreed upon struck, and the captain of the vessel handed an orange to Juan and said, "Mr. Pusong, you may tell us how many seeds this orange contains."

Pusong took the orange and smelled it. Then he opened his book and after a while said, "This orange you have presented me with contains but one seed."

The orange was cut and but the one seed found in it, so Pusong was paid the money. Of course he obtained a great reputation throughout the country, and became very rich.

Juan Pusong's father drove his cows out one day to pasture. Juan slipped secretly from the house, and going to the pasture, took the cows into the forest and tied them there. When his father was going for the cows he met Juan and asked, "Where did you come from?" The boy replied, "I have just come from school. What are you looking for?"

"I am looking for our cows," said his father.

"Why didn't you tell me that before?" asked Juan. "Wait a minute," and he took his little book from his pocket and, looking into it, said, "Our cows are in such a place in the forest, tied together. Go and get them." So his father went to the place where Juan said the cows were and found them. Afterwards it was discovered that Juan could not read even his own name, so his father beat him for the trick he had played.

Pusong had transgressed the law, and was for this reason put into a cage to be in a short time submerged with it into the sea.

Tabloc-laui, a friend of Pusong's, passed by and saw him in the cage. "What are you there for?" Tabloc-laui asked.

"Oh!" answered Pusong, "I am a prisoner here, as you see, because the chief wants me to marry his daughter and I don't want to do it. I am to stay here until I consent."

"What a fool you are!" said Tabloc-laui. "The chief's daughter is pretty, and I am surprised that you are not willing to marry her."

"Hear me, Tabloc-laui!" said the prisoner. "If you want to marry the chief's daughter, let me out and get in here in my place; for tomorrow they will come and ask you if you will consent. Then you will be married at once."

"I am willing!" exclaimed Tabloc-laui. "Get out and I will take your place!"

Next morning the chief ordered his soldiers to take the cage with the prisoner to the sea and submerge it in the water.

Tabloc-laui, on seeing the soldiers coming towards him, thought they would make enquiries of him as Pusong had said.

"I am ready now," he said, "I am ready to be the princess's husband."

"Is this crazy fellow raving?" asked the soldiers. "We are ordered to take you and submerge you in the sea."

"But," objected Tabloc-laui, "I am ready now to marry the chief's daughter."

He was carried to the sea and plunged into the water, in spite of his crying, "I am not Pusong! I am Tabloc-laui!"

The next week the chief was in his boat, going from one fish-trap to another, to inspect them. Pusong swam out to the boat.

The chief, on seeing him, wondered, for he believed that Pusong was dead. "How is this?" he asked. "Did you not drown last week?"

"By no means. I sank to the bottom, but I found that there was no water there. There is another world where the dead live again. I saw your father and he charged me to bid you go to him, and afterwards you will be able to come back here, if you wish to do so." "Is that really true, Pusong?" asked the chief. "Yes, it is really true," was the reply.

"Well, I will go there. I will have a cage made and go through the way you did."

So the next morning the chief was submerged in the water, with the hope of coming back. When a considerable time had elapsed without seeing his return, his servants searched for Pusong, in order to punish him, but he had escaped to the mountains.

There was once a king who had three young and beautiful daughters named Isabel, Catalina and Maria.

In the capital city of the kingdom lived a young man known by the name of Juan Pusong. He had as friends an ape named Amo-Mongo, and a wildcat, whose name was Singalong. The three friends were passing one day in front of the palace, and, seeing the three young ladies, were greatly charmed by their beauty.

Pusong, who posed as a young aristocrat of considerable learning, determined to go before the king and declare his love for the Princess Isabel. The king received him favourably, and offered him a seat; but Juan refused to sit down until he should know the result of his request.

The king was astonished at his manner, and asked him what he wanted. Juan replied that he had presumptuously allowed himself to be charmed by the beauty of the Princess Isabel, and humbly requested the king's consent to their marriage. The king had the princess summoned before him, and in the presence of Pusong asked her if she would accept this man as her husband. She dutifully expressed her willingness to do whatever her father wished, so the king granted the request of Pusong, who was immediately married to Isabel.

When Amo-Mongo saw how successful Pusong had been, he presented himself before the king, as his friend had done, and requested the hand of the Princess Catalina. The king, somewhat unwillingly, gave his consent, and these two were also married.

When Singalong saw to what high positions his friends had attained, he became desirous of like fortune, so he went to the king and obtained his consent to his marriage with the Princess Maria.

All three of the king's sons-in-law lived with their wives at the palace, at the king's expense. The latter seeing that his daughters' husbands were lazy fellows, determined to make them useful, so he sent Pusong and Amo-Mongo out to take charge of his estates in the country, while to Singalong he gave the oversight of the servants who worked in the kitchen of the palace.

Pusong and Amo-Mongo went out to the hacienda with the intention of doing something, but when they arrived there, they found so much to do that they concluded that it would be impossible to attend to everything and so decided to do nothing.

The latter, after merely looking over the estate, entered the forest, in order to visit his relatives there. His fellow monkeys, who knew of his marriage with the princess, believed him to be of some importance, and begged him to save them from the famine which was devastating the forest. This Amo-Mongo, with much boasting of his wealth, promised to do, declaring that at the time of harvest he would give them plenty of rice.

When Pusong and his companion returned to the palace they were asked by the king how many acres they had cleared. They replied that they had cleared and planted about one thousand acres. The king was satisfied with their answer, and, at Amo-Mongo's request, gave orders for a large quantity of rice to be carried from the storehouse to the spot in the forest where his son-in-law had promised the monkeys that they should find it.

On the other hand, Singalong during the day did nothing, and as the king never saw him at work he disliked his third son-in-law very much. Yet every morning there were great piles of fish and vegetables in the palace kitchen. Amo-Mongo, knowing that his brother-in-law usually went out at night in order to bring something home, contrived to get up early and see what there was in the kitchen, so as to present it to the king as the result of his own labours. In this way, Amo-Mongo became each day dearer and dearer to the king, while Singalong became more and more disliked. Maria knew that her husband procured their food in some way, for every morning he said to her, "All that you see here I have brought." However, the king knew nothing of all this.

When the early harvest time came, the king commanded Amo-Mongo to bring rice to make pilipig. (Rice pounded into flakes and toasted, a dish of which Filipinos are very fond.) Amo-Mongo did not know where he could find it, but set out in the direction from which he had seen Singalong coming each morning, and soon came to an extensive rice field bearing an abundant crop. He took a goodly portion of it and, returning to the palace, had the pilipig prepared and set before the king and his household. Everyone ate of it, except Singalong, who was the real owner, and his wife, who had been secretly notified by him of the truth of the matter.

Maria was greatly perplexed by what her husband had told her, so she determined one night to watch him. She discovered that, as soon as the other people were asleep, her husband became transformed into a handsome prince and left the palace, leaving behind him his cat's dress. As soon as he had gone, Maria took the cast-off clothing of her husband and cast it into the fire. Singalong smelt it burning and returned to the palace, where he found his wife and begged her to return to him his cat's dress. This she was unable to do, since it was entirely consumed. As a result, Singalong was obliged to retain the form of a prince, but he was afraid to appear before the king in this guise, and so hid himself.

In the morning, Maria went to the king and told him the truth about her husband. Her father, however, thought that she was crazy, and when she insisted, invited her to accompany him to Amo-Mongo's farm, in order to convince her of her error. Many people went with them, and Amo-Mongo led them to the farm, which was really Singalong's, but told them that it belonged to himself. Besides other things, Singalong had planted many fruits, among them atimon and candol.

Amo-Mongo, seeing the diversity of fruits, began to eat all he could, until he became unable to move a step. Whenever his wife urged him to come away, he would take an atimon under his arm and a candol or so in his hands, until at last his wife, angry at his greediness, gave him a push which caused him to fall headlong, striking his head against a stone and being instantly killed.

Then Singalong, who had secretly followed the crowd from the palace, showed himself to the king in his proper form. After making suitable explanations, he led them to a fine palace in the middle of the hacienda. There they all lived together, but Pusong and his wife, who in former times had treated Singalong very harshly, giving him only the bones and scraps from the table, were now obliged to act as servants in the kitchen of the king's new palace.

Juan Wearing a Monkey's Skin

ONCE UPON A TIME there was a couple who were at first childless. The father was very anxious to have a son to inherit his property: so he went to the church daily, and prayed God to give him a child, but in vain. One day, in his great disappointment, the man exclaimed without thinking, "O great God! let me have a son, even if it is in the form of a monkey!" and only a few days later his wife gave birth to a monkey. The father was so much mortified that he wanted to kill his son; but finally his better reason prevailed, and he spared the child. He said to himself, "It is my fault, I know; but I uttered that invocation without thinking." So, instead of putting the monkey to death, the couple just hid it from visitors; and whenever anyone asked for the child, they merely answered, "Oh, he died long ago."

The time came when the monkey grew to be old enough to marry. He went to his father, and said, "Give me your blessing, father! for I am going away to look for a wife." The father was only too glad to be freed from this obnoxious son, so he immediately gave him his blessing. Before letting him go, however, the father said to the monkey, "You must never come back again to our house."

"Very well, I will not," said the monkey.

The monkey then left his father's house, and went to find his fortune. One night he dreamed that there was a castle in the midst of the sea, and that in this castle dwelt a princess of unspeakable beauty. The princess had been put there so that no one might discover her existence. The monkey, who had been baptized two days after his birth and was named Juan, immediately repaired to the palace of the king. There he posted a letter which read as follows: "I, Juan, know that your Majesty has a daughter."

Naturally the king was very angry to have his secret discovered. He immediately sent soldiers to look for Juan. Juan was soon found, and brought to the palace. The king said to him, "How do you know that I have a daughter? If you can bring her here, I will give her to you for a wife. If not, however, your head shall be cut off from your body."

"O your Majesty!" said Juan, "I am sure that I can find her and bring her here. I am willing to lose my head if within three days I fail to fulfil my promise." After he had said this, Juan withdrew, and sadly went out to look for the hidden princess.

As he was walking along the road, he heard the cry of a bird. He looked up, and saw a bird caught between two boughs so that it could not escape. The bird said to him, "O monkey! if you will but release me, I will give you all I have."

"Oh, no!" said the monkey. "I am very hungry, and would much rather eat you."

"If you will but spare my life," said the bird, "I will give you anything you want."

"On one condition only will I set you free," said the monkey. "You must procure for me the ring of the princess who lives in the midst of the sea."

"Oh, that's an easy thing to do," said the bird. So the monkey climbed the tree and set the bird free.

The bird immediately flew to the island in the sea, where fortunately it found the princess refreshing herself in her garden. The princess was so charmed with the song of the bird, that she looked up, and said, "O little bird! if you will only promise to live with me, I will give you anything you want."

"All right," said the bird. "Give me your ring, and I will forever live with you." The princess held up the ring; and the bird suddenly snatched it and flew away with it. It gave the ring to the monkey, who was, of course, delighted to get it.

Now the monkey jogged along the road until finally he saw three witches. He approached them, and said to them, "You are the very beings for whom I have spent the whole day looking. God has sent me here from heaven to punish you for your evildoings towards innocent persons. So I must eat you up."

Now, witches are said to be afraid of ill-looking persons, although they themselves are the ugliest beings in all the world. So these three were terribly frightened by the monkey's threat, and said, "O sir! spare our lives, and we will do anything for you!"

"Very well, I will spare you if you can execute my order. From this shore you must build a bridge which leads to the middle of the sea, where the castle of the princess is situated."

"That shall be speedily done," replied the witches; and they at once gathered leaves, which they put on their backs. Then they plunged into the water. Immediately after them a bridge was built. Thus the monkey was now able to go to the castle. Here he found the princess. She was very much surprised to see this evil-looking animal before her; but she was much more frightened when the monkey showed her the ring which the bird had given him, and claimed her for his wife. "It is the will of God that you should go with me," said the monkey, after the princess had shown great repugnance towards him. "You either have to go with me or perish." Thinking it was useless to attempt to resist such a mighty foe, the princess finally yielded.

The monkey led her to the king's palace, and presented her before her parents; but no sooner had the king and queen seen their daughter in the power of the beast, than they swooned. When they had recovered, they said simultaneously, "Go away at once, and never come back here again, you girl of infamous taste! Who are you? You are not the princess we left in the castle. You are of villain's blood, and the very air which you exhale does suffocate us. So with no more ado depart at once!"

The princess implored her father to have pity, saying that it was the will of God that she should be the monkey's wife. "Perhaps I have been enchanted by him, for I am powerless to oppose him." But all her remonstrance was in vain. The king shut his ears against any deceitful or flattering words that might fall from the lips of his faithless and disobedient daughter. Seeing that the king was obstinate, the couple turned their backs on the palace, and decided to find a more hospitable home. So the monkey now took his wife to a neighbouring mountain, and here they settled.

One day the monkey noticed that the princess was very sad and pale. He said to her, "Why are you so sad and unhappy, my darling? What is the matter?"

"Nothing. I am just sorry to have only a monkey for my husband. I become sad when I think of my past happiness."

"I am not a monkey, my dear. I am a real man, born of human parents. Didn't you know that I was baptized by the priest, and that my name is Juan?" As the princess would not believe him, the monkey went to a neighbouring hut and there cast off his disguise (*balit cayu*). He at once returned to the princess. She was amazed to see a sparkling youth of not more than twenty years of age – nay, a prince – kneeling before her. "I can no longer keep you in ignorance," he said. "I am your husband, Juan."

"Oh, no! I cannot believe you. Don't try to deceive me! My husband is a monkey; but, with all his defects, I still cling to him and love him. Please go away at once, lest my husband find you here! He will be jealous, and may kill us both."

"Oh, no! my darling, I am your husband, Juan. I only disguised myself as a monkey."

But still the princess would not believe him. At last she said to him, "If you are my real husband, you must give me a proof of the fact." So Juan took her to the place where he had cast off his monkey skin. The princess was now convinced, and said to herself, "After all, I was not wrong in the belief I have entertained from the beginning, that it was the will of God that I should marry this monkey, this man."

Juan and the princess now agreed to go back to the palace and tell the story. So they went. As soon as the king and queen saw the couple, they were very much surprised; but to remove their doubt, Juan immediately related to the king all that had happened. Thus the king and queen were finally reconciled to the at first hated couple. Juan and his wife succeeded to the throne on the death of the king, and lived peacefully and happily during their reign.

The story is now ended. Thus we see that God compensated the father and mother of Juan for their religious zeal by giving them a son, but punished them for not being content with what He gave them by taking the son away from them again, for Juan never recognized his parents.

Juan Wins a Wager for the Governor

JUAN WAS WELL KNOWN for a brave man, though a fool, and the priest and the governor wished to try him on a wager. The governor told him that the priest was dead, and ordered him to watch the body in the church that night. The priest lay down on the bier before the altar, and after Juan came the priest arose.

Juan pushed him down again and ran out of the church and secured a club. Returning, he said to the priest, "You are dead; try to get up again and I will break you to pieces." So Juan proved himself to be a brave man, and the governor won his wager.

The King's Decisions

ONCE A POOR MAN named Juan was without relatives or friends. Life to him was a series of misfortunes. A day often passed without his tasting even a mouthful of food.

One day, weakened with hunger and fatigue, as he was walking along the road, he passed a rich man's house. It so happened that at this time the rich man's food was being cooked. The food smelled so good that Juan's hunger was satisfied merely with the fragrance. When the rich man learned that the smell of his food had satisfied Juan, he demanded money of Juan. Juan refused to give money, however, because he had none, and because he had neither tasted nor touched the rich man's food. "Let's go to the king, then," said Pedro, the rich man, "and have this matter settled!" Juan had no objection to the proposal, and the two set out for the palace.

Soon they came to a place where the mire was knee-deep. There they saw a young man who was trying to help his horse out of a mudhole. "Hey, you lazy fellows! help me to get my horse out of this hole," said Manuel. The three tried with all their might to release the horse. They finally succeeded; but unfortunately Juan had taken hold of the horse's tail, and it was broken off when Juan gave a sudden hard pull.

"You have got to pay me for injuring my horse," said Manuel.

"No, I will not give you any money, because I had no intention of helping you until you asked me to," said Juan.

"Well, the king will have to settle the quarrel." Juan, who was not to be frightened by threats, went with Pedro and Manuel.

Night overtook the three on their way. They had to lodge themselves in the house of one of Pedro's friends. Juan was not allowed to come up, but was made to sleep downstairs.

At midnight the pregnant wife of the host had to make water. She went to the place under which Juan was sleeping. Juan, being suddenly awakened and frightened, uttered a loud shriek; and the woman, also frightened because she thought there were robbers or ghosts about, miscarried. The next morning the husband asked Juan why he had cried out so loud in the night. Juan said that he was frightened.

"You won't fool me! Come with us to the king," said the husband.

When the four reached the palace, they easily gained access to the royal presence. Then each one explained why he had come there.

"I'll settle the first case," said the king. He commanded the servant to fetch two silver coins and place them on the table. "Now, Pedro, come here and smell the coins. As Juan became satisfied with the smell of your food, so now satisfy yourself with the smell of the money." Pedro could not say a word, though he was displeased at the unfavourable decision.

"Now I'll give my decisions on the next two cases. Manuel, you must give your horse to Juan, and let him have it until another tail grows. And you, married man, must let Juan have your wife until she gives birth to another child."

Pedro, Manuel and the married man went home discontented with the decisions of the king – Pedro without having received pay, Manuel without his horse, and the other man without his wife.

King Tasio

JUAN WAS A SERVANT in the palace of King Tasio. One day King Tasio heard Juan discussing with the other servants in the kitchen the management of the kingdom. Juan said that he knew more than anybody else in the palace. The king called Juan, and told him to go down to the seashore and catch the rolling waves.

"You said that you are the wisest man in the palace," said the king. "Go and catch the waves of the sea for me."

"That's very easy, O king!" said Juan, "if you will only provide me with a rope made of sand taken from the seashore."

The king did not know what to answer. He left Juan without saying anything, went into his room, and began to think of some more difficult work.

The next day he called Juan. "Juan, take this small bird and make fifty kinds of food out of it," said the king.

"Yes, sir!" said Juan, "if you will only provide me with a stove, a pan, and a knife made out of this needle," handing a needle to the king, "with which to cook the bird." Again the king did not know what to do. He was very angry at Juan.

"Juan, get out of my palace! Don't you let me see you walking on my ground around this palace without my consent!" said the king.

"Very well, sir!" said Juan, and he left the palace immediately.

The next day King Tasio saw Juan in front of the palace, riding on his *paragos* drawn by a carabao.

"Did I not tell you not to stand or walk on my ground around this palace? Why are you here now? Do you mean to mock me?" shouted the king.

"Well," said Juan, "will your Majesty's eyes please see whether I am standing on your ground or not? This is my ground." And he pointed to the earth he had on his *paragos*. "I took this from my orchard."

"That's enough, Juan," said King Tasio. "I can have no more foolishness."

The king felt very uncomfortable, because many of his courtiers and servants were standing there listening to his talk with Juan.

"Juan, put this squash into this jar. Be careful! See that you do not break either the squash or the jar," said the king, as he handed a squash and a jar to Juan. Now, the neck of the jar was small, and the squash was as big as the jar. So Juan had indeed a difficult task.

Juan went home. He put a very small squash, which he had growing in his garden, inside the jar. He did not, however, cut it from the vine. After a few weeks the squash had grown big enough to fill the jar. Juan then picked off the squash enclosed in the jar, and went to the king. He presented the jar to the king when all the servants, courtiers and visitors from other towns were present. As soon as the king saw the jar with the squash in it, he fainted. It was many hours before he recovered.

The Man in the Shroud

JUAN, BEING A JOKER, once thought to have a little fun at others' expense, so he robed himself in a shroud, placed a bier by the roadside, set candles around it, and lay down so that all who went by should see him and be frightened. A band of robbers went by that way, and seeing the corpse, besought it to give them luck. As it happened, they were more than usually fortunate, and when they returned they began to make offerings to him to secure continuance of their good fortune. As the entire proceeds of their adventures were held in common, they soon began to quarrel over the offerings to be made. The captain became angry, and drew his sword with a threat to run the corpse through for causing so much dissension among his men.

This frightened the sham dead man to such a degree that he jumped up and ran away, and the robbers, who were even more frightened than he, ran the other way, leaving all their plunder.

Juan then returned and gathered all the money and valuables left behind by the robbers, and carried them home. Now he had a friend who was very curious to know how he came into possession of so much wealth, and so Juan told him, only he said nothing about robbers, but told his friend, whose name was Pedro, that the things were the direct reward of God for his piety.

Pedro, being afraid of the woods, decided to lie just inside the church door; besides, that being a more sacred place, he felt sure that God would favour him even more than Juan. He arranged his bier with the candles around him, and lay down to await the shower of money that should reward his devotions. When the sacristan went to the church to ring the bell for vespers, he saw the body lying there, and not knowing of any corpse having been carried in, he was frightened and ran to tell the padre. The padre, when he had seen the body, said it was a miracle, and that it must be buried within the church, for the sanctification of the edifice.

But Pedro, now thoroughly frightened, jumped off the bier and ran away, and the priest and the sacristan ran the other way, so the poor man never received the reward for his piety, and the church was deprived of a new patron saint.

The Miraculous Cow

THERE WAS ONCE A FARMER driving home from his farm in his carreton. He had tied his cow to the back of his cart, as he was accustomed to do every evening on his way home. While he was going along the road, two boys saw him. They were Felipe and Ambrosio. Felipe whispered to Ambrosio, "Do you see the cow tied to the back of that carreton? Well, if you will untie it, I will take it to our house."

Ambrosio approached the carreton slowly, and untied the cow. He handed the rope to Felipe, and then tied himself in the place of the animal.

"Come on, Ambrosio! Don't be foolish! Come on with me!" whispered Felipe impatiently.

"No, leave me alone! Go home, and I will soon be there!" answered the cunning Ambrosio.

After a while the farmer happened to look back. What a surprise for him! He was frightened to find a boy instead of his cow tied to the carreton. "Why are you there? Where is my cow?" he shouted furiously. "Rascal, give me my cow!"

"Oh, don't be angry with me!" said Ambrosio. "Wait a minute, and I will tell you my story. Once, when I was a small boy, my mother became very angry with me. She cursed me, and suddenly I was transformed into a cow; and now I am changed back into my own shape. It is not my fault that you bought me: I could not tell you not to do so, for I could not speak at the time. Now, generous farmer, please give me my freedom! for I am very anxious to see my old home again."

The farmer did not know what to do, for he was very sorry to lose his cow. When he reached home, he told his wife the story. Now, his wife was a kind-hearted woman; so, after thinking a few minutes, she said, "Husband, what can we do? We ought to set him free. It is by the great mercy of God that he has been restored to his former self."

So the wily boy got off. He rejoined his friend, and they had a good laugh over the two simple folks.

The Mona

WHEN THE MONA lived on the earth, there was a certain man who said to his wife, "I want to go out and make some traps."

So that day he went out and made about thirty traps, of sticks with nooses attached, to snare jungle-fowl. His work finished, he returned home. Next day he went out to look at his traps, but found that he had caught not a wild chicken, but a big lizard (palas) with pretty figured patterns on its back. The man said to the lizard, "Halloo!"

Then he released the lizard, and gave him his own carrying-bag and work-knife, and told him to go straight to his house. But the lizard was afraid to go to the man's house, for he suspected that the man wanted to make a meal of him. Instead, he ran up a tree, taking with him the knife and the bag. The tree overhung a clear brook, and the lizard could see his reflection (alung) in the water.

No fowl could the man snare that day, and he went home. As soon as he reached the house, he said to his wife, "Are you all done cleaning that lizard?"

"What lizard are you talking about?" returned the woman. "There's no lizard here."

"I sent one here," insisted the man, "and I'm hungry."

"We have no lizard," repeated his wife.

In a hot temper the man went back to his traps, and there saw the tracks of the lizard, leading not towards his house, but exactly in the opposite direction. Following the tracks, he reached the brook, and at once caught sight of the lizard's reflection in the water. Immediately the man jumped into the water, grasping for the image of the slippery lizard; but he had to jump out again with empty hands. He tried again. Hour after hour he kept on jumping, until he got so wet and cold that he had to give it up and go home.

"The lizard is right over there in the brook," he told his wife; "but I could not get hold of him."

"I'll go and look at him with you," she said.

So together they reached the brook; and the woman glanced first into the water, and then up into the tree.

"You foolish man," she smiled. "Look in the tree for your lizard. That's just his shadow (alung) in the water."

The man looked up, and saw the lizard in the tree. Then he started to climb up the trunk, but found himself so chilled and stiff from jumping into the water, that he kept slipping down whenever he tried to climb. Then the woman took her turn, and got part way up the tree. The man looked up at his wife, and noticed that she had sores on parts of her body where she could not see them, and he called to her, "Come down! don't climb any higher; you've got sores." So she climbed down.

Then her husband wanted to get some medicine out of his bag to give her for the sores; but the lizard had his bag.

"Throw down my bag and knife to me!" he shouted up to the lizard, "because I must get busy about fixing medicine for my wife." And the lizard threw down to him his knife and his bag.

As soon as they got home, the man made some medicine for his wife; but the sores did not heal. Then he went to his friend Tuglay and said, "What is the medicine for my wife?"

Tuglay went home with the man; and when they reached the house, he told him what he was about to do. "Look!" said the Tuglay.

Then the man looked, and saw the Tuglay go to his wife and consort with her.

And the husband let him do it, for he said to himself, "That is the medicine for my wife."

When the Tuglay was done with the woman, he said, "Go now to your wife."

Then the man went to her, and said, "This is the best of all." After that, the man cared for nothing except to be with his wife. He did not even care to eat. He threw out of the house all the food they had: the rice, the sugarcane, the bananas, and all of their other things. He threw them far away. But after they had taken no food for several days, the man and the woman began to grow thin and weak. Still they did not try to get food, because they wanted only to gratify their passion for each other. At last both of them got very skinny, and finally they died.

Sagacious Marcela

LONG, LONG BEFORE the Spaniards came, there lived a man who had a beautiful, virtuous and, above all, clever daughter. He was a servant of the king. Marcela, the daughter, loved her

father devotedly, and always helped him with his work. From childhood she had manifested a keen wit and undaunted spirit. She would even refuse to obey unjust orders from the king. No question was too hard for her to answer, and the king was constantly being surprised at her sagacity.

One day the king conceived a plan by which he might test the ingenious Marcela. He bade his servants procure a tiny bird and carry it to her house. "Tell her," said the king, "to make twelve dishes out of that one bird."

The servants found Marcela sewing. They told her of the order of the king. After thinking for five minutes, she took one of her pins, and said to the servants, "If the king can make twelve spoons out of this pin, I can also make twelve dishes out of that bird." On receiving the answer, the king realized that the wise Marcela had gotten the better of him; and he began to think of another plan to puzzle her.

Again he bade his servants carry a sheep to Marcela's house. "Tell her," he said, "to sell the sheep for six *reales*, and with the money this very same sheep must come back to me alive."

At first Marcela could not make out what the king meant for her to do. Then she thought of selling the wool only, and not the whole sheep. So she cut off the wool and sold it for six *reales*, and sent the money with the live sheep back to the king. Thus she was again relieved from a difficulty.

The king by this time realized that he could not beat Marcela in points of subtlety. However, to amuse himself, he finally thought of one more scheme to test her sagacity. It took him two weeks to think it out. Summoning a messenger, he said to him, "Go to Marcela, and tell her that I am not well, and that my physician has advised me to drink a cup of bull's milk. Therefore she must get me this medicine, or her father will lose his place in the palace." The king also issued an order that no one was to bathe or to wash anything in the river, for he was going to take a bath the next morning.

As soon as Marcela had received the command of the king and had heard of his second order, she said, "How easy it will be for me to answer this silly order of the king!" That night she and her father killed a pig, and smeared its blood over the sleeping-mat, blanket and pillows. When morning came, Marcela took the stained bedclothing to the source of the river, where the king was bathing. As soon as the king caught sight of her, he said in a voice of thunder, "Why do you wash your stuff in the river when you know I ordered that nobody should use the river today but me?"

Marcela replied, "It is the custom, my lord, in our country, to wash the mat, pillows, and other things stained with blood, immediately after a person has given birth to a child. As my father gave birth to a child last night, custom forces me to disobey your order, although I do it much against my will."

"Nonsense!" said the king. "The idea of a man giving birth to a child! Absurd! Ridiculous!"

"My lord," said Marcela, "it would be just as absurd to think of getting milk from a bull."

Then the king, recollecting his order, said, "Marcela, as you are so witty, clever and virtuous, I will give you my son for your husband."

The Seven Crazy Fellows

ONCE THERE WERE LIVING in the country in the northern part of Luzon seven crazy fellows, named Juan, Felipe, Mateo, Pedro, Francisco, Eulalio and Jacinto. They were happy all the day long.

One morning Felipe asked his friends to go fishing. They stayed at the Cagayan River a long time. About two o'clock in the afternoon Mateo said to his companions, "We are hungry; let us go home!"

"Before we go," said Juan, "let us count ourselves, to see that we are all here!" He counted; but because he forgot to count himself, he found that they were only six, and said that one of them had been drowned. Thereupon they all dived into the river to look for their lost companion; and when they came out, Francisco counted to see if he had been found; but he, too, left himself out, so in they dived again. Jacinto said that they should not go home until they had found the one who was lost. While they were diving, an old man passed by. He asked the fools what they were diving for. They said that one of them had been drowned.

"How many were you at first?" said the old man.

They said that they were seven.

"All right," said the old man. "Dive in, and I will count you." They dived, and he found that they were seven. Since he had found their lost companion, he asked them to come with him.

When they reached the old man's house, he selected Mateo and Francisco to look after his old wife; Eulalio he chose to be water-carrier; Pedro, cook; Jacinto, wood-carrier; and Juan and Felipe, his companions in hunting.

When the next day came, the old man said that he was going hunting, and he told Juan and Felipe to bring along rice with them. In a little while they reached the mountains, and he told the two fools to cook the rice at ten o'clock. He then went up the mountain with his dogs to catch a deer. Now, his two companions, who had been left at the foot of the mountain, had never seen a deer. When Felipe saw a deer standing under a tree, he thought that the antlers of the deer were the branches of a small tree without leaves: so he hung his hat and bag of rice on them, but the deer immediately ran away. When the old man came back, he asked if the rice was ready. Felipe told him that he had hung his hat and the rice on a tree that ran away. The old man was angry, and said, "That tree you saw was the antlers of a deer. We'll have to go home now, for we have nothing to eat."

Meanwhile the five crazy fellows who had been left at home were not idle. Eulalio went to get a pail of water. When he reached the well and saw his image in the water, he nodded, and the reflection nodded back at him. He did this over and over again; until finally, becoming tired, he jumped into the water, and was drowned. Jacinto was sent to gather small sticks, but he only destroyed the fence around the garden. Pedro cooked a chicken without removing the feathers. He also let the chicken burn until it was as black as coal. Mateo and Francisco tried to keep the flies off the face of their old mistress. They soon became tired, because the flies kept coming back; so they took big sticks to kill them with. When a fly lighted on the nose of the old woman, they struck at it so hard that they killed her. She died with seemingly a smile on her face. The two fools said to each other that the old woman was very much pleased that they had killed the fly.

When the old man and his two companions reached home, the old man asked Pedro if there was any food to eat. Pedro said that it was in the pot. The old man looked in and saw the charred chicken and feathers. He was very angry at the cook. Then he went in to see his wife, and found her dead. He asked Mateo and Francisco what they had done to the old woman. They said that they had only been killing flies that tried to trouble her, and that she was very much pleased by their work.

The next thing the crazy fellows had to do was to make a coffin for the dead woman; but they made it flat, and in such a way that there was nothing to prevent the corpse from falling off. The old man told them to carry the body to the church; but on their way they ran, and the body rolled off the flat coffin. They said to each other that running was a good thing, for it made their burden lighter.

When the priest found that the corpse was missing, he told the six crazy fellows to go back and get the body. While they were walking towards the house, they saw an old woman picking up sticks by the roadside.

"Old woman, what are you doing here?" they said. "The priest wants to see you."

While they were binding her, she cried out to her husband, "Ah! here are some bad boys trying to take me to the church." But her husband said that the crazy fellows were only trying to tease her. When they reached the church with this old woman, the priest, who was also crazy, performed the burial ceremony over her. She cried out that she was alive; but the priest answered that since he had her burial fee, he did not care whether she was alive or not. So they buried this old woman in the ground.

When they were returning home, they saw the corpse that had fallen from the coffin on their way to the church. Francisco cried that it was the ghost of the old woman. Terribly frightened, they ran away in different directions, and became scattered all over Luzon.

The Story of Zaragoza

YEARS AND YEARS AGO there lived in a village a poor couple, Luis and Maria. Luis was lazy and selfish, while Maria was hard-working and dutiful. Three children had been born to this pair, but none had lived long enough to be baptized. The wife was once more about to be blessed with a child, and Luis made up his mind what he should do to save its life. Soon the day came when Maria bore her second son. Luis, fearing that this child, like the others, would die unchristened, decided to have it baptized the very next morning. Maria was very glad to know of her husband's determination, for she believed that the early deaths of their other children were probably due to delay in baptizing them.

The next morning Luis, with the infant in his arms, hastened to the church; but in his haste he forgot to ask his wife who should stand as godfather. As he was considering this oversight, a strange man passed by, whom he asked, "Will you be so kind as to act as my child's godfather?"

"With all my heart," was the stranger's reply.

They then entered the church, and the child was named Luis, after his father. When the services were over, Luis entreated Zaragoza – such was the name of the godfather – to dine at his house. As Zaragoza had just arrived in that village for the first time, he was but too ready to accept the invitation. Now, Zaragoza was a kind-hearted man, and soon won the confidence of his host and hostess, who invited him to remain with them for several days. Luis and Zaragoza became close friends, and often consulted each other on matters of importance.

One evening, as the two friends were conversing, their talk turned upon the affairs of the kingdom. Luis told his friend how the king oppressed the people by levying heavy taxes on all sorts of property, and for that reason was very rich. Zaragoza, moved by the news, decided to avenge the wrongs of the people. Luis hesitated, for he could think of no sure means of punishing the tyrannical monarch. Then Zaragoza suggested that they should try to steal the king's treasure, which was hidden in a cellar of the palace. Luis was much pleased with the project, for he thought that it was Zaragoza's plan for them to enrich themselves and live in comfort and luxury.

Accordingly, one evening the two friends, with a pickaxe, a hoe and a shovel, directed their way towards the palace. They approached the cellar by a small door, and then began to dig in the ground at the foot of the cellar wall. After a few hours of steady work, they succeeded in making an excavation leading into the interior. Zaragoza entered, and gathered up as many bags of money as he and Luis could carry. During the night they made several trips to the cellar, each time taking back to their house as much money as they could manage. For a long time the secret way was not discovered, and the two friends lost no opportunity of increasing their already great hoard. Zaragoza gave away freely much of his share to the poor; but his friend was selfish, and kept constantly admonishing him not to be too liberal.

In time the king observed that the bulk of his treasure was considerably reduced, and he ordered his soldiers to find out what had caused the disappearance of so much money. Upon close examination, the soldiers discovered the secret passage; and the king, enraged, summoned his counsellors to discuss what should be done to punish the thief.

In the meantime the two friends were earnestly discussing whether they should get more bags of money, or should refrain from making further thefts. Zaragoza suggested that they would better first get in touch with the secret deliberations of the court before making another attempt. Luis, however, as if called by fate, insisted that they should make one more visit to the king's cellar, and then enquire about the unrest at court. Persuaded against his better judgement, Zaragoza followed his friend to the palace, and saw that their secret passage was in the same condition as they had lately left it. Luis lowered himself into the hole; but lo! the whiz of an arrow was heard, and then a faint cry from Luis.

"What is the matter? Are you hurt?" asked Zaragoza.

"I am dying! Take care of my son!" These were Luis's last words.

Zaragoza knew not what to do. He tried to pull up the dead body of his friend; but in vain, for it was firmly caught between two heavy blocks of wood, and was pierced by many arrows. But Zaragoza was shrewd; and, fearing the consequences of the discovery of Luis's corpse, he cut off the dead man's head and hurried home with it, leaving the body behind. He broke the fatal news to Maria, whose grief was boundless. She asked him why he had mutilated her husband's body, and he satisfied her by telling her that they would be betrayed if Luis were recognized. Taking young Luis in her arms, Maria said, "For the sake of your godson, see that his father's body is properly buried."

"Upon my word of honour, I promise to do as you wish," was Zaragoza's reply.

Meantime the king was discussing the theft with his advisers. Finally, wishing to identify the criminal, the king decreed that the body should be carried through the principal streets of the city and neighbouring villages, followed by a train of soldiers, who were instructed to arrest any person who should show sympathy for the dead man. Early one morning the military procession started out, and passed through the main streets of the city. When the procession arrived before Zaragoza's house, it happened that Maria was at the window, and, seeing the body of her husband, she cried, "O my husband!"

Seeing the soldiers entering their house, Zaragoza asked, "What is your pleasure?"

"We want to arrest that woman," was the answer of the chief of the guard.

"Why? She has not committed any crime."

"She is the widow of that dead man. Her words betrayed her, for she exclaimed that the dead man was her husband."

"Who is her husband? That remark was meant for me, because I had unintentionally hurt our young son," said Zaragoza smiling.

The soldiers believed his words, and went on their way. Reaching a public place when it was almost night, they decided to stay there until the next morning. Zaragoza saw his opportunity. He disguised himself as a priest and went to the place, taking with him a bottle of wine mixed with a strong narcotic. When he arrived, he said that he was a priest, and, being afraid of robbers, wished to pass the night with some soldiers. The soldiers were glad to have with them, as they thought, a pious man, whose stories would inspire them to do good. After they had talked a while, Zaragoza offered his bottle of wine to the soldiers, who freely drank from it. As was expected, they soon all fell asleep, and Zaragoza succeeded in stealing the corpse of Luis. He took it home and buried it in that same place where he had buried the head.

The following morning the soldiers woke up, and were surprised to see that the priest and the corpse were gone. The king soon knew how his scheme had failed. Then he thought of another plan. He ordered that a sheep covered with precious metal should be let loose in the streets, and that it should be followed by a spy, whose duty it was to watch from a distance, and, in case anyone attempted to catch the sheep, to ascertain the house of that person, and then report to the palace.

Having received his orders, the spy let loose the sheep, and followed it at a distance. Nobody else dared even to make a remark about the animal; but when Zaragoza saw it, he drove it into his yard. The spy, following instructions, marked the door of Zaragoza's house with a cross, and hastened to the palace. The spy assured the soldiers that they would be able to capture the criminal; but when they began to look for the house, they found that all the houses were similarly marked with crosses.

For the third time the king had failed; and, giving up all hopes of catching the thief, he issued a proclamation pardoning the man who had committed the theft, provided he would present himself to the king within three days. Hearing the royal proclamation, Zaragoza went before the king, and confessed that he was the perpetrator of all the thefts that had caused so much trouble in the court. True to his word, the king did not punish him. Instead, the king promised to give Zaragoza a title of nobility if he could trick Don Juan, the richest merchant in the city, out of his most valuable goods.

When he knew of the desire of the king, Zaragoza looked for a fool, whom he could use as his instrument. He soon found one, whom he managed to teach to say "*Si*" (Spanish for "yes") whenever asked a question. Dressing the fool in the guise of a bishop, Zaragoza took a carriage and drove to the store of D. Juan. There he began to ask the fool such questions as these: "Does your Grace wish to have this? Does not your Grace think that this is cheap?" to all of which the fool's answer was "Si." At last, when the carriage was well loaded, Zaragoza said, "I will first take these things home, and then return with the money for them;" to which the fool replied, "Si." When Zaragoza reached the palace with the rich goods, he was praised by the king for his sagacity.

After a while D. Juan the merchant found out that what he thought was a bishop was really a fool. So he went to the king and asked that he be given justice. Moved by pity, the king restored all the goods that had been stolen, and D. Juan wondered how his Majesty had come into possession of his lost property.

Once more the king wanted to test Zaragoza's ability. Accordingly he told him to bring to the palace an old hermit who lived in a cave in the neighbouring mountains. At first Zaragoza tried to persuade Tubal to pay the visit to the king, but in vain. Having failed in his first attempt, Zaragoza determined to play a trick on the old hermit. He secretly placed an iron cage near the mouth of Tubal's cave, and then in the guise of an angel he stood on a high cliff and shouted,

"Tubal, Tubal, hear ye me!"

Tubal, hearing the call, came out of his cave, and, seeing what he thought was an angel, knelt down. Then Zaragoza shouted,

"I know that you are very religious, and have come to reward your piety. The gates of heaven are open, and I will lead you thither. Go enter that cage, and you will see the way to heaven."

Tubal meekly obeyed; but when he was in the cage, he did not see the miracle he expected. Instead, he was placed in a carriage and brought before the king. Thoroughly satisfied now, the king released Tubal, and fulfilled his promise to Zaragoza. Zaragoza was knighted, and placed among the chief advisers of the kingdom. After he had been raised to this high rank, he called to his side Maria and his godson, and they lived happily under the protection of one who became the most upright and generous man of the realm.

Suan Eket

MANY YEARS AGO there lived in the country of Campao a boy named Suan. While this boy was studying in a private school, it was said that he could not pronounce the letter x very well – he called it "eket." So his schoolmates nicknamed him "Suan Eket."

Finally Suan left school, because, whenever he went there, the other pupils always shouted at him, "Eket, eket, eket!" He went home, and told his mother to buy him a pencil and a pad of paper. "I am the wisest boy in our town now," said he.

One night Suan stole his father's plough, and hid it in a creek near their house. The next morning his father could not find his plough.

"What are you looking for?" said Suan.

"My plough," answered his father.

"Come here, Father! I will guess where it is." Suan took his pencil and a piece of paper. On the paper he wrote figures of various shapes. He then looked up, and said,

"Ararokes, ararokes,
Na na nakawes
Ay na s'imburnales,"

which meant that the plough had been stolen by a neighbour and hidden in a creek. Suan's father looked for it in the creek near their house, and found it. In great wonder he said, "My son is truly the wisest boy in the town." News spread that Suan was a good guesser.

One day as Suan was up in a guava tree, he saw his uncle Pedro ploughing. At noon Pedro went home to eat his dinner, leaving the plough and the carabao in the field. Suan got down from the tree and climbed up on the carabao's back. He guided it to a very secret place in the mountains and hid it there. When Pedro came back, he could not find his carabao. A man who was passing by said, "Pedro, what are you looking for?"

"I am looking for my carabao. Somebody must have stolen it." "Go to Suan, your nephew," said the man. "He can tell you who stole your carabao." So Pedro went to Suan's house, and told him to guess who had taken his carabao.

Suan took his pencil and a piece of paper. On the paper he wrote some round figures. He then looked up, and said,

"Carabaues, carabaues,
Na nanakawes
Ay na sa bundokes,"

which meant that the carabao was stolen by a neighbour and was hidden in the mountain. For many days Pedro looked for it in the mountain. At last he found it in a very secret place. He then went to Suan's house, and told him that the carabao was truly in the mountain. In great wonder he said, "My nephew is surely a good guesser."

One Sunday a proclamation of the king was read. It was as follows: "The princess's ring is lost. Whoever can tell who stole it shall have my daughter for his wife; but he who tries and fails loses his head."

When Suan's mother heard it, she immediately went to the palace, and said, "King, my son can tell you who stole your daughter's ring."

"Very well," said the king, "I will send my carriage for your son to ride to the palace in."

In great joy the woman went home. She was only ascending the ladder when she shouted, "Suan Suan, my fortunate son!"

"What is it, Mother?" said Suan.

"I told the king that you could tell him who stole the princess's ring."

"Foolish mother, do you want me to die?" said Suan, trembling.

Suan had scarcely spoken these words when the king's carriage came. The coachman was a courtier. This man was really the one who had stolen the princess's ring. When Suan was in the carriage, he exclaimed in great sorrow, "Death is at hand!" Then he blasphemed, and said aloud to himself, "You will lose your life now."

The coachman thought that Suan was addressing him. He said to himself, "I once heard that this man is a good guesser. He must know that it was I who stole the ring, because he said that my death is at hand." So he knelt before Suan, and said, "Pity me! Don't tell the king that it was I who stole the ring!"

Suan was surprised at what the coachman said. After thinking for a moment, he asked, "Where is the ring?"

"Here it is."

"All right! Listen, and I will tell you what you must do in order that you may not be punished by the king. You must catch one of the king's geese tonight, and make it swallow the ring."

The coachman did what Suan had told him to do. He caught a goose and opened its mouth. He then dropped the ring into it, and pressed the bird's throat until it swallowed the ring.

The next morning the king called Suan, and said, "Tell me now who stole my daughter's ring."

"May I have a candle? I cannot guess right if I have no candle," said Suan.

The king gave him one. He lighted it and put it on a round table. He then looked up and down. He went around the table several times, uttering Latin words. Lastly he said in a loud voice, "Mi domine!"

"Where is the ring?" said the king.

Suan replied,

"Singsing na nawala
Ninakao ang akala
Ay nas' 'big ng gansa,"

which meant that the ring was not stolen, but had been swallowed by a goose. The king ordered all the geese to be killed. In the crop of one of them they found the ring. In great joy the king patted Suan on the back, and said, "You are truly the wisest boy in the world."

The next day there was a great entertainment, and Suan and the princess were married.

* * *

In a country on the other side of the sea was living a rich man named Mayabong. This man heard that the King of Campao had a son-in-law who was a good guesser. So he filled one of his cascos with gold and silver, and sailed to Campao. He went to the palace, and said, "King, is it true that your son-in-law is a good guesser?"

"Yes," said the king.

"Should you like to have a contest with me? If your son-in-law can tell how many seeds these melons I have brought here contain, I will give you that casco filled with gold and silver on the sea; but if he fails, you are to give me the same amount of money as I have brought."

The king agreed. Mayabong told him that they would meet at the public square the next day.

When Mayabong had gone away, the king called Suan, and said, "Mayabong has challenged me to a contest. You are to guess how many seeds the melons he has contain. Can you do it?" Suan was ashamed to refuse; so, even though he knew that he could not tell how many seeds a melon contained, he answered, "Yes."

When night came, Suan could not sleep. He was wondering what to do. At last he decided to drown himself in the sea. So he went to the shore and got into a tub. "I must drown myself far out, so that no one may find my body. If they see it, they will say that I was not truly a good guesser," he said to himself. He rowed and rowed until he was very tired. It so happened that he reached the place where Mayabong's casco was anchored. There he heard somebody talking. "How many seeds has the green melon?" said one. "Five," answered another. "How many seeds has the yellow one?" – "Six."

When Suan heard how many seeds each melon contained, he immediately rowed back to shore and went home.

The next morning Suan met Mayabong at the public square, as agreed. Mayabong held up a green melon, and said, "How many seeds does this melon contain?"

"Five seeds," answered Suan, after uttering some Latin words.

The melon was cut, and was found to contain five seeds. The king shouted, "We are right!"

Mayabong then held up another melon, and said, "How many does this one contain?"

Seeing that it was the yellow melon, Suan said, "It contains six."

When the melon was cut, it was found that Suan was right again. So he won the contest.

Now, Mayabong wanted to win his money back again. So he took a bottle and filled it with dung, and covered it tightly. He challenged the king again to a contest. But when Suan refused this time, because he had no idea as to what was in the bottle, the king said, "I let you marry my daughter, because I thought that you were a good guesser. Now you must prove that you are. If you refuse, you will lose your life."

When Mayabong asked what the bottle contained, Suan, filled with rage, picked it up and hurled it down on the floor, saying, "I consider that you are all waste to me." When the bottle was broken, it was found to contain waste, or dung. In great joy the king crowned Suan to succeed him. Thus Suan lived happily the rest of his life with his wife the princess.

Teofilo the Hunchback, and the Giant

ONCE THERE LIVED a hunchback whose name was Teofilo. He was an orphan, and used to get his food by wandering through the woods. He had no fixed home. Sometimes he even slept under large trees in the forest. His one blind eye, as well as his crooked body, would make almost anyone pity his miserable condition.

One day, while he was wandering through the woods looking for something to eat, he found a piece of large rope. He was very glad; for he could sell the rope, and in that way get money to buy food. Walking a little farther, he found a gun leaning against a fence. This gun, he supposed, had been left there by a hunter. He was glad to have it, too, for protection. Finally, while crossing a swampy place, he saw a duck drinking in the brook. He ran after the duck, and at last succeeded in catching it. Now he was sure of a good meal.

But it had taken him a long time to capture the duck. Night soon came on, and he had to look for a resting place. Fortunately he came to a field, and his eye caught a glimpse of light on the other side. He went towards the light, and found it to come from a house, all the windows of which were open. He knocked at the door, but nobody answered; so he just pushed it open and entered. He then began to feel very comfortable. He prepared his bed, and then went to sleep. He did not know that he was in a giant's house.

At midnight Teofilo was awakened by a loud voice. He made a hole in the wall and looked out. There in the dark he saw a very tall man, taller even than the house itself. It was the giant. The giant said, "I smell someone here." He tried to open the door, but Teofilo had locked it.

"If you are really a strong man and braver than I," said the giant, "let me see your hair!"

Teofilo then threw out the piece of rope. The giant was surprised at its size. He then asked to see Teofilo's louse, and Teofilo threw out the duck. The giant was terrified, for he had never seen such a large louse before. Finally the giant said, "Well, you seem to be larger than I. Let me hear your voice!"

Teofilo fired his gun. When the giant heard the gun and saw it spitting fire, he trembled, for he thought that the man's saliva was burning coals. Afraid to challenge his strange guest any more, the giant ran away and disappeared forever.

And so Teofilo the hunchback lived happily all the rest of his days in the giant's house without being troubled by anyone.

Magic, the Supernatural & the Divine

MANY TALES OF MAGIC and the supernatural in the Philippines are taken as fact or lived experience, as folk culture is deeply intertwined with everyday life. For instance, the Bagobo tales concerning the *buso*, a type of demonic spirit that brings evil and ill fortune to the community, has deeply impacted their religious rituals, indigenous medicine practices and their funerary rites. A good example of this would be 'The Buso-Child', which explains that if a Bagobo woman did not sleep with sharp blades beside her, the *buso* would transform her child (much like the changeling tale) into a weak and frail baby, unable to fulfil their duties to the community. Similarly, 'The Buso-Monkey' shows how the malevolent spirit can transform a dead creature into a zombie-like state.

Other stories of magic are focused on the great deeds of legendary people, such as the tale of 'Aponibolinayen and the Sun' and 'The Malaki's Sister and the Basolo' whose feats of strength and heroism were magical in nature. However, not all tales of the supernatural and the divine date from precolonial times. The presence of Spain ensured the spread of Catholicism across the archipelago, and many of these magical stories, such as 'The Priest, the Servant Boy and the Child Jesus', are also tinged with Christian didacticism.

Aponibolinayen and the Sun

ONE DAY APONIBOLINAYEN and her sister-in-law went out to gather greens. They walked to the woods to the place where the siksiklat grew, for the tender leaves of this vine are very good to eat. Suddenly, while searching about in the underbrush, Aponibolinayen cried out with joy, for she had found the vine, and she started to pick the leaves. Pull as hard as she would, however, the leaves did not come loose, and all at once the vine wound itself around her body and began carrying her upward.

Far up through the air she went until she reached the sky, and there the vine set her down under a tree. Aponibolinayen was so surprised to find herself in the sky that for some time she just sat and looked around, and then, hearing a rooster crow, she arose to see if she could find it. Not far from where she had sat was a beautiful spring surrounded by tall betel nut trees whose tops were pure gold. Rare beads were the sands of the spring, and the place where the women set their jars when they came to dip water was a large golden plate. As Aponibolinayen stood admiring the beauties of this spring, she beheld a small house nearby, and she was filled with fear lest the owner should find her there. She looked about for some means of escape and finally climbed to the top of a betel nut tree and hid.

Now the owner of this house was Ini-init, the Sun, but he was never at home in the daylight, for it was his duty to shine in the sky and give light to all the world. At the close of the day when the Big Star took his place in the sky to shine through the night, Ini-init returned to his house, but early the next morning he was always off again.

From her place in the top of the betel nut tree, Aponibolinayen saw the Sun when he came home at evening time, and again the next morning she saw him leave. When she was sure that he was out of sight she climbed down and entered his dwelling, for she was very hungry. She cooked rice, and into a pot of boiling water she dropped a stick which immediately became fish, so that she had all she wished to eat. When she was no longer hungry, she lay down on the bed to sleep.

Now late in the afternoon Ini-init returned from his work and went to fish in the river near his house, and he caught a big fish. While he sat on the bank cleaning his catch, he happened to look up towards his house and was startled to see that it appeared to be on fire. He hurried home, but when he reached the house he saw that it was not burning at all, and he entered. On his bed he beheld what looked like a flame of fire, but upon going closer he found that it was a beautiful woman fast asleep.

Ini-init stood for some time wondering what he should do, and then he decided to cook some food and invite this lovely creature to eat with him. He put rice over the fire to boil and cut into pieces the fish he had caught. The noise of this awakened Aponibolinayen, and she slipped out of the house and back to the top of the betel nut tree. The Sun did not see her leave, and when the food was prepared he called her, but the bed was empty and he had to eat alone. That night Ini-init could not sleep well, for all the time he wondered who the beautiful woman could be. The next morning, however, he rose as usual and set forth to shine in the sky, for that was his work.

That day Aponibolinayen stole again to the house of the Sun and cooked food, and when she returned to the betel nut tree she left rice and fish ready for the Sun when he came home. Late in the afternoon Ini-init went into his home, and when he found pots of hot rice and fish over the fire he was greatly troubled. After he had eaten he walked a long time in the fresh air. "Perhaps it is done by the lovely woman who looks like a flame of fire," he said. "If she comes again I will try to catch her."

The next day the Sun shone in the sky as before, and when the afternoon grew late he called to the Big Star to hurry to take his place, for he was impatient to reach home. As he drew near the house he saw that it again looked as if it was on fire. He crept quietly up the ladder, and when he had reached the top he sprang in and shut the door behind him.

Aponibolinayen, who was cooking rice over the fire, was surprised and angry that she had been caught; but the Sun gave her betel nut which was covered with gold, and they chewed together and told each other their names. Then Aponibolinayen took up the rice and fish, and as they ate they talked together and became acquainted.

After some time Aponibolinayen and the Sun were married, and every morning the Sun went to shine in the sky, and upon his return at night he found his supper ready for him. He began to be troubled, however, to know where the food came from, for though he brought home a fine fish every night, Aponibolinayen always refused to cook it.

One night he watched her prepare their meal, and he saw that, instead of using the nice fish he had brought, she only dropped a stick into the pot of boiling water.

"Why do you try to cook a stick?" asked Ini-init in surprise.

"So that we can have fish to eat," answered his wife.

"If you cook that stick for a month, it will not be soft," said Ini-init. "Take this fish that I caught in the net, for it will be good."

But Aponibolinayen only laughed at him, and when they were ready to eat she took the cover off the pot and there was plenty of nice soft fish. The next night and the next, Aponibolinayen cooked the stick, and Ini-init became greatly troubled for he saw that though the stick always supplied them with fish, it never grew smaller.

Finally he asked Aponibolinayen again why it was that she cooked the stick instead of the fish he brought, and she said:

"Do you not know of the woman on earth who has magical power and can change things?"

"Yes," answered the Sun, "and now I know that you have great power."

"Well, then," said his wife, "do not ask again why I cook the stick."

And they ate their supper of rice and the fish which the stick made.

One night not long after this Aponibolinayen told her husband that she wanted to go with him the next day when he made light in the sky.

"Oh, no, you cannot," said the Sun, "for it is very hot up there, and you cannot stand the heat."

"We will take many blankets and pillows," said the woman, "and when the heat becomes very great, I will hide under them."

Again and again Ini-init begged her not to go, but as often she insisted on accompanying him, and early in the morning they set out, carrying with them many blankets and pillows.

First, they went to the East, and as soon as they arrived the Sun began to shine, and Aponibolinayen was with him. They travelled towards the West, but when morning had passed into noontime and they had reached the middle of the sky Aponibolinayen was so hot that she melted and became oil. Then Ini-init put her into a bottle and wrapped her in the blankets and pillows and dropped her down to earth.

Now one of the women of Aponibolinayen's town was at the spring dipping water when she heard something fall near her. Turning to look, she beheld a bundle of beautiful blankets and pillows which she began to unroll, and inside she found the most beautiful woman she had ever seen. Frightened at her discovery, the woman ran as fast as she could to the town, where she called the people together and told them to come at once to the spring. They all hastened to the spot and there they found Aponibolinayen for whom they had been searching everywhere.

"Where have you been?" asked her father; "we have searched all over the world and we could not find you.'

"I have come from Pindayan," answered Aponibolinayen. "Enemies of our people kept me there till I made my escape while they were asleep at night."

All were filled with joy that the lost one had returned, and they decided that at the next moon they would perform a ceremony for the spirits and invite all the relatives who were mourning for Aponibolinayen.

So they began to prepare for the ceremony, and while they were pounding rice, Aponibolinayen asked her mother to prick her little finger where it itched, and as she did so a beautiful baby boy popped out. The people were very much surprised at this, and they noticed that every time he was bathed the baby grew very fast so that, in a short time, he was able to walk. Then they were anxious to know who was the husband of Aponibolinayen, but she would not tell them, and they decided to invite everyone in the world to the ceremony that they might not overlook him.

They sent for the betel nuts that were covered with gold, and when they had oiled them they commanded them to go to all the towns and compel the people to come to the ceremony.

"If anyone refuses to come, grow on his knee," said the people, and the betel nuts departed to do as they were bidden.

As the guests began to arrive, the people watched carefully for one who might be the husband of Aponibolinayen, but none appeared and they were greatly troubled. Finally they went to the old woman, Alokotan, who was able to talk with the spirits, and begged her to find what town had not been visited by the betel nuts which had been sent to invite the people. After she had consulted the spirits the old woman said:

"You have invited all the people except Ini-init who lives up above. Now you must send a betel nut to summon him. It may be that he is the husband of Aponibolinayen, for the siksiklat vine carried her up when she went to gather greens."

So a betel nut was called and bidden to summon Ini-init.

The betel nut went up to the Sun, who was in his house, and said:

"Good morning, Sun. I have come to summon you to a ceremony which the father and mother of Aponibolinayen are making for the spirits. If you do not want to go, I will grow on your head."

"Grow on my head," said the Sun. "I do not wish to go."

So the betel nut jumped upon his head and grew until it became so tall that the Sun was not able to carry it, and he was in great pain.

"Oh, grow on my pig," begged the Sun. So the betel nut jumped upon the pig's head and grew, but it was so heavy that the pig could not carry it and squealed all the time. At last the Sun saw that he would have to obey the summons, and he said to the betel nut:

"Get off my pig and I will go."

So Ini-init came to the ceremony, and as soon as Aponibolinayen and the baby saw him, they were very happy and ran to meet him. Then the people knew that this was the husband of Aponibolinayen, and they waited eagerly for him to come up to them. As he drew near, however, they saw that he did not walk, for he was round; and then they perceived that he was not a man but a large stone. All her relatives were very angry to find that Aponibolinayen had married a stone; and they compelled her to take off her beads and her good clothes, for, they said, she must now dress in old clothes and go again to live with the stone.

So Aponibolinayen put on the rags that they brought her and at once set out with the stone for his home. No sooner had they arrived there, however, than he became a handsome man, and they were very happy.

"In one moon," said the Sun, "we will make a ceremony for the spirits, and I will pay your father and mother the marriage price for you."

This pleased Aponibolinayen very much, and they used magic so that they had many neighbours who came to pound rice for them and to build a large spirit house.

Then they sent oiled betel nuts to summon their relatives to the ceremony. The father of Aponibolinayen did not want to go, but the betel nut threatened to grow on his knee if he did not. So he commanded all the people in the town to wash their hair and their clothes, and when all was ready they set out.

When they reached the town they were greatly surprised to find that the stone had become a man, and they chewed the magic betel nuts to see who he might be. It was discovered that he was the son of a couple in Aponibolinayen's own town, and the people all rejoiced that this couple had found the son whom they had thought lost. They named him Aponitolau, and his parents paid the marriage price for his wife – the spirit house nine times full of valuable jars.

After that all danced and made merry for one moon, and when the people departed for their homes Ini-init and his wife went with them to live on the earth.

The Battle of the Enchanters

THERE WAS ONCE a poor boy who was very ambitious to learn, and with the consent of his parents he bound himself to an enchanter who was a very wise man. The boy remained with him for a very long time, until at last his master sent him home, saying that he could teach him nothing more. The boy went home, but there he found nothing in the way of adventure, so he proposed to his father that he should become a horse, which his father could sell for twenty pesos to his late teacher. He cautioned his father that, as soon as he received the money for the horse, he should drop the halter as if by accident.

The young man then became a horse, and his father took him to the enchanter, who gave him twenty pesos. As soon as the money was in the father's hand, he dropped the halter, and the horse at once became a bird which flew away. The enchanter metamorphosed himself into a hawk and followed. The bird was so hard pressed by the hawk that it dived into the sea and became a fish. The hawk followed and became a shark. The fish, being in danger from the shark, leaped out on to the dry ground and took the shape of a crab, which hid in a spring where a princess was bathing. The shark followed in the shape of a cat, which began to search under the stones for the crab, but the crab escaped by changing itself into a ring on the finger of the princess.

Now it chanced that the father of the princess was very sick, and the enchanter went to the palace and offered to cure him for the ring on the finger of the princess. To this the king agreed, but the ring begged the princess not to give him directly to the enchanter, but to let him fall on the floor. The princess did this, and as the ring touched the floor it broke into a shower of rice. The enchanter immediately took the form of a cock and industriously pecked at the grains on the floor. But as he pecked, one of the grains changed to a cat which jumped on him and killed him.

The young man then resumed his own form, having proven himself a greater man than his master.

Buso and the Woman

IN A LITTLE HOUSE there lived a man and his wife together. One night, after they had been married for a long time, the man told his wife that he would like to go fishing.

"Oh, yes! my husband," said the woman eagerly. "Go, and bring me some nice fish tomorrow, so that we can have a good meal."

The man went out that same night to fish. And his wife was left alone in the house.

In the night, while her husband was away, the Buso came, and tried to pass himself off as her husband, saying, "You see I am back. I got no fish, because I was afraid in the river." Then the Buso-man made a great fire, and sat down by it.

But the woman did not believe that it was her husband. So she hid her comb in a place on the floor, and she said to her comb, "If the Buso calls me, do you answer. Tell him that I have run away because I have great fear of the Buso."

Then, when the Buso called, the comb answered just as the woman had told it. By and by the Buso went away. In the morning, the man came back from fishing, because daylight had come. And he had a fine catch of fish. Then the woman told him all that had happened, and the man never again let his wife sleep alone in the house. After that, everything went well; for Buso was afraid of the man, and never again attempted to come there.

The Buso-Child

DATU AYO WAS a great man among the Bagobo, well known throughout the mountain-country for his bravery and his riches. He had gathered in his house many products of Bagobo workmanship in textiles and brass and fine weapons. At his death, human sacrifices of slaves were offered up for him. It was not many years ago that he went down to the great city of the dead, and many of his children and grandchildren are living now. His sons like to think about their father's renown; and, as a reminder, the eldest son, Kawayun, always kept in his medicine case two of the incisor teeth of the great Ayo, until he needed money, and sold the medicine case with its contents. It had made Kawayun happy to look at his father's teeth.

When Datu Ayo died, his wife was about to become a mother. Now, the Bagobo women know that, when they become pregnant, they must be very careful to protect themselves from the evil Buso. On going to bed at night, an expectant mother places near her the woman's knife (gulat), the kampilan, and all the other knives, to frighten the Buso away. Failing this, the Buso will come to the woman while she sleeps, and change her baby into a Buso-child. One night, the wife of Datu Ayo lay down to sleep without putting any knives near her; and that very night the Buso came, and he transformed her child into a Buso-child. She did not know when he came, nor did she even think that a Buso had been near her, until her baby was born.

Everybody around the woman at the birth saw that something was the matter with the child. It was little and frail, and as weak as threads of cotton. Its body was flat, and its legs and arms were helpless and flabby. Then all the men said, "That is a Buso-child."

As the little boy grew old enough to creep, he moved just like a fish, with a sort of wriggling motion. He could not stand on his feet, for his legs were too weak to support his body; and he could not sit down, but only lie flat. He could never be dressed in umpak and saroa'r, and his body remained small and puny.

Now the boy is more than fourteen years old, but he cannot walk a step. He understands very well what is said to him, and he can talk, though not distinctly. When he hears it said that somebody is dead, he breaks into laughter, and keeps on laughing. This trait alone would stamp him as a Buso-child.

The Buso-Monkey

ONE DAY A MAN went out, carrying seventeen arrows, to hunt monkeys; but he found none. Next day he went again, and, as he walked along on the slope of the mountain called Malagu'san, he heard the sound of the chattering of monkeys in the trees. Looking up, he saw the great monkey sitting on an aluma'yag tree. He took a shot at the monkey, but his arrow

missed; and the next time he had no better luck. Twice eight he tried it; but he never hit the mark. The monkey seemed to lead a charmed life. Finally he took his seventeenth and last arrow, and brought down his game; the monkey fell down dead. But a voice came from the monkey's body that said, "You must carry me."

So the man picked up the monkey, and started to go back home; but on the way the monkey said, "You are to make a fire, and eat me up right here."

Then the man laid the monkey on the ground. Again came the voice, "You will find a bamboo to put me in; by and by you shall eat me."

Off went the man to find the bamboo called laya, letting the monkey lie on the ground, where he had dropped it.

He walked on until he reached a forest of bamboo. There, swinging on a branch of the laya, was a karirik bird. And the bird chirped to the man, "Where are you going?"

The man answered, "I am looking for bamboo to put the monkey in."

But the karirik bird exclaimed, "Run away, quick! for by and by the monkey will become a buso. I will wait here, and be cutting the laya; then, when the monkey calls you, I will answer him."

In the meantime the monkey had become a great buso. He had only one eye, and that stood right in the middle of his forehead, looking just like the big bowl called langungan (the very bad buso have only one eye; some have only one leg).

After the Buso-monkey had waited many hours for the man to come back, he started out to look for him. When he reached the forest of laya, he called to the man, "Where are you?"

Then the karirik bird answered from the tree, "Here I am, right here, cutting the bamboo."

But the man had run away, because the bird had sent him off, and made him run very fast.

As soon as the bird had answered the Buso, it flew off to another bamboo tree, and there the Buso spied it, and knew that he had been fooled; and he said, "It's a man I want; you're just a bird. I don't care for you."

Directly then the Buso began to smell around the ground where the man had started to run up the mountainside, and, as quick as he caught the scent, he trailed the man. He ran and ran, and all the time the man was running too; but soon the Buso began to gain on him. After a while, when the Buso had come close upon him, the man tried to look for some cover. He reached a big rock, and cried out, "O rock! will you give me shelter when the Buso tries to eat me?"

"No," replied the rock; "for, if I should help you, the Buso would break me off and throw me away."

Then the man ran on; and the Buso came nearer and nearer, searching behind every rock as he rushed along, and spying up into every tree, to see if, perchance, the man were concealed there.

At last the man came to the lemon tree called kabayawa, that has long, sharp thorns on its branches. And the man cried out to the lemon tree, "Could you protect me, if I were to hide among your leaves and flowers?"

Instantly the lemon tree answered, "Come right up, if you want to." Then the man climbed the tree, and concealed himself in the branches, among the flowers. Very soon the Buso came under the lemon tree, and shouted to it, "I smell a man here. You are hiding him."

The Kabayawa said, "Sure enough, here's a man! You just climb up and get him."

Then the Buso began to scramble up the tree; but as he climbed, the thorns stuck their sharp points into him. The higher he climbed, the longer and sharper grew the thorns of the tree, piercing and tearing, until they killed the Buso.

It is because the monkey sometimes turns into a Buso that many Bagobo refuse to eat monkey. But some of the mountain Bagobo eat monkey to keep off sores.

The Buso's Basket

TWO CHILDREN WENT out into the field to tend their rice plants. They said these words to keep the little birds away from the grain:

"One, one, maya bird,
Yonder in the north;
Keep off from eating it,
This my rice."

Just then they heard the sound of a voice, calling from the great pananag tree, "Wait a minute, children, until I make a basket for you."

"What is that?" said the boy to his sister.

"Oh, nothing!" answered the little girl. "It's the sound of something."

Then the children called to their father and mother; but only from the pananag tree the answer came, "Just wait till I finish this basket to hold you in."

Down, then, from the tree came the great Buso, with a big, deep basket (such as women carry bananas and camotes in) hanging from his shoulders. The frightened children did not dare to run away; and Buso sat down near by in the little hut where the rice was kept. Soon he said to the children, "Please comb out my nice hair."

But, when they tried to comb his hair, they found it swarming with big lice and worms.

"Well, let's go on now," said the Buso. Then he stuffed the children into his deep burden-basket, and swung the basket upon his back.

On the instant the little girl screamed out, "Wait a minute, Buso! I've dropped my comb. Let me down to pick it up."

So the Buso sat down on the ground, and let the girl climb out of the basket. He sat waiting for her to find her comb; but all the time she was picking up big stones, and putting them into the basket. Her brother got out of the basket too, and then both girl and boy climbed up into a tall betel nut tree, leaving Buso with a basket full of stones on his back.

Up to his house in the pananag tree went Buso with the heavy basket. When his wife saw him, she laughed and shouted very loud. She was glad, because she thought there was a man in the basket, all ready to eat. But, when Buso slipped the basket down from his shoulders, there was no human flesh in it, but only big stones.

Then the angry Buso hurried back to look for the two children. At last he caught sight of them far up in the betel nut tree, and wondered how he could get them. Now, at the foot of the tree there was a growth of the wild plant called "bagkang;" and Buso said words to make the bagkang grow faster and taller:

"Tubu, tubu, bagkang,
Grow, grow, bagkang,
Baba, baba mamaa'n" (Handle, handle, betel nut).

But the children, in their turn, said:

"Tubu, tubu, mamaa'n,
Grow, grow, betel nut,
Baba, baba bagkang" (Handle, handle, bagkang).

By and by, when the bagkang stems had grown so tall as almost to reach the clusters of betel nuts at the top of the trunk, the boy and girl said to each other, "Let us pick betel nuts, and throw them down on the bagkang."

And as soon as they began to pick, the betel nuts became so big and heavy that the bagkang plants fell down when the betel nuts dropped on them.

Then the Buso went away; and the children climbed down in haste, ran home, and told their mother and father how the Buso had tried to carry them off.

Camanla and Parotpot

CAMANLA WAS A VERY poor but very busy man, and always praising his own work. When he talked with other people he ended every third or fourth word with "la," which was the last syllable of his name and is a word of praise.

One day he made a boat, and when it was finished he began to talk to it. These were his words: "My boat, la, you may go, la, to find a pretty lady, la, for my wife, la, to make me happy, la." Then his boat started to sail without anybody to manage it. When she reached a large town she stopped in the river, near where the pretty daughters of some rich men of the town were taking a walk. They were accustomed to take any boat they might find and use it when they wished to cross the river, returning in the same way.

As Camanla's boat was there and looked very fine, the young ladies decided to cross the river in it. The youngest was the first to jump into the boat. When the little boat felt that someone had come on board, she ran away, carrying the lady.

When Camanla saw his boat coming, he began to praise it, saying, "My boat, la, is coming, la, to bring me, la, my pretty lady, to marry me, la." Very soon the boat anchored, and he went down to receive the lady, whom he soon married. Then was Camanla happy, but one day he had no food to give his wife, so he made a little taon, or fish trap, and said to it, "My pretty taon, la, you may go, la, to the river, la, to get me some fish, la." The taon then walked towards the river, and soon came back, full of fish. Camanla was an object of envy to all the world.

His happiness was soon heard of by his friend Parotpot, who became very envious. At last he went to Camanla's house. When he met his friend, he said to him, "You are very happy, my friend, and I envy you." Camanla replied, "Yes, I am very fortunate. I have my little boat that sails every day to get my food, and a little taon that goes to the river and brings me fine fish."

Parotpot returned sadly home. He concluded to build a boat like his friend's, but Parotpot, when he talked, ended every third or fourth word with "pot" (pronounced po), the ending of his name: This word has a scornful meaning. When the boat was finished, he began to talk to it as follows: "My boat, pot, you may go, pot, to find me a wife, pot, prettier than my friend's wife, pot." The boat sailed away, and reached a large river, just as some men were looking for a boat to take across the body of their grandmother, in order to bury it in the cemetery of the town. When they saw the boat they were glad to get across the river so easily, so they lifted the body and placed it in the boat. When the boat felt that something was on board, she sailed swiftly towards home, leaving the men behind. Parotpot was watching, and when he saw the boat coming, he began to talk thus: "My boat, pot, is coming, pot, to bring me, pot, a pretty lady, pot, to marry me, pot." But, alas! a dead grandmother, instead of a pretty lady! He was so angry that he seized his bolo and chopped the boat to pieces, leaving the body to float away.

But Parotpot thought that he might succeed better with a fish-trap, like his friend Camanla's. When he had finished it, he sent it to the river, saying, "My taon, pot, go now to the river, pot, and catch many fishes, pot, for my dinner, pot." The taon went. It was Sunday and the people of the town were killing cattle for their Sunday dinner, and throwing the waste into the river. All this filth floated into the taon and filled it. Then it ran back home. While the taon had been gone, Parotpot had been making preparations for a great dinner. He cooked the rice and washed the dishes, and then invited his friends to come to his house and share his excellent dinner. When he saw the taon coming, he said, "My taon, pot, is coming now, pot, to bring me many fine fish, pot, for my dinner, pot." When his neighbours saw what was in the taon, they laughed, and Parotpot said, "I can never be as happy as my friend Camanla." Then he took the taon and threw it into the fire.

Catalina of Dumaguete

MANY YEARS AGO there lived in Dumaguete a poor tuba seller named Banog, who made his daily rounds to the houses just as the milkman does in far-off America. But instead of a rattling wagon he had only a long bamboo from which he poured the drink, and in place of sweet milk he left the sap of the coconut tree.

The bad custom of mixing tuñgud, a kind of red bark, with the sap, and thus making of it a strong liquor, had not yet been known, so Banog, though poor, was respected, and the people tried in every way to help him and his daughter Catalina.

Catalina was a beautiful girl of sixteen and very good and industrious, but with many strange ways. She scarcely ever spoke a word and spent most of her time in looking out over the sea. Sometimes she would suddenly stand erect and, clasping her hands, would remain for a long time looking up at the sky as if she saw something that no one else could see. On account of these strange manners the people thought her a wonderful girl and she was supposed to have mysterious powers.

One day many ships came up from the island of Mindanao and hundreds of fierce Moros landed. Shouting and waving their terrible knives, they fell upon the peaceful people and killed many, among them poor Banog. Then they robbed and burned the houses and, seizing all the women they could find, set sail for their great southern island. Among the prisoners was Catalina. With her eyes fixed on the sky she sat very quiet and still in the bow of one of the boats, and though her companions spoke often to her she made no reply.

Suddenly she sprang into the water and a wonderful thing occurred, for, instead of sinking, she walked lightly over the waves towards the distant shore. The Moros were so astonished that they did not try to stop her and she reached the land safely.

Many people who had hidden in the forests ran out to meet her but she spoke to no one. With her eyes still fixed above she walked through the burning town and along the road to Dalugdug, the Thunder mountain, that lies behind Dumaguete.

On Dalugdug there lived a terrible Sigbin. Its body was like that of a monstrous crow, but just under its neck were two long legs like those of a grasshopper, which enabled it to leap great distances without using its wings. It ate anyone who came near its home, so when the people saw Catalina start to climb the mountain they begged her to come back. She paid no heed to their cries, however, but went up higher and higher, till her white dress seemed merely a speck on the mountainside.

All at once she seemed to stop and raise her hands. Then a fearful shriek was heard, and the fierce Sigbin came rushing down the mountain. It appeared to be greatly frightened, for it took tremendous leaps and screamed as if in terror. Over the heads of the people it jumped, and, reaching the shore, cleared the narrow channel and disappeared among the mountains of the island of Cebu.

When the people saw that the Sigbin had gone they ran up the mountain and searched everywhere for Catalina, but they could find no trace of her. Sorrowfully they returned to their homes and busied themselves in building new houses and in making their town beautiful once more.

Several years passed in peace and then again the Moro boats came up from Mindanao. The men hurriedly gathered on the beach to meet them, and the women and children hid in the coconut groves.

This time the Moros had no quick and easy victory, for the Visayans, armed with bolos and remembering their lost wives and sisters, fought furiously, and for a time drove the enemy before them. But more Moro boats arrived and numbers told against the defenders. Slowly but surely they fell fighting until but a few remained.

Suddenly a bridge of clouds unfolded from Dalugdug to the town, and across it came the lost Catalina holding a beehive in her hands. Then she spoke and thousands of bees flew from the hive to the ground. Again she spoke and waved her hand, and the bees changed into little black men with long sharp spears, who charged the Moros and killed every one of them.

Then Catalina, the hive still in her hand, went back over the bridge and disappeared once more in the mountain.

The people came out of their hiding places, crowding around the little black men and questioning them, but they received no answer. Instead the little warriors gathered together and ran into the forest and up the mountainside, where they were soon lost to view.

Such is the story of Catalina. Since that time Dumaguete has been safe from the Moros. The Sigbin has never returned to Negros. It still lives in the mountains of Cebu and the people are so afraid of it that they lock themselves in their houses after dark and can hardly be induced to come out. Up in the mountains of Negros live the little black men. They are called Negritos and are very savage and wild.

The saviour of Dumaguete still lives in Dalugdug and is worshipped by the people. And in the town, now grown into a big busy city, the old people for years to come will tell their grandchildren the story of Catalina.

The Child Saint

ONCE THERE WAS a child who was different from other children. She was very quiet and patient, and never spoke unless she was spoken to. Her mother used to urge her to play in the streets with the other children, but she always preferred to

sit in the corner quietly and without trouble to anyone. When the time came for the child to enter school, she begged her mother to get her a book of doctrines and let her learn at home. So her mother got a book of doctrines for her, and she was able to read at once without being taught. Day after day she sat in the corner reading her books and meditating.

When she became a little larger she asked to have a little room built away from the house, where she might remain free from the intrusion of any earthly thought.

Her mother had this done, and there in the tight little room with no one to see her she sat. She never tasted the food or drink placed at her door, and finally her mother, becoming alarmed, made a tiny hole and peeped through the wall. There sat the child reading her book, with a huge man standing beside her, and all manner of beasts and serpents filling the little room.

More frightened than ever, the mother ran to the priest, who told her that those were devils tempting the child, but not to fear, for she would certainly become a saint. And it was so, for afterwards the evil shapes were gone. Then the priest and the people built a costly shrine and placed her in it, and there the people used to go and ask her to intercede for them. But at last the shrine was found empty, and surely she was taken alive into heaven and is now a saint.

The Covetous King and the Three Children

THERE WERE ONCE three orphan children, the oldest of whom was perhaps ten years old, and the others but little things, almost babies. They had a tiny little tumbledown house to live in, but very little to eat. Said the eldest to his little brother and sister, "I will go yonder on the sands laid bare by the falling tide, and it may be that I shall find something that we can eat." The little children begged to go too, and they all set out over the sands. Soon they found a large living shell. "Thanks be to God," said the boy, for he was well instructed,

"we shall have something to eat." "Take me home, but do not cook me," said the shell, "and I will work for you." Now this was probably the Holy Virgin herself, in the form of a shell, who had taken pity on the poor children. They took the shell home, and there it spoke again. "Put me into the rice pot, cover me up, and you shall turn out plenty of boiled rice for all of you." And they did so, and the boiled rice came from the pot. "Now put me into the other pot, and take out ulam." And they took out ulam in abundance. "Have you a clothes chest?" asked the shell; but there was none, so they put it into a box, and the box became filled with clothing. Then the shell filled the spare room with rice, and last of all filled another large box with money.

Now the king of this city was a cruel man, and he sent for the children and told them that they must give up their money, their rice and all to him and be poor again. "O dear king," said the oldest child, "will you not leave us a little for our living?" "No," replied the king, "I will give you as much boiled rice as you need, and you ought to be glad that you get it."

So the king sent ten soldiers to move the rice and the money, but, as soon as they got it to the king's house, it returned to the children. The soldiers worked a whole week without getting a grain of rice or a piece of money to stay in the king's house. Then because they were about to die from fatigue, the king sent ten more, and these too failed. Then the king went himself, but when he tried to move the money he fell down dead. The children, relieved from persecution, lived long and happy lives and were always rich and influential people.

The Faithlessness of Sinogo

YEARS AND YEARS AGO, when Maguayan ruled the sea and the terrible Captan launched his thunderbolts from above, the water and air were filled with swimming and flying monsters. Those that lived in the air were armed with great

teeth and sharp claws; but, though they were fierce and savage, they lived together in peace, for they feared the anger of their master Captan.

In the sea, however, all was not so peaceful, for some of the monsters were so huge and savage and so confident in their strength that Maguayan could do nothing with them. He lived in constant fear of attack from these fierce subjects and finally, in despair, called on Captan to help him in his trouble.

Accordingly Captan sent his swift messengers to every part of the earth, air and sea, and ordered that a council of all the creatures in the world should be held. He named the little island of Caueli in the centre of the Sulu Sea as the meeting place, and commanded all to hasten there without delay.

Soon the members of the council began to arrive, and the sky was darkened by flying monsters, and the water boiled as the terrible reptiles of the sea rushed to the place appointed.

In a short time the little island was crowded with these dreadful creatures. There were huge Buayas from Mindanao, fierce Tic-bolans from Luzon, savage Sigbins from Negros and Bohol, hundreds of Unglocs from Panay and Leyte, and great Uak Uaks and other frightful monsters from Samar and Cebu. They grouped themselves in a large circle around a golden throne on which sat Captan and Maguayan, and while waiting the commands of their master filled the air with shrieks and howls.

At length Captan raised his hand and the noise instantly stopped. Then he announced his decree. He said that Maguayan was his brother god and should be treated with the same respect. He commanded all his subjects to obey the god of the sea and told them that he would kill with a thunderbolt any that disobeyed this order. Then he desired all to return to their own regions, and again the air was filled with a noise of thunder and the sea roared and foamed as the monsters went back to their homes.

Soon there remained on the island only Captan, Maguayan and three messengers of Captan, who were called Sinogo, Dalagan and Guidala. These were giants in size and had large wings which enabled them to fly with great swiftness. They had long spears and sharp swords and were very brave and powerful. Of the three, Dalagan was the swiftest, Guidala the bravest, and Sinogo the handsomest and best loved by Captan.

When all the creatures were gone Maguayan thanked Captan, but the great god said that he had only done his duty in helping his brother. Then he gave Maguayan a little golden shell and explained to him its wonderful power. Maguayan had but to put it in his mouth and he could change his form to that of any creature he pleased. In case a monster, defying Captan's orders, should attack him, he had simply to change himself into a stronger monster of twice the size of his enemy, and then fight and kill him easily.

Again Maguayan thanked his brother god and, taking the shell, placed it on the throne beside him. Then Captan ordered his messengers to bring food and drink, and soon the two gods were feasting merrily.

Now it happened that Sinogo had been standing behind the throne and had heard all that had been said. He was filled with a desire to own the wonderful shell, and in spite of the many favours he had received from Captan he resolved to steal it. The more he thought of its great power, the more he longed for it. With it he could rule the earth and sea as a god, and, by hiding, he might avoid the anger of Captan. So he watched for an opportunity to make away with it. Finally his chance came. While handing Maguayan some food, he slyly caught up the shell, and soon afterwards quietly slipped away.

For some time his absence was not discovered, but all at once Captan called for his favourite messenger and, receiving no reply, ordered Dalagan to search for him. Soon Dalagan returned and reported that Sinogo could not be found on the island. At the same time Maguayan noticed that the golden shell was gone.

Then Captan knew that his messenger had stolen the shell and escaped. He flew into a great rage and swore he would kill Sinogo. He ordered Dalagan and Guidala to hasten to the north in search of the faithless messenger and to bring him back a prisoner.

Swiftly northward over the blue sea flew the messengers, and near the island of Guimaras caught sight of Sinogo. He saw his pursuers and flew all the swifter, but he was no match for them in speed. Nearer and nearer they came and then, drawing their swords, rushed forward to seize him.

But Sinogo was not to be easily caught. Quick as a flash, he placed the shell in his mouth and dived down into the water, at the same time changing himself into a huge crocodile-shaped Buaya with scales like armour of steel.

In vain Dalagan and Guidala rained blows on the monster. The swords could not pierce the heavy scales.

Up through Guimaras Strait the chase went on, and Sinogo tore up the water in his flight. So great was the disturbance of the ocean that, as they rounded the northern coast of Negros, the waves dashed completely over the little island of Bacabac, sweeping away the hills and bringing the land to the level of the sea.

Still the rapid flight went on. Straight for Bantayan headed Sinogo, but suddenly changing his course he dashed into the narrow channel between Negros and Cebu. Then Dalagan, leaving Guidala to continue the chase alone, flew swiftly back to Caueli and told Captan that Sinogo was in the little strait. Up sprang the god and, flying directly east, he posted himself at the southern entrance of the channel. In his hand he held an enormous thunderbolt, and thus armed he waited for the appearance of Sinogo.

Down into the narrow entrance sped the faithless messenger, tearing up the water in his mad flight, while the brave Guidala struck in vain at his huge body. Suddenly a roar of thunder sounded and the thunderbolt fell on the back of the monster, bearing him down beneath the waves and then, stiffening like a bar of iron, pinning him to the bottom far below. In vain he struggled to free himself; the bar held him fast and sure. In his struggles the shell fell from his mouth, but a little Tamban caught it and brought it safely to Captan.

Thousands of years have passed, but far under the water, like a fly on a pin, Sinogo struggles in the form of a huge Buaya. The water bubbles around him and for three miles little whirlpools go racing up the channel. And the native in his little sacayan avoids the narrow entrance where the water boils and foams, for Sinogo still twists and squirms, and the Liloan is a thing to be feared and dreaded.

How Iro Met the S'irang

NOT LONG AGO, a young man named Iro went out, about two o'clock in the afternoon, to get some tobacco from one of the neighbours. Not far from his house, he saw his friend Atun coming along; and Atun said to him, "I've got some tobacco hidden away in a place in the woods. Let us go and get it."

So they went along together. When they reached the forest, Atun disappeared, and Iro could not see which way he had gone. Then he concluded that it was not Atun, but a S'iring, whom he had met. He started for home, and reached there about eight o'clock in the evening. To his astonishment, he saw Atun sitting there in the house. Confused and wondering, he asked Atun, "Did you carry me away?"

But his friend Atun laughed, and said, "Where should I carry you? I have not been anywhere."

Then Iro was convinced that a S'iring had tried to lure him into the forest.

When you have a companion, the S'iring cannot hurt you.

Hidden Treasure

THERE WERE ONCE a husband and his wife who were very poor. They had a little plot of ground that helped to sustain them, but as the man was sick the woman went to work alone.

As she was weeding in the fields she found a malapad, and after a little she found another, and so on until she had a sec-apat. With this she returned home and bought rice, but she was afraid to tell her husband lest he be jealous.

The next day she went to work and on this day she found a silver peso. As she reached the edge of the field a voice spoke to her saying, "Tell no one of your good fortune, not even your husband, and you shall have more treasure." Afterwards she went to the field, and daily she found a peso until she had five pesos, which she hid in a safe place.

On the seventh day she went to the field, but found nothing. She went to the edge of the field to boil her rice, and was blowing her fire when she heard the same voice again saying, "Never mind boiling your rice, but dig there under your pallok, and you will find more than enough. Tell no one, not even your husband, of what you find." She dug down and there she found a great jar filled to the brim with gold pieces. She took one or two, and hastily covered up the rest and went home. Like a good wife she disliked to keep a secret from her husband, and finally she took him off to a quiet place and told him of their good fortune.

He, overjoyed, could not restrain himself and went into the village and told everyone of the treasure trove. Then they went to dig it up, but it was no longer there. Even the gold and the five pesos already saved and hidden in another secret place were gone, and they were as poor as they had been before.

How foolish they were to disobey the command of the voice!

How Jackyo Became Rich

A LONG TIME AGO there was a young man whose name was Jackyo. He was very poor, and by his daily labour could earn barely enough for his food and nothing at all for his clothes. He had a little farm at some distance from the village in which he lived, and on it raised a few poor crops.

One pleasant afternoon Jackyo started off to visit his farm. It was late when he reached it, and after he had finished inspecting his crops, he turned back homewards. But the bright day had gone and the sun had set. Night came on quickly, and the way was dark and lonely.

At last he could no longer see the road. Not a star was to be seen, and the only sounds he heard were the sad twitterings of the birds and soft rustling of the leaves as they were moved by the wind.

At last he entered a thick forest where the trees were very big. "What if I should meet some wild beast," thought Jackyo; but he added half aloud, "I must learn to be brave and face every danger."

It was not long before he was very sure that he could hear a deep roar. His heart beat fast, but he walked steadily forward, and soon the roar was repeated, this time nearer and more distinctly, and he saw in the dim light a great wild ox coming towards him.

He found a large hole in the trunk of a huge tree. "I will pass the night here in this tree," he said to himself.

In a little while an old man appeared. His body was covered with coarse hair and he was very ugly. He looked fiercely at Jackyo from head to foot and said, "What are you thinking of to come in here? Do you not know that this is the royal castle of the king of evil spirits?"

Jackyo became more frightened than before and for a long time he could not speak, but at last he stammered, "Excuse me, sir, but I cannot go home on account of the dark night. I pray you to let me rest here for a short time."

"I cannot let you stay here, because our king is not willing to help anyone who does not belong to his kingdom. If he did so, his kingdom would be lost. But what is your name? Do you know how to sing?" said the old man.

"My name is Jackyo, and I know a little bit about singing," replied Jackyo.

"Well," said the old man, "if you know any song, sing for me." Now Jackyo knew but one song, and that was about the names of the days of the week except Sunday. He did not like to sing it, but the old man urged him, saying, "If you do not sing, I will cut your head off." So Jackyo began to sing.

It happened that the king of the evil spirits, whose name was Mensaya, heard Jackyo's song and was very much interested in it. He called a servant, named Macquil, and said, "Macquil, go downstairs and see who is singing down there, and when you find him, bring him to me."

Jackyo went before the king, bowed to the floor, touching the carpet with his forehead, and stood humbly before the king.

"Let me hear your song," said the king. So Jackyo, with great respect, sang the only song he knew. Here it is:

Mon-day, Tues-day, Wednesday, Thurs-day, Fri-day, Sat-ur-day.

While he was singing, all the evil spirits in the cave gathered around him to hear his song, and Mensaya asked him to sing it over and over again. They were all so pleased with it that Mensaya ordered Macquil to give Jackyo a large quantity of gold and silver as a reward for his beautiful song.

When the morning came Jackyo returned home, full of joy, and became known as the richest man in the village.

How the Farmer Deceived the Demon

VERY MANY YEARS AGO, in a faraway land where the trees never changed their green leaves and where the birds always sang, there lived on an island a farmer with a large family. Though all alone on the island and knowing nothing of people in the outer world, they were always happy – as happy as the laughing rills that rippled past their home. They had no great wealth, depending from year to year on the crops which the father raised. They needed no money, for they lacked nothing; and they never sold their produce, for no people were near to buy.

One day in the middle of the year, after the crops were well started, a loud, unusual roar was heard. Suddenly a stiff gale blew up from the southwest, and with it came clouds which quickly hid the entire sky. The day turned to night. The birds ceased to sing and went to their nests. The wild beasts ran to their caves. The family sought shelter in the house from a heavy downpour of rain which continued for many days and nights. So long did it last that they became very anxious about the condition of things around them.

On the eighth day the birds again began to sing, and the sun was, as usual, bright. The farmer arose early and went out to look at his fields, but, lo! his crop was all destroyed. He went back to the house and told the family that the water-god was angry and had washed away all that he had hoped to have for the coming year.

What were they to do? The supply in the house was getting low and it was too late to raise another crop. The father worried night and day, for he did not know how he could keep his children from starvation.

One day he made a long journey and came into a place that was strange to him. He had never before seen the like of it. But in the midst of a broad meadow he saw a tree with spreading branches like an elm, and as his legs and back were stiff from walking, he went over and sat down under it. Presently, looking up, he discovered that on the tree were large red fruits. He climbed up and brought some down, and after satisfying his hunger he fell asleep.

He had not slept long when he was awakened by a loud noise. The owner of the place was coming. He was fearful to look upon. His body was like that of a person, but he was of enormous size; and he had a long tail, and two horns growing out of his head. The farmer was frightened and did not know what to do. He stood motionless till the master came up and began to talk to him. Then he explained that he had come there in search of food to keep his family alive. The monster was delighted to hear this, for he saw that he had the man and the man's family in his power. He told the traveller that in return for a certain promise he would help him out of his troubles.

The demon, as he was called by some travellers to that land, showed the farmer a smooth, round stone, which, he said, gave its possessor the power of a magician. He offered to lend this to the farmer for five years, if at the expiration of that time the farmer and family would become his slaves. The farmer consented.

Then the demon was glad. He said to the farmer, "You must squeeze the stone when you wish to become invisible; and must put it in your mouth when you wish to return to human form."

The man tried the power of the magic stone. He squeezed it, and instantly became invisible to the demon; but he bade him farewell, and promised to meet him in the same place at the appointed time.

In this invisible form the man crossed the water that washed the shore of the island on which he lived. There he found a people who lived in communities. He wanted something to eat, so he went into the shops; but he found that a restaurant owned by a Chinaman was the one to which most people of the city went. He put the stone in his mouth, thus appearing in visible form, and, entering the restaurant, ordered the best food he could find. He finished his meal quickly and went out. The waiter, perceiving that he did not pay, followed him. The man had no money; so he squeezed the stone and shot up into the air without being seen. The Chinaman, alarmed by the cry of the waiter, came out and ran in all directions, trying to find and catch the man. No one could find him; and the people thought he must indeed be a fast runner to escape so quickly, for they did not know of the gift of the demon.

Not far from that place he saw groups of men and women going in and out of a large building. It was a bank. The farmer went in to see what he could find. There he saw bags of money, gold and silver. He chuckled with joy at this opportunity. In order to use his hands freely, he put the stone in his mouth; but before he could fill all his pockets with money, he was discovered by the two guards, who began to pound him on the head. He struggled to save his life, and finally took the stone out of his mouth and squeezed it. Instantly he vanished from their sight; but he was vexed at the beating he had received, so he carried off all the gold they had in the bank. The people inside as well as outside the building became crazy. They ran about in all directions, not knowing why. Some called the firemen, thinking the bank was on fire; but nothing had happened, except that the farmer was gone and the two guards were "half dead frightened". They danced up and down the streets in great excitement, but could not utter a word.

Straight home went the farmer, not stopping by the way. His wife and children were awaiting him. He gave them the money, and told them all about the fortune which he had gotten from the man on their own island – told all his secrets. Prosperous they became, and with the money which he had brought they purchased all they needed from the city just opposite them.

The time passed so pleasantly that the man was surprised to discover that his promise would be due in two more days. He made preparations to go back to the land of his master. Arrived there, he met the same monster under the same tree. The demon was displeased to see the old man alone, without the family which also had been promised. He told the man that he would shut him in a cave and then would go and capture those left at home.

But the farmer would not go to the cave. The demon tried to pull him into a deep hole. Both struggled; and at last the farmer squeezed the magic stone and disappeared. He took a green branch of the tree and beat the demon. The demon surrendered. He begged for mercy.

The farmer went home, and from that day thought no more of the demon. He knew that while he held the stone the monster would never come to trouble him. And the family lived on in peace and happiness, as they had done before the water-god became angry with them.

How the World Was Made

THOUSANDS OF YEARS AGO there was no land nor sun nor moon nor stars, and the world was only a great sea of water, above which stretched the sky. The water was the kingdom of the god Maguayan, and the sky was ruled by the great god Captan.

Maguayan had a daughter called Lidagat, the sea, and Captan had a son known as Lihangin, the wind. The gods agreed to the marriage of their children, so the sea became the bride of the wind.

Three sons and a daughter were born to them. The sons were called Licalibutan, Liadlao and Libulan, and the daughter received the name of Lisuga.

Licalibutan had a body of rock and was strong and brave; Liadlao was formed of gold and was always happy; Libulan was made of copper and was weak and timid; and the beautiful Lisuga had a body of pure silver and was sweet and gentle. Their parents were very fond of them, and nothing was wanting to make them happy.

After a time Lihangin died and left the control of the winds to his eldest son Licalibutan. The faithful wife Lidagat soon followed her husband, and the children, now grown up, were left without father or mother. However, their grandfathers, Captan and Maguayan, took care of them and guarded them from all evil.

After a time, Licalibutan, proud of his power over the winds, resolved to gain more power, and asked his brothers to join him in an attack on Captan in the sky above. At first they refused; but when Licalibutan became angry with them, the amiable Liadlao, not wishing to offend his brother, agreed to help. Then together they induced the timid Libulan to join in the plan.

When all was ready the three brothers rushed at the sky, but they could not beat down the gates of steel that guarded the entrance. Then Licalibutan let loose the strongest winds and blew the bars in every direction. The brothers rushed into the opening, but were met by the angry god Captan. So terrible did he look that they turned and ran in terror; but Captan, furious at the destruction of his gates, sent three bolts of lightning after them.

The first struck the copper Libulan and melted him into a ball. The second struck the golden Liadlao and he too was melted. The third bolt struck Licalibutan and his rocky body broke into many pieces and fell into the sea. So huge was he that parts of his body stuck out above the water and became what is known as land.

In the meantime the gentle Lisuga had missed her brothers and started to look for them. She went towards the sky, but as she approached the broken gates, Captan, blind with anger, struck her too with lightning, and her silver body broke into thousands of pieces.

Captan then came down from the sky and tore the sea apart, calling on Maguayan to come to him and accusing him of ordering the attack on the sky. Soon Maguayan appeared and answered that he knew nothing of the plot as he had been asleep far down in the sea. After a time he succeeded in calming the angry Captan. Together they wept at the loss of their grandchildren, especially the gentle and beautiful Lisuga; but with all their power they could not restore the dead to life. However, they gave to each body a beautiful light that will shine forever.

And so it was that golden Liadlao became the sun and copper Libulan the moon, while the thousands of pieces of silver Lisuga shine as the stars of heaven. To wicked Licalibutan the gods gave no light, but resolved to make his body support a new race of people. So Captan gave Maguayan a seed and he planted it on the land, which, as you will remember, was part of Licalibutan's huge body. Soon a bamboo tree grew up, and from the hollow of one of its branches a man and a woman came out. The man's name was Sicalac, and the woman was called Sicabay. They were the parents of the human race. Their first child was a son whom they called Libo; afterwards they had a daughter who was known as Saman. Pandaguan was a younger son and he had a son called Arion.

Pandaguan was very clever and invented a trap to catch fish. The very first thing he caught was a huge shark. When he brought it to land, it looked so great and fierce that he thought it was surely a god, and he at once ordered his people to worship it. Soon all gathered around and began to sing and pray to the shark. Suddenly the sky and sea opened, and the gods came out and ordered Pandaguan to throw the shark back into the sea and to worship none but them.

All were afraid except Pandaguan. He grew very bold and answered that the shark was as big as the gods, and that since he had been able to overpower it he would also be able to conquer the gods. Then Captan, hearing this, struck Pandaguan with a small thunderbolt, for he did not wish to kill him but merely to teach him a lesson. Then he and Maguayan decided to punish these people by scattering them over the earth, so they carried some to one land and some to another. Many children were afterwards born, and thus the earth became inhabited in all parts.

Pandaguan did not die. After lying on the ground for thirty days he regained his strength, but his body was blackened from the lightning, and all his descendants ever since that day have been black.

His first son, Arion, was taken north, but as he had been born before his father's punishment he did not lose his colour, and all his people therefore are white.

Libo and Saman were carried south, where the hot sun scorched their bodies and caused all their descendants to be of a brown colour.

A son of Saman and a daughter of Sicalac were carried east, where the land at first was so lacking in food that they were compelled to eat clay. On this account their children and their children's children have always been yellow in colour.

And so the world came to be made and peopled. The sun and moon shine in the sky and the beautiful stars light up the night. All over the land, on the body of the envious Licalibutan, the children of Sicalac and Sicabay have grown great in numbers. May they live forever in peace and brotherly love!

Juan Manalaksan

ONCE UPON A TIME there lived in a certain village a brave and powerful datu who had only one son. The son was called Pedro. In the same place lived a poor woodcutter whose name was Juan Manalaksan. Pedro was rich, and had no work to do. He often diverted himself by hunting deer and wild boar in the forests and mountains. Juan got his living by cutting trees in the forests.

One day the datu and his son went to the mountain to hunt. They took with them many dogs and guns. They did not take any food, however, for they felt sure of catching something to eat for their dinner. When they reached the mountain, Pedro killed a deer. By noon they had become tired and hungry, so they went to a shady place to cook their game. While he was eating, Pedro choked on a piece of meat. The father cried out loudly, for he did not know what to do for his dying son. Juan, who was cutting wood near by, heard the shout. He ran quickly to help Pedro, and by pulling the piece of meat out of his throat he saved Pedro's life. Pedro was grateful, and said to Juan, "Tomorrow come to my palace, and I will give you a reward for helping me."

The next morning Juan set out for the palace. On his way he met an old woman, who asked him where he was going.

"I am going to Pedro's house to get my reward," said Juan.

"Do not accept any reward of money or wealth," said the old woman, "but ask Pedro to give you the glass which he keeps in his right armpit.

The glass is magical. It is as large as a peso, and has a small hole in the centre. If you push a small stick through the hole, giants who can give you anything you want will surround you." Then the old woman left Juan, and went on her way.

As soon as Juan reached the palace, Pedro said to him, "Go to that room and get all the money you want."

But Juan answered, "I do not want you to give me any money. All I want is the glass which you keep in your right armpit."

"Very well," said Pedro, "here it is." When Juan had received the glass, he hurried back home.

Juan reached his hut in the woods, and found his mother starving. He quickly thought of his magic glass, and, punching a small stick through the hole in the glass, he found himself surrounded by giants.

"Be quick, and get me some food for my mother!" he said to them. For a few minutes the giants were gone, but soon they came again with their hands full of food. Juan took it and gave it to his mother; but she ate so much that she became sick, and died.

In a neighbouring village ruled another powerful datu, who had a beautiful daughter. One day the datu fell very ill. As no doctor could cure him, he sent his soldiers around the country to say that the man who could cure him should have his daughter for a wife. Juan heard the news, and, relying on his charm, went to cure the datu. On his way, he asked the giants for medicine to cure the sick ruler. When he reached the palace, the datu said to him, "If I am not cured, you shall be killed." Juan agreed to the conditions, and told the datu to swallow the medicine which he gave him. The datu did so, and at once became well again.

The next morning Juan was married to the datu's daughter. Juan took his wife to live with him in his small hut in the woods.

One day he went to the forest to cut trees, leaving his wife and magic glass at home. While Juan was away in the forest, Pedro ordered some of his soldiers to go get the woodcutter's wife and magic glass. When Juan returned in the evening, he found wife and glass gone. One of his neighbours told him that his wife had been taken away by some soldiers. Juan was very angry, but he could not avenge himself without his magical glass.

At last he decided to go to his father-in-law and tell him all that had happened to his wife. On his way there, he met an old *mankukulam*, who asked him where he was going. Juan did not tell her, but related to her all that had happened to his wife and glass while he was in the forest cutting trees. The *mankukulam* said that she could help him. She told him to go to a certain tree and catch the king of the cats. She furthermore advised him, "Always keep the cat with you." Juan followed her advice.

One day Pedro's father commanded his soldiers to cut off the ears of all the men in the village, and said that if anyone refused to have his ears cut off, he should be placed in a room full of rats. The soldiers did as they were ordered, and in time came to Juan's house; but, as Juan was unwilling to lose his ears, he was seized and placed in a room full of rats. But he had his cat with him all the time. As soon as he was shut up in the room, he turned his cat loose. When the rats saw that they would all be killed, they said to Juan, "If you will tie your cat up there in the corner, we will help you get whatever you want."

Juan tied his cat up, and then said to the rats, "Bring me all the glasses in this village." The rats immediately scampered away to obey him. Soon each of them returned with a glass in its mouth. One of them was carrying the magical glass. When Juan had his charm in his hands again, he pushed a small stick through the hole in the glass, and ordered the giants to kill Pedro and his father, and bring him his wife again.

Thus Juan got his wife back. They lived happily together till they died.

The Juan Who Visited Heaven

THERE WAS ONCE an old couple who always prayed for a child, for they had always been childless. No matter how it looked, whether deformed or ugly, they must have a child. So after a short time they saw that their prayers would be answered, and in the course of nature a child was born, but the mother died at the birth.

The newborn child ran to the church, climbed into the tower, and began to hammer on the bells. The priest, hearing the noise, sent the sacristan to see what was the matter. The sacristan went, and seeing there a little child, asked what he was doing and told him to stop, for the priest would be angry; but the ringing of the bells went on. Then the priest went up. "Little boy," he said, "what is your name?" "Juan," said the child. "Why are you ringing the church bells?" "Because my mother is dead." "When did she die?" "Only now." "If you stop ringing the bells she shall have a fine funeral and you shall live with me and be as my son," said the priest. "Very well, sir, if you will let me stay in the church all I wish." To this the priest assented. The dead woman was buried with all the pomp of music, candles and bells, and the boy went to live in the convent. Always after his school was done he would be in the church. The father did everything that was possible for him, for he knew that he was not a natural child.

After a time the padre sent for him to get his dinner, but he would not leave the church, so the priest had a good dinner cooked and sent it down to the church, but he told the sacristan to watch the church and see what happened. The sacristan watched and soon saw the statue of Jesus eating with the boy. This he told the padre, and the child's dinner was always sent to the church after that. One day not long after he went to the priest and said, "Master, my friend down at the church wants me to go away with him." "Where are you going?" "My friend wants me to go to heaven with him."

The priest consented and the little boy and the Lord Jesus went away together. As they walked the little boy saw that two roads ran along together, one thorny and the other smooth. Asked the boy of his companion, "Friend, why is this road where we walk so thorny, and that other yonder so smooth?" Said the Lord, "Hush, child, it is not fitting to disturb the peace of this place, but I will tell you. This is the path of the sinless and is thorny, but that smooth way yonder is the way of the sinners and never reaches heaven."

Again they came to a great house filled with young men and women who were all working hammering iron. Said the little boy, "Who are those who labour with the hammer?" "Hush, child, they are the souls of those who died unmarried."

They journeyed on, and on one side were bush pastures filled with poor cattle while on the opposite side of the road were pastures dry and bare where the cattle were very fat. The child enquired the meaning of the mystery. The Lord answered him, "Hush, child! These lean cattle in the rich pastures are the souls of sinners, while those fat cattle on dry and sunburnt ground are the souls of sinless ones."

After a while they crossed a river, one part of which was ruby red and the other spotless white. "Friend, what is this?" asked the boy. "Hush, child, the red is the blood of your mother whose life was given for yours, and the white is the milk which she desired to give to you, her child," said the Lord.

At last they came to a great house having seven stories, and there on a table they saw many candles, some long, some short, some burned out. Said Juan, "Friend, what are all these candles?" "Hush, child, those are the lives of your friends." "What are those empty candlesticks?" "Those are your mother and your uncle, who are dead." "Who is this long one?" "That is your father, who has long to live." "Who is this very short one?" "That is your master, who will die soon." "May I put in another?" "Yes, child, if you wish." So he changed it for a long one, and with his heavenly companion he returned to earth.

There he told his master, the padre, all that he had seen and heard and how he had changed the candles; and he and his master lived together a very long time. And in the fulness of time the padre died, but Juan went to heaven one day with his Lord and never returned.

The King and the Dervish

ONCE THERE LIVED a young and brave king with his gentle and loving wife. Both had enjoyed an easy, comfortable and, best of all, happy life. The king ruled his people well. The queen was a good wife as well as a good sovereign: she always cheered her husband when he was sad.

One day a dervish came to the palace. He told the king that he possessed magical power, and straightway they became friends. This dervish had the power to leave his body and enter that of a dead animal or person. Now, the king was fond of hunting, and once he took his new friend with him to shoot deer. After a few hours of hard chasing, they succeeded in killing a buck. To show his power, the dervish left his body and entered that of the dead deer. Then he resumed his former shape. The king was very anxious to be able to do the same thing; whereupon the dervish gave him minute instructions, and taught him the necessary charms. Then the king left his body, and took possession of that of the deer. In an instant the dervish entered the king's body and went home as the monarch. He gave orders that a deer with certain marks should be hunted out and killed. The true king was very unhappy, especially when he saw his own men chasing him to take his life.

In his wanderings through the forest, he saw a dead nightingale. He left the deer's body and entered the bird's. Now he was safe, so he flew to his palace. He sang so sweetly that the queen ordered her attendants to catch him. He gladly allowed himself to be caught, and to be cared for by the queen. Whenever the dervish took the bird in his hands, the bird pecked him; but the beautiful singer always showed signs of satisfaction when the queen smoothed his plumage.

Not long after the bird's capture, a dog died in the palace. The king underwent another change: he left the bird's body and entered that of the dog. On waking up in the morning, the queen found that her pet was dead. She began to weep. Unable to see her so sad, the dervish comforted her, and told her that he would give the bird life again. Consequently he left the king's body and entered the bird's. Seeing his chance, the real king left the dog's body and resumed his original form. He then went at once to the cage and killed the ungrateful bird, the dervish.

The tender queen protested against the king's act of cruelty; but when she heard that she had been deceived by the dervish, she died of grief.

Legend of Prince Oswaldo

ONCE UPON A TIME, on a moonlight night, three young men were walking monotonously along a solitary country road. Just where they were going nobody could tell: but when they

came to a place where the road branched into three, they stopped there like nails attracted by a powerful magnet. At this crossroads a helpless old man lay groaning as if in mortal pain. At the sight of the travellers he tried to raise his head, but in vain. The three companions then ran to him, helped him up, and fed him a part of the rice they had with them.

The sick old man gradually regained strength, and at last could speak to them. He thanked them, gave each of the companions a hundred pesos, and said, "Each one of you shall take one of these branch-roads. At the end of it is a house where they are selling something. With these hundred pesos that I am giving each of you, you shall buy the first thing that you see there." The three youths accepted the money, and promised to obey the old man's directions.

Pedro, who took the left branch, soon came to the house described by the old man. The owner of the house was selling a raincoat. "How much does the coat cost?" Pedro asked the landlord.

"One hundred pesos, no more, no less."

"Of what value is it?" said Pedro.

"It will take you wherever you wish to go." So Pedro paid the price, took the raincoat, and returned.

Diego, who took the middle road, arrived at another house. The owner of this house was selling a book. "How much does your book cost?" Diego enquired of the owner.

"One hundred pesos, no more, no less."

"Of what value is it?"

"It will tell you what is going on in all parts of the world." So Diego paid the price, took the book, and returned.

Juan, who took the third road, reached still another house. The owner of the house was selling a bottle that contained some violet-coloured liquid. "How much does the bottle cost?" said Juan.

"One hundred pesos, no more, no less."

"Of what value is it?"

"It brings the dead back to life," was the answer. Juan paid the price, took the bottle, and returned.

The three travellers met again in the same place where they had separated; but the old man was now nowhere to be found. The first to tell of his adventure was Diego. "Oh, see what I have!" he shouted as he came in sight of his companions. "It tells everything that is going on in the world. Let me show you!" He opened the book and read what appeared on the page: "'The beautiful princess of Berengena is dead. Her parents, relatives and friends grieve at her loss.'"

"Good!" answered Juan. "Then there is an occasion for us to test this bottle. It restores the dead back to life. Oh, but the kingdom of Berengena is far away! The princess will be long buried before we get there."

"Then we shall have occasion to use my raincoat," said Pedro. "It will take us wherever we wish to go. Let us try it! We shall receive a big reward from the king. We shall return home with a *casco* full of money. To Berengena at once!" He wrapped the raincoat about all three of them, and wished them in Berengena. Within a few minutes they reached that country. The princess was already in the church, where her parents were weeping over her. Everybody in the church was in deep mourning.

When the three strangers boldly entered the church, the guard at the door arrested them, for they had on red clothes. When Juan protested, and said that the princess was not dead, the guard immediately took him to the king; but the king, when he heard what Juan had said, called him a fool.

"She is only sleeping," said Juan. "Let me wake her up!"

"She is dead," answered the king angrily. "On your life, don't you dare touch her!"

"I will hold my head responsible for the truth of my statement," said Juan. "Let me wake her up, or rather, not to offend your Majesty, restore her to life!"

"Well, I will let you do as you please," said the king; "but if your attempt fails, you will lose your head. On the other hand, should you be successful, I will give you the princess for a wife, and you shall be my heir."

Blinded by his love for the beautiful princess, Juan said that he would restore her to life. "May you be successful!" said the king; and then, raising his voice, he continued, "Everybody here present is to bear witness that I, the King of Berengena, do hereby confirm an agreement with this unknown stranger. I will allow this man to try the knowledge he pretends to possess of restoring the princess to life. But there is this condition to be understood: if he is successful, I will marry him to the princess, and he is to be my heir; but should he fail, his head is forfeit."

The announcement having been made, Juan was conducted to the coffin. He now first realized what he was undertaking. What if the bottle was false? What if he should fail? Would not his head be dangling from the ropes of the scaffold, to be hailed by the multitude as the remains of a blockhead, a dunce and a fool? The coffin was opened. With these meditations in his mind, Juan tremblingly uncorked his bottle of violet liquid, and held it under the nose of the princess. He held the bottle there for some time, but she gave no signs of life. An hour longer, still no trace of life. After hours of waiting, the people began to grow impatient. The king scratched his head, the guards were ready to seize him; the scaffold was waiting for him. "Nameless stranger!" thundered the king, with indignant eyes, "upon your honour, tell us the truth! Can you do it, or not? Speak. I command it!"

Juan trembled all the more. He did not know what to say, but he continued to hold the bottle under the nose of the princess. Had he not been afraid of the consequences, he would have given up and entreated the king for mercy. He fixed his eyes on the corpse, but did not speak. "Are you trying to joke us?" said the king, his eyes flashing with rage. "Speak! I command!"

Just as Juan was about to reply, he saw the right hand of the princess move. He bade the king wait. Soon the princess moved her other hand and opened her eyes. Her cheeks were fresh and rosy as ever. She stared about, and exclaimed in surprise, "Oh, where am I? Where am I? Am I dreaming? No, there is my father, there is my mother, there is my brother." The king was fully satisfied. He embraced his daughter, and then turned to Juan, saying, "Stranger, can't you favour us now with your name?"

With all the rustic courtesy he knew, Juan replied to the king, told his name, and said that he was a poor labourer in a *barrio* far away. The king only smiled, and ordered Juan's clothes to be exchanged for prince's garments, so that the celebration of his marriage with the princess might take place at once. "Long live Juan! Long live the princess!" the people shouted.

When Diego and Juan heard the shout, they could not help feeling cheated. They made their way through the crowd, and said to the king, "Great Majesty, pray hear us! In the name of justice, pray hear us!"

"Who calls?" asked the king of a guard near by. "Bring him here!" The guard obeyed, and led the two men before the king.

"What is the matter?" asked the king of the two.

"Your Majesty shall know," responded Diego. "If it had not been for my book, we could not have known that the princess was dead. Our home is far away, and it was only because of my magic book that we knew of the events that were going on here."

"And his Majesty shall be informed," seconded Pedro, "that Juan's good luck is due to my raincoat. Neither Diego's book nor Juan's bottle could have done anything had not my raincoat carried us here so quickly. I am the one who should marry the princess."

The king was overwhelmed: he did not know what to do. Each of the three had a good reason, but all three could not marry the princess. Even the counsellors of the king could not decide upon the matter.

While they were puzzling over it, an old man sprang forth from the crowd of spectators, and declared that he would settle the difficulty. "Young men," he said, addressing Juan, Pedro and Diego, "none of you shall marry the princess. You, Juan, shall not marry her, because you intended to obtain your fortunes regardless of your companions who have been helping you to get them. And you, Pedro and Diego, shall not have the princess, because you did not accept your misfortune quietly and thank God for it. None of you shall have her. I will marry her myself."

The princess wept. How could the fairest maiden of Berengena marry an old man? "What right have you to claim her?" said the king in scorn.

"I am the one who showed these three companions where to get their bottle, raincoat and book," said the old man. "I am the one who gave each of them a hundred pesos. I am the capitalist: the interest is mine." The old man was right; the crowd clapped their hands; and the princess could do nothing but yield. Bitterly weeping, she gave her hand to the old man, who seemed to be her grandfather, and they were married by the priest. The king almost fainted.

But just now the sun began to rise, its soft beams filtering through the eastern windows of the church. The newly married couple were led from the altar to be taken home to the palace; but just as they were descending the steps that led down from the altar, the whole church was flooded with light. All present were stupefied. The glorious illumination did not last long. When the people recovered, they found that their princess was walking with her husband, not an old man, however, but a gallant young prince. The king recognized him. He kissed him, for they were old-time acquaintances. The king's new son-in-law was none other than Prince Oswaldo, who had just been set free from the bonds of enchantment by his marriage. He had been a former suitor of the princess, but had been enchanted by a magician.

With magnificent ceremony the king's son-in-law was conducted to the royal residence. He was seated on the throne, the crown and sceptre were transferred to him, and he was hailed as King Oswaldo of Berengena.

The Malaki's Sister and the Basolo

THERE IS A CERTAIN mountain that has a sharp, long crest like a kampilan. Up on this mountain stretched many fields of hemp, and groves of coconut palms, that belonged to the Malaki and his sister.

Near to these hemp fields lived the Basolo-man, under a tall barayung tree. His little house was full of venison and pig meat and lard, and he kept a dog to hunt pigs and deer. Although his hut looked small and poor, the Basolo possessed treasures of brass and beads and fine textiles. He had a kabir, from which darted fork lightning; and in the bag was a betel box and a necklace of pure gold.

One day when the Malaki's sister went to look at her hemp, she felt curious to go inside the Basolo's house. The Basolo was lying on the floor, fast asleep, when the woman entered. She looked at the things in the house, and saw hanging on the wall the Basolo's bag with the lightning playing on it. Now the bag was an old one, and had a lot of mud in it; but the woman thought it must be full of gold, because the lightning never ceased to flash from it. So she crept across the floor, and took the bag from off the end of the bamboo slat on which it hung. Still the Basolo slept, and still the lightning continued to play upon the bag. The woman looked inside the bag and saw a fine gold betel box, and when she lifted the lid, there in the box lay a necklace of pure gold. Swiftly she closed the box, and stealthily drew it out of the bag. Into the folds of her hemp skirt she slipped the precious box with the gold necklace inside, and very quietly ran down the bamboo ladder at the house door.

When she got home, her brother smiled, and said to her, "What has happened to you, my sister?"

Bright flashes of lightning seemed to be coming from the girl. She looked almost as if she were made of gold, and the lightning could not escape from her. Then she took out the betel box and the necklace, and showed them to her brother, saying that she had found them in the Basolo's hut.

The Basolo awoke, and found his brass katakia and his fine necklace gone.

"Who has been here?" he cried.

In a frenzy he hunted through his kabir, throwing out of it his old work-knife and his rusty spearhead and all the poor things that he kept in his bag. Then he began to moan and weep for his betel box and gold necklace.

By and by he started out to find his lost things. In the soft soil close to the house, he found the footprints of the woman; and, following the prints, he traced her to the Malaki's house. Right there the footprints ended. The Basolo stood at the foot of the steps, and called, "Who has been in my house?"

Then he ran up the ladder and rushed into the house, screaming to the Malaki's sister, "Give me back my gold necklace! If you don't give it back, I'll marry you."

Quick came the woman's answer, "I don't like you, and I will not marry you."

But her brother was angry because she refused to marry the Basolo. At last she agreed to the match, and said to the Basolo, "Yes, I will marry you; but I can't let you live in my house. You must stay in your own house over yonder."

So the Basolo and the Malaki's sister agreed to meet and try each other (talabana). Then the Basolo went home.

Not long after this, there came a day when many men went out to hunt the wild pig and the deer. And from her house the woman heard the sound of many men gathering in the meadow. There were Malaki T'oluk Waig and other malaki, who were there ready for the chase. And the girl thought, "I will go out and see the men."

Immediately she hurried to dress herself carefully. She put on nine waists one over another, and similarly nine skirts (panapisan); and then she girded herself with a chain of brass links that went a thousand times round her waist. Over her left shoulder she hung her small beaded basket (kambol) that was decorated with row upon row of little tinkling bells, a million in all, and each bell as round as a pea.

But the Basolo knew that the girl was dressing to go out, and he was angry that she should want to go where there were so many men gathered. In order to keep watch on her movements, he climbed up into a hiding place behind the great leaves of an areca palm, and waited. Presently he saw the woman walking to the meadow. And she stayed there just one night. But the Malaki was alarmed when he found that his sister had gone out to see the men. And after he had taken off his clothes, he began to put them on again to follow his sister.

Then, when the girl's brother and all the other malaki had assembled in the meadow, the Basolo came down from the tree and went home. When he got into his house, he took off his coat, and became a Malaki T'oluk Waig. His body shone like the sun (you could hardly look at him), and all his garments were of gold. He had on nine jackets, one over another, and nine pairs of trousers. Then he called for his horse, whose name was Kambeng Diluk; and Kambeng neighed into the air, and waited, prancing, before the house. Soon the Malaki T'oluk Waig mounted his horse, and sitting on a saddle of mirrored glass, he rode towards the meadow. Then Kambeng Diluk began to run, just like the wind.

When they reached the meadow, there were many people there. The Malaki's wife was sitting on the grass, with men grouped around her, and she was laughing with them. But she did not recognize her husband when he came riding up. After everybody had arrived, they set fire to the long grass, and burned off the meadow, so as to bring the wild pigs and the deer out of the brush. Then many men entered the chase and ran their horses; but none could catch the deer or the wild boar, except only the great Malaki, who had been the Basolo: he alone speared much game.

When the burning of the meadow and the hunt were finished, many men wanted to marry the Malaki T'oluk Waig's wife, and many of them embraced her. But the Malaki T'oluk Waig stood up, fierce with passion. His body was almost like a flame to look at. And he fought the other malaki, and killed many, until at last all were dead but one, and that was the woman's brother.

When all was done, the Malaki mounted his horse and rode back to his home. His house was all of gold, and yet it looked just like a mean little hut nestled under the barayung tree. Then the Malaki picked up his coat and put it on: at once he became a Basolo again. He then went over to the woman's house and waited there for her to come back. By and by she came loitering along, crying all the way, because she was afraid to meet her husband. But the Basolo stayed right along in the house, and lived with the woman and her brother. Then, after they had tried each other, they were married with Bagobo ceremony. The Basolo took off his coat, and again became a Malaki T'oluk Waig. They lived well in their house, and they had a big hacienda of hemp and coconuts and banana plants.

Mangita and Larina

MANY YEARS AGO there lived on the banks of the Laguna de Bai a poor fisherman whose wife had died, leaving him two beautiful daughters named Mangita and Larina.

Mangita had hair as black as night and dark skin. She was as good as she was beautiful, and was loved by all for her kindness. She helped her father mend the nets and make the torches to fish with at night, and her bright smile lit up the little nipa house like a ray of sunshine.

Larina was fair and had long golden hair of which she was very proud. She was different from her sister, and never helped with the work, but spent the day combing her hair and catching butterflies. She would catch a pretty butterfly, cruelly stick a pin through it, and fasten it in her hair. Then she would go down to the lake to see her reflection in the clear water, and would laugh to see the poor butterfly struggling in pain. The people disliked her for her cruelty, but they loved Mangita very much. This made Larina jealous, and the more Mangita was loved, the more her sister thought evil of her.

One day a poor old woman came to the nipa house and begged for a little rice to put in her bowl. Mangita was mending a net and Larina was combing her hair in the doorway. When Larina saw the old woman she spoke mockingly to her and gave her a push that made her fall and cut her head on a sharp rock; but Mangita sprang to help her, washed the blood away from her head, and filled her bowl with rice from the jar in the kitchen.

The poor woman thanked her and promised never to forget her kindness, but to her sister she spoke not a word. Larina did not care, however, but laughed at her and mocked her as she painfully made her way again down the road. When she had gone Mangita took Larina to task for her cruel treatment of a stranger; but, instead of doing any good, it only caused Larina to hate her sister all the more.

Some time afterwards the poor fisherman died. He had gone to the big city down the river to sell his fish, and had been attacked with a terrible sickness that was raging there.

The girls were now alone in the world.

Mangita carved pretty shells and earned enough to buy food, but, though she begged Larina to try to help, her sister would only idle away the time.

The terrible sickness now swept everywhere and poor Mangita, too, fell ill. She asked Larina to nurse her, but the latter was jealous of her and would do nothing to ease her pain. Mangita grew worse and worse, but finally, when it seemed as if she would soon die, the door opened and the old woman to whom she had been so kind came into the room. She had a bag of seeds in her hand, and taking one she gave it to Mangita, who soon showed signs of being better, but was so weak that she could not give thanks.

The old woman then gave the bag to Larina and told her to give a seed to her sister every hour until she returned. She then went away and left the girls alone.

Larina watched her sister, but did not give her a single seed. Instead, she hid them in her own long hair and paid no attention to Mangita's moans of pain.

The poor girl's cries grew weaker and weaker, but not a seed would her cruel sister give her. In fact, Larina was so jealous that she wished her sister to die.

When at last the old woman returned, poor Mangita was at the point of death. The visitor bent over the sick girl and then asked her sister if she had given Mangita the seeds. Larina showed her the empty bag and said she had given them as directed. The old woman searched the house, but of course could not find the seeds. She then asked Larina again if she had given them to Mangita. Again the cruel girl said that she had done so.

Suddenly the room was filled with a blinding light, and when Larina could see once more, in place of the old woman stood a beautiful fairy holding the now well Mangita in her arms.

She pointed to Larina and said, "I am the poor woman who asked for rice. I wished to know your hearts. You were cruel and Mangita was kind, so she shall live with me in my island home in the lake. As for you, because you tried to do evil to your good sister, you shall sit at the bottom of the lake forever, combing out the seeds you have hidden in your hair." Then, she clapped her hands and a number of elves appeared and carried the struggling Larina away.

"Come," said the fairy to Mangita, and she carried her to her beautiful home, where she lives in peace and happiness.

As for Larina, she sits at the bottom of the lake and combs her hair. As she combs a seed out, another comes in, and every seed that is combed out becomes a green plant that floats out of the lake and down the Pasig.

And to this day people can see them, and know that Larina is being punished for her wickedness.

The Manglalabas

ONCE UPON A TIME, in the small town of Balubad, there was a big house. It was inhabited by a rich family. When the head of the family died, the house was gloomy and dark. The family wore black clothes, and were sad.

Three days after the death of the father, the family began to be troubled at night by a manglalabas. He threw stones at the house, broke the water jars and moved the beds. Some pillows were even found in the kitchen the next day. The second night, Manglalabas visited the house again. He pinched the widow; but when she woke up, she could not see anything. Manglalabas also emptied all the water jars. Accordingly the family decided to abandon the house.

A band of brave men in that town assembled, and went to the house. At midnight the spirit came again, but the brave men said they were ready to fight it. Manglalabas made a great deal of noise in the house. He poured out all the water, kicked the doors and asked the men who they were. They answered, "We are fellows who are going to kill you." But when the spirit approached them, and they saw that it was a ghost, they fled. From that time on, nobody was willing to pass a night in that house.

In a certain *barrio* of Balubad there lived two queer men. One was called Bulag, because he was blind; and the other, Cuba, because he was hunchbacked. One day these two arranged to go to Balubad to beg. Before they set out, they agreed that the blind man should carry the hunchback on his shoulder to the town. So they set out. After they had crossed the Balubad River, Cuba said, "Stop a minute, Bulag! here is a hatchet." Cuba got down and picked it up. Then they proceeded again. A second time Cuba got off the blind man's shoulder, for he saw an old gun by the roadside. He picked this up also, and took it along with him.

When they reached the town, they begged at many of the houses, and finally they came to the large abandoned house. They did not know that this place was haunted by a spirit. Cuba said, "Maybe no one is living in this house;" and Bulag replied, "I think we had better stay here for the night."

As they were afraid that somebody might come, they went up into the ceiling. At midnight they were awakened by Manglalabas making a great noise and shouting, "I believe that there are some new persons in my house!" Cuba, frightened, fired the gun. The ghost thought that the noise of the gun was someone crying. So he said, "If you are truly a big man, give me some proof."

Then Cuba took the handle out of the hatchet and threw the head down at the ghost. Manglalabas thought that this was one of the teeth of his visitor, and, convinced that the intruder was a powerful person, he said, "I have a buried treasure near the barn. I wish you to dig it up. The reason I come here every night is on account of this treasure. If you will only dig it up, I will not come here anymore."

The next night Bulag and Cuba dug in the ground near the barn. There they found many gold and silver pieces. When they were dividing the riches, Cuba kept three-quarters of the treasure for himself. Bulag said, "Let me see if you have divided fairly," and, placing his hands on the two piles, he found that Cuba's was much larger.

Angry at the discovery, Cuba struck Bulag in the eyes, and they were opened. When Bulag could see, he kicked Cuba in the back, and straightway his deformity disappeared. Therefore they became friends again, divided the money equally, and owned the big house between them.

The Passing of Loku

HUNDREDS OF YEARS AGO a very wicked king named Loku ruled the Philippines. He was cruel and unjust, and condemned to death all who refused to do his bidding. He had vast armies and made war on all until his name was feared everywhere.

His power was very great. He conquered every nation that opposed him and killed so many people that the god, viewing the slaughter from his throne above, sent an angel to order him to cease from warfare and to rule the land in peace.

Loku was in his palace, planning an assault on his neighbours, when a soft light filled the chamber, and a beautiful angel appeared and delivered the mandate of the master.

The cruel king paid no heed, but dismissed the holy messenger in scorn. "Tell your master," said he, "to deliver his message in person. I do not deal with messengers. I am Loku. All fear my name. I am the great Loku."

Hardly had he spoken when the palace shook to its foundations and a mighty voice thundered, "Is it thus thou slightest my word? Thou art Loku. All shall indeed know thy name. From every crevice thou shalt forever cry it in a form that suits thy ill nature."

The courtiers, alarmed by the shock, rushed to the king's chamber, but Loku was nowhere to be found. The royal robes lay scattered on the floor and the only living thing to be seen was an ugly lizard that blinked at them from among the plans on the table.

They searched far and wide, and when no trace of the king could be found the courtiers divided the kingdom and ruled so wisely and well that there was peace for many years.

As for Loku, you may still hear him fulfilling his punishment. From crack and crevice, tree and shrub, he calls his name from dark till dawn: "Lok-u! Lok-u! Lok-u!"

And he must cry it forever.

The Priest, the Servant Boy and the Child Jesus

THERE WAS ONCE a priest who had for his servant a very good boy. One day the padre wanted the boy, and, after looking everywhere for him, went to church. Opening the door quietly, he looked in and there he saw that the statue of the child Jesus

had left its shrine and was down on the floor talking and playing with the boy. The priest slipped softly away and ordered a very fine dinner cooked for the lad. When the boy returned to the convent, the padre asked him where he had been. "I have been down to the church playing with a friend." "Very well, there is your dinner. If you play with your friend again, ask him if I shall go to glory in heaven when I am dead." The boy took his dinner to the church and ate, sharing it with the child Jesus.

"Tell me, friend," said he to his heavenly companion, "will my master, the priest, go to glory in heaven?"

"No," said the child Jesus, "because he has neglected his father and mother." When the boy carried these words to the priest he became very sad, and asked the lad to enquire whether he might atone for his wrong by doing good to other old people. "No," came the answer. "It must be his father and mother who shall receive their dues, and it may be that he shall enter heaven alive."

So the priest sent for his poor old father and mother, and lavished on them every care, suffering no one else to do the least thing for them. At last the old people died, and the priest was very sad. Then one night, as he slept, came soft and very beautiful music around about and within the convent, and the boy awoke the priest to listen. "Oh," said the padre, "it is perhaps the angels come to carry us alive to heaven." And it was so. The angels carried the boy and the priest, his master, to be in glory in heaven.

The Silent Lover

A LONG TIME AGO, when the world was young, there lived a very bashful young man. Not far from his house there lived the most beautiful young woman in the world. The young woman had many suitors but rejected all, wishing only for the love of the bashful young man. He in his turn was accustomed

to follow her about, longing for courage to declare his love, but bashfulness always sealed his lips.

At last, despairing of ever making his unruly tongue tell of his passion, he took a dagger and, following her to the bathing place on the riverbank, he cut out his own heart, cast it at her feet, and fell down lifeless. The girl fled, terrified, and a crow pounced upon the heart, and carried it to a hollow dao tree, when it fell from his beak into the hollow and there remained. But the love for the girl was so strong in the heart that it became reanimated and clothed again with humanity in the form of a little child. A hunter, pursuing the wild boar with dogs, found the child crying from hunger at the foot of the dao tree and, being childless, took it home, and he and his old wife cared for it as their own. The young woman, knowing now the love of the young man, lived for his memory's sake, a widow, rejecting all suitors.

But from the child was never absent the image of his loved one, and at last his love so wrought on his weak frame that he sickened. Knowing that his end was near, he begged of his foster mother that, after his death, she should leave him, and not be surprised if she could not find him on her return. He also asked that on the third day she should take whatever she should find in a certain compartment of the great chest and give it to the girl without price. All this she promised, realizing fully that this was not a natural child.

At last he died, and when his foster mother left the body, his great love reanimated the body and it crept into the chest, becoming there transformed into a beautifully carved casket of fragrant wood.

Obedient to his wishes, on the third day the old woman carried the casket to the girl, giving it to her without price.

When the girl took the casket into her hands, its charm fascinated her, and she clasped it tight and covered it with kisses. At last the spell was broken by the magic of her kisses, and the casket whispered softly to her, "I am thy true love. I was the heart of him who killed himself for love of thee, and I was the youth who died for love of thee, but at last I am contented. In life and death we shall never more be separated." And it was so, for the woman lived to a great age, carrying the casket always with her, inhaling its fragrance with her kisses, and when she died it was buried with her.

The S'iring

THE S'IRING IS the ugly man that has long nails and curly hair. He lives in the forest trees. If a boy goes into the forest without a companion, the S'iring tries to carry him off. When you meet a S'iring, he will look like your father, or mother, or some friend; and he will hide his long nails behind his back, so that you cannot see them. It is the S'iring who makes the echo (a'u'd). When you talk in a loud voice, the S'iring will answer you in a faint voice, because he wants to get you and carry you away.

There was once a boy who went without a companion into the forest, and he met a man who looked just like his own father, but it was a S'iring; and the S'iring made him believe that he was his father. The S'iring said to the boy, "Come, you must go with me. We will shoot some wild birds with our bow and arrows."

And the boy, not doubting that he heard his father's voice, followed the S'iring into the deep forest. After a while, the boy lost his memory, and forgot the way to his own house. The S'iring took him up on a high mountain, and gave him food; but the poor boy had now lost his mind, and he thought the food was a millipede one fathom long, or it seemed to him the long, slim worm called liwati.

So the days went on, the boy eating little, and growing thinner and weaker all the time. When he met any men in the forest, he grew frightened, and would run away. When he had been a long time in the forest, the S'iring called to him and said, "We will move on now."

So they started off again. When they reached the high bank of a deep and swift-flowing river, the S'iring scratched the boy with his long nails. Straightway the boy felt so tired that he could no longer stand on his legs, and then he dropped down into the ravine. He fell on the hard rocks, so that his bones were broken, and his skull split open.

All this time, the mother at home was mourning for her son, and crying all day long. But soon she arranged a little shrine (tambara) under the great tree, and, having placed there a white bowl with a few betel nuts and some buyo leaf as an offering for her son, she crouched on the ground and prayed for his life to the god in the sky.

Now, when the S'iring heard her prayer, he took some betel nuts, and went to the place where the boy's body lay. On the parts where the bones were broken, he spat betel nut, and did the same to the boy's head. Immediately the boy came to life, and felt well again. Then the S'iring took him up, and carried him to the shrine where the mother was praying; but she could not see the S'iring nor her boy. She went home crying.

That night, as the woman slept, she dreamed that a boy came close to her, and spoke about her son. "Tomorrow morning," he said, "you must pick red peppers, and get a lemon, and carry them to the shrine, and burn them in the fire."

Next morning, the woman hastened to gather the peppers, and get a lemon, and with happy face she ran to the shrine under the big tree. There she made a fire, and burned the lemon and the red peppers, as the dream had told her. And, as soon as she had done this, her son appeared from under the great tree. Then his mother caught him in her arms, and held him close, and cried for joy.

When you lose your things, you may be sure that the S'iring has hidden them. What you have to do is to burn some red peppers with beeswax (tadu ka petiukan), and observe carefully the direction in which the smoke goes. The way the smoke goes points out where your things are hidden, because the S'iring is afraid of the wax of bees. He is afraid, too, of red peppers and of lemons.

Story of Lumabat and Wari

TUGLAY AND TUGLIBUNG had many children. One of them was called Lumabat. There came a time when Lumabat quarrelled with his sister and was very angry with her. He said, "I will go to the sky, and never come back again."

So Lumabat started for the sky-country, and many of his brothers and sisters went with him. A part of their journey lay over the sea, and when they had passed the sea, a rock spoke to them and said, "Where are you going?"

In the beginning, all the rocks and plants and the animals could talk with the people. Then one boy answered the rock, "We are going to the sky-country."

As soon as he had spoken, the boy turned into a rock. But his brothers and sisters went on, leaving the rock behind.

Presently a tree said, "Where are you going?"

"We are going to the sky," replied one of the girls.

Immediately the girl became a tree. Thus, all the way along the journey, if anyone answered, he became a tree, or stone, or rock, according to the nature of the object that put the question.

By and by the remainder of the party reached the border of the sky. They had gone to the very end of the earth, as far as the horizon. But here they had to stop, because the horizon kept moving up and down (supa-supa). The sky and the earth would part, and then close together again, just like the jaws of an animal in eating. This movement of the horizon began as soon as the people reached there.

There were many young men and women, and they all tried to jump through the place where the sky and the earth parted. But the edges of the horizon are very sharp, like a kampilan, and they came together with a snap whenever anybody tried to jump through; and they cut him into two pieces. Then the parts of his body became stones, or grains of sand. One after another of the party tried to jump through, for nobody knew the fate of the one who went before him.

Last of all, Lumabat jumped – quick, quicker than the rest; and before the sharp edges snapped shut, he was safe in heaven. As he walked along, he saw many wonderful things. He saw many kampilans standing alone, and fighting, and that without any man to hold them. Lumabat passed on by them all. Then he came to the town where the bad dead live. The town is called "Kilut." There, in the flames, he saw many spirits with heavy sins on them. The spirits with little sins were not in the flames; but they lay, their bodies covered with sores, in an acid that cuts like the juice of a lemon. Lumabat went on, past them all.

Finally he reached the house of Diwata, and went up into the house. There he saw many diwata, and they were chewing betel nut, And one diwata spat from his mouth the isse that he had finished chewing. When Lumabat saw the isse coming from the mouth of the god, it looked to him like a sharp knife. Then Diwata laid hold of Lumabat, and Lumabat thought the god held a sharp knife in his hand. But it was no knife: it was just the isse. And Diwata rubbed the isse on Lumabat's belly, and with one downward stroke he opened the belly, and took out Lumabat's intestines (betuka).

Then Lumabat himself became a god. He was not hungry anymore, for now his intestines were gone. Yet if he wanted to eat, he had only to say, "Food, come now!" and at once all the fish were there, ready to be caught. In the sky-country, fish do not have to be caught. And Lumabat became the greatest of all the diwata.

Now, when Lumabat left home with his brothers and sisters, one sister and three brothers remained behind. The brother named Wari felt sad because Lumabat had gone away. At last he decided to follow him. He crossed the sea, and reached the border of the sky, which immediately began to make the opening and shutting motions. But Wari was agile, like his brother Lumabat; and he jumped quick, just like Lumabat, and got safe into heaven. Following the same path that his brother had taken, he reached the same house. And again Diwata took the isse, and attempted to open Wari's belly; but Wari protested, for he did not like to have his intestines pulled out. Therefore the god was angry at Wari.

Yet Wari stayed on in the house for three days. Then he went out on the atad that joined the front and back part of the god's house, whence he could look down on the earth. He saw his home town, and it made him happy to look at his fields of sugarcane and bananas, his groves of betel and coconuts. There were his bananas ripe, and all his fruits ready to be plucked. Wari gazed, and then he wanted to get back to earth again, and he began to cry; for he did not like to stay in heaven and have his intestines taken out, and he was homesick for his own town.

Now, the god was angry at Wari because he would not let him open his belly. And the god told Wari to go home, and take his dogs with him. First the god fixed some food for Wari to eat on his journey. Then he took meadow grass (karan), and tied the long blades together, making a line long enough to reach down to earth. He tied Wari and the dogs to one end of the line; but before he lowered the rope, he said to Wari, "Do not eat while you are up in the air, for if you eat, it will set your dogs to quarrelling. If I hear the sound of dogs fighting, I shall let go the rope."

But while Wari hung in the air, he got very hungry, and, although he had been let down only about a third of the distance from heaven to earth, he took some of his food and ate it. Immediately the dogs began to fight. Then Diwata in the sky heard the noise, and he dropped the rope of meadow grass. Then Wari fell down, down; but he did not strike the ground, for he was caught in the branches of the tree called lanipo. It was a tall tree, and Wari could not get down. He began to utter cries; and all night he kept crying, "Aro-o-o-o-i!" Then he turned into a kulago bird. At night, when you hear the call of the kulago bird, you know that it is the voice of Wari.

The kulago bird has various sorts of feathers, feathers of all kinds of birds and chickens; it has the hair of all animals and the hair of man. This bird lives in very high trees at night, and you cannot see it. You cannot catch it. Yet the old men know a story about a kulago bird once having been caught while it was building its nest. But this was after there came to be many people on the earth.

The three dogs went right along back to Wari's house. They found Wari's sister and two brothers at home, and stayed there with them. After a while, the woman and her two brothers had many children.

"In the beginning," say the old men, "brother and sister would marry each other, just like pigs. This was a very bad custom."

Story of Duling and the Tagamaling

BEFORE THE WORLD was made, there were Tagamaling. The Tagamaling is the best Buso, because he does not want to hurt man all of the time. Tagamaling is actually Buso only part of the time; that is, the month when he eats people. One month he

eats human flesh, and then he is Buso; the next month he eats no human flesh, and then he is a god. So he alternates, month by month. The month he is Buso, he wants to eat man during the dark of the moon; that is, between the phases that the moon is full in the east and new in the west.

The other class of Buso, however, wants human flesh all of the time. They are the Tigbanua', the chief of whom is Datu of all the Buso. A Tigbanua' lives in his own house, and goes out only to eat the bodies of the dead.

The Tagamaling makes his house in trees that have hard wood, and low, broad-spreading branches. His house is almost like gold, and is called "Palimbing," but it is made so that you cannot see it; and, when you pass by, you think, "Oh! what a fine tree with big branches," not dreaming that it is the house of a Tagamaling. Sometimes, when you walk in the forest, you think you see one of their houses; but when you come near to the place, there is nothing. Yet you can smell the good things to eat in the house.

Once a young man named Duling, and his younger brother, went out into the woods to trap wild chickens. Duling had on his back a basket holding a decoy cock, together with the snares of running-nooses and all the parts of the trap. While they were looking for a good spot to drive in the stakes for the snare, they heard the voice of Tagamaling in the trees, saying, "Duling, Duling, come in! My mother is making a little fiesta here."

The boys looked up, and could see the house gleaming there in the branches, and there were two Tagamaling-women calling to them. In response to the call, Duling's younger brother went up quickly into the house; but Duling waited on the ground below. He wanted the Tagamaling-girls to come down to him, for he was enamoured (kalatugan) of them. Then one girl ran down to urge Duling to come up into the tree. And as soon as she came close to him, he caught her to his breast, and hugged her and caressed her.

In a moment, Duling realized that the girl was gone, and that he was holding in his arms a nanga bush, full of thorns. He had thought to catch the girl, but, instead, sharp thorns had pricked him full of sores. Then from above he heard the woman's voice, tauntingly sweet, "Don't feel bad, Duling; for right here is your younger brother."

Yet the young man, gazing here and there, saw around him only tall trees, and could not catch a glimpse of the girl who mocked him.

Immediately, Duling, as he stood there, was turned into a rock. But the little brother married the Tagamaling-girl.

There is a place high up in the mountains of Mindanao, about eight hours' ride west of Santa Cruz, where you may see the rock, and you will know at once that it is a human figure. There is Duling, with the trap and the decoy cock on his shoulder. You may see the cock's feathers too.

The Tobacco of Harisaboqued

LONG BEFORE THE STRANGE men came over the water from Spain, there lived in Negros, on the mountain of Canlaon, an old man who had great power over all the things on the earth. He was called Harisaboqued, King of the Mountain.

When he wished anything done he had but to tap the ground three times and instantly a number of little men would spring from the earth to answer his call. They would obey his slightest wish, but as he was a kind old man and never told his dwarfs to do anything wrong, the people who lived near were not afraid. They planted tobacco on the mountainside and were happy and prosperous.

The fields stretched almost to the top of the mountain and the plants grew well, for every night Harisaboqued would order his dwarfs to attend to them, and though the tobacco was high up it grew faster and better than that planted in the valley below.

The people were very grateful to the old man and were willing to do anything for him; but he only asked them not to plant above a line he had ordered his little men to draw around the mountain near the top. He wished that place for himself and his dwarfs.

All obeyed his wish and no one planted over the line. It was a pretty sight to see the long rows of tobacco plants extending from the towns below far up to the line on the mountainside.

One day Harisaboqued called the people together and told them that he was going away for a long time. He asked them again not to plant over the line, and told them that if they disregarded this wish he would carry all the tobacco away and permit no more to grow on the mountainside until he had smoked what he had taken. The people promised faithfully to obey him. Then he tapped on the ground, the earth opened, and he disappeared into the mountain.

Many years passed and Harisaboqued did not come back. All wondered why he did not return and at last decided that he would never do so. The whole mountainside was covered with tobacco and many of the people looked with greedy eyes at the bare ground above the line, but as yet they were afraid to break their promise.

At last one man planted in the forbidden ground, and, as nothing happened, others did the same, until soon the mountain was entirely covered with the waving plants. The people were very happy and soon forgot about Harisaboqued and their promise to him.

But one day, while they were laughing and singing, the earth suddenly opened and Harisaboqued sprang out before them. They were very much frightened and fled in terror down the mountainside. When they reached the foot and looked back they saw a terrible sight. All the tobacco had disappeared and, instead of the thousands of plants that they had tended so carefully, nothing but the bare mountain could be seen.

Then suddenly there was a fearful noise and the whole mountain top flew high in the air, leaving an immense hole from which poured fire and smoke.

The people fled and did not stop until they were far away. Harisaboqued had kept his word.

Many years have come and gone, but the mountain is bare and the smoke still rolls out of the mountain top. Villages have sprung up along the sides, but no tobacco is grown on the mountain. The people remember the tales of the former great crops and turn longing eyes to the heights above them, but they will have to wait. Harisaboqued is still smoking his tobacco.

The Tuglibung and the Tuglay

BEFORE TIME BEGAN, an old woman (Tuglibung) and an old man (Tuglay) lived in a town at the centre of the world. There came a season of drought, when their bananas spoiled, and all their plants died from the hot sun. Tuglibung and Tuglay were very hungry, and looked skinny, because they had nothing to eat.

One night as the old man slept, he dreamed that a little boy with white hair came close to him, and said, "Much better it would be, if you would stay here no longer; much better, that you go to the T'oluk Waig ('water sources'), where there is a good place to live."

So the old folks started on their journey to the source of the rivers. On their way, they stopped at one place that seemed good, and stayed for about a month; but there was little to eat, and they were always hungry. At last, one day, the man climbed up into a tall tree, whence he could see the whole earth, even to the border of the sky. Far away he could see a little smoke, just like a cigarette. Then he climbed down the tree in a hurry, and told his wife what he had seen.

"I will go and find out where that smoke comes from," he said, "and see if I can get some bananas and things – all we can eat."

So the man started out and travelled a long way, leaving his wife at home. As he approached the place where he had seen the smoke, he found himself in a vast field full of fruit trees and sugarcane plants. The sugarcane grew as big as trees; the bananas were as huge as the trunks of coconut palms; and the papaya fruit was the size of a great clay jar. He walked on until he reached a very large meadow, full of long wavy grass, where there were many horses and carabao and other animals. Soon after he left the meadow grass, he could make out, some distance ahead of him, a big house with many smaller houses grouped around it. He was so scared that he could not see the houses very well. He kept his eyes on the ground at his feet.

When he came up to the big house, he saw lying under it piles of human bones. He then knew that the Datu of the Buso lived there. In all the other houses there were buso living too. But he went bravely up the steps of the big house, and sat down on the floor. Right away, while he sat there, the children of Buso wanted to eat him. But Tuglay said, "No, no! don't eat me, because I just came to get bananas of many different kinds."

Then the man made a bargain with the Datu of the Buso, and said, "Give me some bananas, and I will pay you two children for them. Come to my house in nine days, and you shall have one boy and one girl for the bananas." But Tuglay had no children.

Then the Buso gave Tuglay a basket of bananas, and let him go away.

Now, while her husband was away, the woman gave birth to twins, a boy and a girl. And when the man got home he was pleased, and said, "Oh! that's fine! You got some babies while I was away."

But the man felt very sorry to think of giving his children to the Buso, and he went from place to place, hoping to find some friend who would help him. All the time, the days of the falla ("time of contract") were slipping by. He could get nobody to help him. Now it lacked only two of the nine days' falla. And while the children were asleep, Tuglay said to his wife, "Let us run away, and leave our babies here asleep, because tomorrow the Buso will come."

Then Tuglay and Tuglibung ran away, and left their children. They ran and ran until they reached the T'oluk Waig; but they could not get away from the falla. The nine days of falla had caught up with them.

At home, the children woke up and found no mother and father there, and they began to cry. They thought they would run after their parents. So they left the house, and forded the river, and began to run.

When the nine days were up, the Buso came to Tuglay's house for his pay. When he found nobody at home, he ran after the children, carrying with him many iron axes and big bolos, and accompanied by a crowd of other buso. In all there were three thousand buso – two thousand walking, and one thousand flying. The children had the start; but the three thousand buso kept gaining on them, until they were close behind.

As they ran, the little boy said to his sister, "When we get to that field over there, where there are ripe bananas, you must not speak a word."

But when they reached the banana tree, the girl-child cried out,

"Brother, I want to eat a banana."

Then she ate a banana; but she felt so weak she could run no longer. She just lay down and died. Then the boy-child looked about for a place to put his sister's body. He looked at the fine branched trees, full of fruit, and saw that each single fruit was an agong, and the leaves, mother-of-pearl.

To one of the trees, the boy said, "May I put my sister here?" And the tree said that he might do it.

Then the boy laid his sister on a branch of the tree, because the child was dead.

After this, the boy ran back towards the Buso who led the rest, and called out to him, "I'm going to run very fast. Chase me now, and catch me if you can!"

So the boy ran, and the Buso chased him. Hard pressed, the boy sprang towards a big rock, and shouted to it, "O rock, help me! The Buso will catch me."

"Come up!" said the rock, "I'll help you, if I can."

But when the boy climbed up, he found that it was not a rock, but a fine house, that was giving him shelter. In that house lived the Black Lady (Bia t' metum), and she received the boy kindly.

As soon as the Buso came up to the rock, he smiled, and said, "The boy is here all right! I'll break the rock with my axe."

But when he tried to break the rock with axe and poko, the hard stone resisted; and the Buso's tools were blunted and spoiled.

Meantime, in the Black Lady's house the boy was getting ready for a fight, because the Black Lady said, "Go down now; they want you down there."

Then with sharp sword and long spear, bearing a fine war shield, and wearing earplugs of shining ivory, the boy went down to meet the Buso. When he went down the steps, all the other buso had come, and were waiting for him in front of the house. Then they all went to fighting the one boy, and he met them all alone. He fought until every one of the three thousand buso fell down dead. At last, one only of the buso stood up, and he was the great Datu of Buso. But even he fell down before that mighty boy, for none could conquer the boy. He was matulus. After all was done, the boy married the Black Lady, and lived well in her house.

The Two Wives and the Witch

THERE WAS ONCE a man who had a wife that was not pretty. He became tired of looking at her, and so went away and married another wife.

His first wife was in great sorrow, and wept every day. One day as she was crying by the well, where she had gone for water, a woman asked her, "Why are you weeping?" The wife answered, "Because my husband has left me and gone to live with another wife." "Why?" said the witch, for that is what the woman was.

"Because I have not a pretty face," answered the wife. While she was talking the witch touched the wife's face, and then she said, "I cannot stay here any longer," and went off.

When the wife reached home she looked in the glass and saw that her face had been changed until it was the most beautiful in the town. Very soon a rumour spread through the town that in such and such a house there was living a very beautiful woman. Many young men went to see the pretty woman, and all were pleased with her beauty.

The bad husband went also. He was astonished that his wife was not at home, and that a pretty woman was living there alone. He bowed to the lady and avowed his love. The lady at first refused to believe him, and said, "If you will leave the woman who is now your wife and come to live with me right along I will take you for my husband." The man agreed, and went to live with the pretty woman.

The other woman was very angry when she heard the news, for it was reported that the pretty woman was the man's first wife, who had been changed by a witch. She determined to try what the witch could do for her, and went to get water at the same well.

The witch appeared and asked, "Why are you weeping, my good woman?" The woman told her that her husband had gone away to live with the pretty woman. As she was speaking, the witch touched her face, and said, "Go home, my good woman, and do not weep, for your husband will come very soon to see you."

When she heard this she ran home as fast as she could. All the people whom she met on the road were afraid of her, because she was so ugly. Her nose was about two feet long, her ears looked like large handkerchiefs, and her eyes were as big as saucers. Nobody recognized her, not even her mother. All were afraid of such a creature. When she saw in the glass how ugly she was, she refused to eat, and in a few days she died.

The White Squash

IN A QUEER LITTLE BAMBOO house in front of a big garden lived a man and his wife all alone. They had always been kind and good to everyone, but still they were not happy, because the child for which they longed had never come to them. Each day for many years they had prayed for a son or a daughter, but their prayers had been unanswered. Now that they were growing old they believed that they must always live alone.

In the garden near their house this couple grew fine white squash, and as the vines bore the year around, they had never been in need of food. One day, however, they discovered that no new squash had formed to take the place of those they had picked, and for the first time in many seasons they had no vegetables.

Each day they examined the vines, and though the big, yellow flowers continued to bloom and fade, no squash grew on the stems. Finally, one morning after a long wait, the woman cried out with delight, for she had discovered a little green squash. After examining it, they decided to let it ripen that they might have the seeds to plant. They eagerly watched it grow, and it became a beautiful white vegetable, but by the time it was large enough for food they were so hungry that they decided to eat it.

They brought a large knife and picked it, but scarcely had they started to open it when a voice cried out from within, "Please be careful that you do not hurt me."

The man and woman stopped their work, for they thought that a spirit must have spoken to them. But when the voice again called and begged them to open the squash, they carefully opened it, and there inside was a nice baby boy. He could already stand alone and could talk. And the man and his wife were overjoyed.

Presently the woman went to the spring for a jar of water, and when she had brought it she spread a mat on the floor and began to bathe the baby. As the drops of water fell off his body, they were immediately changed to gold, so that when the bath was finished gold pieces covered the mat. The couple had been so delighted to have the baby that it had seemed as if there was nothing more to wish for, but now that the gold had come to them also they were happier than ever.

The next morning the woman gave the baby another bath, and again the water turned to gold. They now had enough money to build a large house. The third morning she brought water for his bath again, but he grew very sad and flew away. At the same time all the gold disappeared also, and the man and his wife were left poor and alone.

Fables & Animal Tales

A PLETHORA OF ANIMAL TALES and fables are spread across the different regions of the Philippines, but they usually have at least two purposes in common. The first is to show human characteristics to non-human characters, and to emphasize specific traits that are either enviable or problematic. The second is to show a moral aspect of a situation, and use that to teach a lesson. Perhaps one of the most popular animal tales is 'The Monkey and the Turtle', popularized by Jose Rizal though his illustrations of the story in the 1890s. Here a version of the tale, called 'Story of Ca Matsin and Ca Boo-Ug', involves more characters and more violence than the Rizal retelling.

Other animal tales usually explain a natural phenomenon or form of animal behaviour, highlighting the ways in which the natural world is tied to folk narratives. Stories such as 'The Battle of the Crabs' explain the actions of fiddler crabs and their movements between shore and sea; 'How the Lizards got their Markings' similarly explains why monitor lizards have ugly markings on their backs. Eugenio notes that in many folk stories Philippine rural life is highlighted, and that the monkey is usually the 'helpful animal' in many of these tales.

Alelu'k and Alebu'tud

ALELU'K AND ALEBU'TUD lived together in their own house. They had no neighbours. One day Alelu'k said to his wife, "I must go and hunt some pigs."

Then he started out to hunt, taking with him his three dogs. He did not find any wild pigs; but before long he sighted a big deer with many-branched antlers. The dogs gave chase and seized the deer, and held it until the man came up and killed it with the sharp iron spike that tipped his long staff (tidalan). Then the man tied to the deer's antlers a strong piece of rattan, and dragged it home.

When he reached his house, his wife met him joyfully; and they were both very happy, because they had now plenty of meat. They brought wood and kindled a fire, and fixed over the fire a frame of wood tied to upright posts stuck into the ground. On the frame they laid the body of the deer to singe off the hair over the flames. And when the hair was all burned off, and the skin clean, Alelu'k began to cut off pieces of venison, and Alebu'tud got ready the big clay pot, and poured into it water to boil the meat. But there was only a little water in the house, so Alubu'tud took her bucket (sekkadu), and hurried down to the river. When she reached there, she stood with her bare feet in the stream, and dipped the bucket into the stream, and took it out full of water. But, just as she turned to climb up the riverbank, an enormous fish jumped out of the river, seized her, dragged her down, and devoured her.

At home, Alelu'k was watching for his wife to come back bringing the water. Day after day he waited for her, and all day long he was crying from sorrow.

The man (Alelu'k) symbolizes a big black ant that makes its nest in a hollow tree. The woman (Alebu'tud) is a little worm that lives in the palma brava tree. The fish is another man who carried off Alelu'k's wife.

Arnomongo and Iput-Iput (The Ape and the Firefly)

ONE EVENING THE FIREFLY was on his way to the house of a friend, and as he passed the ape's house, the latter asked him, "Mr. Firefly, why do you carry a light?" The firefly replied, "Because I am afraid of the mosquitoes." "Oh, then you are a coward, are you?" said the ape. "No, I am not," was the answer. "If you are not afraid," asked the ape, "why do you always carry a lantern?" "I carry a lantern so that when the mosquitoes come to bite me I can see them and defend myself," replied the firefly. Then the ape laughed aloud, and on the next day he told all his neighbours that the firefly carried a light at night because he was a coward.

When the firefly heard what the ape had said, he went to his house. It was night and the ape was asleep, but the firefly flashed his light into his face and awakened him. The firefly was very angry and said, "Why did you spread the report that I was a coward? If you wish to prove which of us is the braver, I will fight you on the plaza next Sunday evening."

The ape enquired, "Have you any companions?" "No," replied the firefly, "I will come alone." Then the ape laughed at the idea of such a little creature presuming to fight with him, but the firefly continued, "I shall be expecting you on the plaza about six o'clock next Sunday afternoon." The ape replied, "You had better bring someone to help you, as I shall bring my whole company, about a thousand apes, each as big as myself." This he said, thinking to frighten the strange little insect, who seemed to him to be crazy. But the firefly answered, "I shall not need any companions, but will come alone. Goodbye."

When the firefly had gone, the ape called together his company, and told them about the proposed fight. He ordered them to get each one a club about three feet long and to be on the plaza at six o'clock the next Sunday evening. His companions were greatly amazed, but as they were used to obeying their captain, they promised to be ready at the appointed time and place.

On Sunday evening, just before six o'clock, they assembled on the plaza, and found the firefly already waiting for them. Just then the church bells rang the Angelus, so the firefly proposed that they should all pray. Immediately after the prayer, the firefly signified that he was ready to begin. The ape had drawn up his company in line, with himself at the head. Suddenly the firefly lighted upon the ape's nose. The ape next in line struck at the firefly, but succeeded only in striking the captain such a terrible blow on the nose as to kill him. The firefly meanwhile, seeing the blow coming, had jumped upon the nose of the second ape, who was killed by the next in line just as the captain had been killed; and so on down the whole line, until there was but one ape left. He threw down his club and begged the firefly to spare him. The firefly graciously allowed him to live, but since that time the apes have been in mortal terror of the fireflies.

The Battle of the Crabs

ONE DAY THE LAND CRABS had a meeting. One of them said, "What shall we do with the waves? They sing all the time so loudly that we cannot possibly sleep well at night." "Do you not think it would be well for all of us males to go down and fight them?" asked the eldest of the crabs. "Yes," all replied. "Well, tomorrow all the males must get ready to go."

The next day they started to go down to the sea. On the way they met the shrimp. "Where are you going, my friends?" asked the shrimp. The crabs answered, "We are going to fight the waves, because they will not let us sleep at night."

"I don't think you will win the battle," said the shrimp. "The waves are very strong, while your legs are so weak that your bodies bend almost to the ground when you walk," and he laughed. The crabs were so angry at his scorn that they ran at the shrimp and pinched him until he promised to help them in the battle.

When they reached the shore, the crabs looked at the shrimp and said, "Your face is turned the wrong way, friend shrimp," and they laughed at him, for crabs are much like other people, and think they are the only ones who are right. "Are you ready to fight with the waves? What weapon have you?"

"My weapon," replied the shrimp, "is a spear on my head." Just then he saw a large wave coming, and ran away; but the crabs, who were all looking towards the shore, did not see it, and were killed.

The wives of the dead crabs wondered why their husbands did not come home. They thought the battle must be a long one, and decided to go down and help their husbands. As they reached the shore and entered the water to look for their husbands, the waves killed them.

A short time afterwards, thousands of little crabs, such as are now called fiddlers, were found near the shore. When these children were old enough to walk, the shrimp often visited them and related to them the sad fate of their parents. And so, if you will watch carefully the fiddlers, you will notice that they always seem ready to run back to the land, where their forefathers lived, and then, as they regain their courage, they rush down, as if about to fight the waves. But they always lack the courage to do so, and continually run back and forth. They live neither on dry land, as their ancestors did, nor in the sea, like the other crabs, but up on the beach, where the waves wash over them at high tide and try to dash them to pieces.

The Crow and the Golden Trees

THE LIVER OF THE CROW is "medicine" for many pains and for sickness. On this account the Bagobo kills the crow so that he may get his liver for "medicine". The liver is good to

eat, either cooked or raw. If you see a crow dead, you can get its liver and eat some of it, and it will be "medicine" for your body.

The crow never makes its nest in low-growing trees, but only in tall, big trees. Far from here, the old men say, in the land where the sun rises, there are no more living trees; for the scorching heat of the sun has killed them all, and dried up the leaves. There they stand, with naked branches, all bare of leaves. Only two trees there have not died from the heat. The trunks of these trees are of gold, and all their leaves of silver. But if any bird lights on one of these trees, it falls down dead. The ground under the two trees is covered with the bones of little birds and big birds that have died from perching on the trees with the golden trunks and the silver leaves. These two trees are full of a resin that makes all the birds die. Only the crow can sit on the branches, and not die. Hence the crow alone, of all the birds, remains alive in the land of the sunrise.

No man can get the resin from these trees. But very long ago, in the days of the Mona, there came a Malaki T'oluk Waig to the trees. He had a war shield that shone brightly, for it had a flame of fire always burning in it. And this Malaki came to the golden trees and took the precious resin from their trunks.

The Eagle and the Hen

ONE DAY THE EAGLE declared his love for the hen. He flew down to search for her, and when he had found her he said, "I wish you to be my mate."

The hen answered, "I am willing, but let me first grow wings like yours, so I can fly as high as you." The eagle replied, "I will do so, and as a sign of our betrothal I will give you this ring. Take good care of it until I come again."

The hen promised to do so, and the eagle flew away.

The next day the cock met the hen. When he saw the ring around her neck he was very much surprised and said, "Where did you get that ring? I think you are not true to me. Do you not remember your promise to be my mate? Throw away that ring." So she did.

At the end of a week the eagle came with beautiful feathers to dress the hen. When she saw him she became frightened and hid behind the door. The eagle entered, crying, "How are you, my dear hen? I am bringing you a beautiful dress," and he showed it to the hen. "But where is your ring? Why do you not wear it?" The hen could not at first answer, but after a little she tried to deceive the eagle, and said, "Oh, pardon me, sir! Yesterday as I was walking in the garden I met a large snake, and I was so frightened that I ran towards the house. When I reached it I found that I had lost the ring, and I looked everywhere for it; but alas! I have not yet found it."

The eagle looked keenly at the hen and said, "I would never have believed that you would behave so badly. I promise you that, whenever you have found my ring, I will come down again and take you for my mate. As a punishment for breaking your promise you shall always scratch the ground and look for the ring, and all your chickens that I find I will snatch away from you. That is all. Goodbye." Then he flew away.

And ever since, all the hens all over the world have been scratching to find the eagle's ring.

How the Lizards Got Their Markings

ONE DAY THE CHAMELEON (palas) and the Monitor lizard (ibid) were out in a deep forest together. They thought they would try scratching each other's backs to make pretty figures on them.

First the Chameleon said to the Monitor lizard, "You must scratch a nice pattern on my back."

So the Monitor went to work, and the Chameleon had a fine scratching. Monitor made a nice, even pattern on his back.

Then Monitor asked Chameleon for a scratching. But no sooner had Chameleon begun to work on Monitor's back than there came the sound of a dog barking. A man was hunting in the forest with his dog. The sharp barks came nearer and nearer to the two lizards; and the Chameleon got such a scare that his fingers shook, and the pretty design he was making went all askew. Then he stopped short and ran away, leaving the Monitor with a very shabby marking on his back.

This is the reason that the monitor lizard is not so pretty as the chameleon.

The Living Head

THERE ONCE LIVED a man and his wife who had no children. They earnestly desired to have a son, so they prayed to their God, Diva, that he would give them a son, even if it were only a head.

Diva pitied them, and gave them a head for a son. Head, for that was his name, grew up, and gradually his father and mother ceased to think of his misfortune, and grew to love him very much.

One day Head saw the chief's daughter pass the house, and fell in love with her. "Mother," he said, "I am in love with the chief's daughter and wish to marry her. Go now, I pray you, to the chief and ask him to give me his daughter to be my wife." "Dear Head," answered his mother, "it is of no use to go on such an errand, the chief's daughter will surely not be willing to marry only a head." But Head insisted, so, in order to quiet him, his mother went to the chief and made known her son's desire. Of course she met with a refusal, and returned home and told Head the result of her errand.

Head went downstairs into the garden and began to sink into the ground.

"Head, come up," said his mother, "and let us eat."

"Sink! sink! sink!" cried Head.

"Head, come up and let us eat!" repeated his mother.

"Sink! sink! sink!" was Head's answer, and he continued to sink until he could no longer be seen. His mother tried in vain to take him out. After a while a tree sprang up just where Head had sunk, and in a short time it bore large, round fruit, almost as large as a child's head. This is the origin of the orange tree.

Lucas the Rope-Maker

LUIS AND ISCO were intimate friends. They lived in a country called Bagdad. Though these two friends had been brought up together in the same school, their ideas were different. Luis believed that gentleness and kindness were the second heaven, while Isco's belief was that wealth was the source of happiness and peace in life.

One day, while they were eating, Isco said, "Don't you believe, my friend, that a rich man, however cruel he may be, is known everywhere and has great power over all his people? A poor man may be gentle and kind, but then he is disdainfully looked upon by his neighbours."

"Oh," answered Luis, "I know it, but to me everybody is the same. I love them all, and I am not enchanted by anything that glisters."

"My friend," said Isco, "our conversation is becoming serious. Let us take a walk this afternoon and see how these theories work out in the lives of men."

That afternoon Luis and Isco went to a town called Cohija. On their way they saw a rope-maker, Lucas by name, who by his condition showed his great suffering from poverty. He approached Lucas and gave him a roll of paper money, saying, "Now, Lucas, take this money and spend it judiciously."

Lucas was overjoyed: he hardly knew what to do. When he reached home, he related to his wife Zelima what had happened to him. As has been said, Lucas was very poor and was a rope-maker. He had six little children to support; but he had no money with which to feed them, nor could he get anything from his rope-making. Some days he could not sell even a yard of rope. When Lucas received the money from Luis, and had gone home and told his wife, he immediately went out again to buy food. He had one hundred pesos in paper money. He bought two pounds of meat and a roll of *cañamo*; and as there was some more money left, he put it in one of the corners of his hat. Unfortunately, as he was walking home, an eagle was attracted by the smell of the meat, and began flying about his head. He frightened the bird away; but it flew so fast that its claws became entangled in his hat, which was snatched off his head and carried away some distance. When he searched for the money, it was gone. He could not find it anywhere.

Lucas went home very sad. When his wife learned the cause of his sorrow, she became very angry. She scolded her husband roundly. As soon as the family had eaten the meat Lucas bought, they were as poor as before. They were even pale because of hunger.

One day Luis and Isco decided to visit Lucas and see how he was getting along. It happened that while they were passing in the same street as before, they saw Lucas weeping under a mango tree near his small house. "What is the matter?" said Luis. "Why are you crying?"

Poor Lucas told them all that had happened to him – how the money was lost, and how his wife had scolded him. At first Luis did not believe the rope-maker's story, and became angry at him. At last, however, when he perceived that Lucas was telling the truth, he pardoned him and gave him a thousand pesos.

Lucas returned home with delight, but his wife and children were not in the house. They were out asking alms from their neighbours. Lucas then hid the bulk of the money in an empty jar in the corner of the room, and then went out to buy food for his wife and children. While he was gone, his wife and children returned. They had not yet eaten anything.

Not long afterwards a man came along selling rice. Zelima said to him, "Sir, can't you give us a little something to appease our hunger? I'll give you some *darak* in exchange."

"Oh, yes!" said the man, "I'll give you some rice, but you do not need to give me anything."

Zelima took the rice gladly; and as she was looking for something with which to repay the man, she happened to see the empty jar in which her husband had secretly put his money. She filled the jar with *darak* and gave it to the rice-seller.

When Lucas came home, he was very happy. He told his wife about the money he had hidden. But when he found out that the money was gone, he was in despair: he did not know what to do. He scolded his wife for her carelessness. As he could not endure to see the suffering of his children, he tried to kill himself, but his children prevented him. At last he concluded to be quiet; for he thought, "If I hurt my wife, and she becomes sick, I can't stand it. I must take care of her."

Two months passed by, and Luis and Isco again visited their friend Lucas. While they were walking in the street, Luis found a big piece of lead. He picked it up and put it in his pocket. When they reached Lucas's house, they were astonished to see him in a more wretched condition than before. Luis asked what was the matter. Lucas related to him all that had occurred; but Luis just said, "Oh, no! you are fooling us. We will not believe you." Lucas was very sad. He asked pardon of Luis for his carelessness, and said, "Don't increase the burden of my suffering by your scolding!"

Now, Luis was by nature gentle and pitiful. He could not endure to see his friend suffering. So he gave him the lead he had found in the street, saying, "Now, take care of that! Maybe your wealth will come from it." Luis accepted the lead unwillingly, for he thought that Luis was mocking him.

When Lucas went into the house, he threw the lead away in the corner, and went to sleep. During the night a neighbour knocked at their door, asking for a piece of lead for her husband. The neighbour said, "My husband is going fishing early in the morning, and he asked me to buy him some lead for his line, but I forgot it. I know he will scold me if I don't have some ready for him." Lucas, who was wakened by the talk, told his wife to get the lead he had thrown in the corner.

When Zelima found it, she gave it to their neighbour, who went away happy, promising that she would bring them the first fish her husband should catch.

The next morning Lucas woke very late. The neighbour was already there with a big fish, and Zelima was happy at having so much to eat. While she was cleaning the fish, she found a bright stone inside it. As she did not know of the value of the stone, she gave it to her youngest son to play with; but when the other children saw it, they quarrelled with their brother, and tried to take it away from him. Lucas, too, was ignorant of the fact that the stone was worth anything.

In front of their house lived a rich man named Don Juan. When he heard the noise of his neighbour's children quarrelling, he sent his wife to see what was the matter. Don Juan's wife saw the stone, and wanted to have it very much. She asked Zelima to sell it to her, but Zelima said that she would wait and ask her husband. The rich man's wife went home and told her husband about the jewel. He went to Lucas's house, and offered the rope-maker a thousand pesos for the stone; but Lucas refused, for now he suspected that it was worth more than that. At last he sold it for twenty thousand pesos.

Lucas was now a rich man. He bought clothes for his wife and children, renewed his house, which was falling to pieces, and bought a machine for making rope. As his business increased, he bought another machine. But although Lucas was the richest man in town, he was very kind. His house was open to every comer. He supported crippled persons, and gave alms to the poor.

When Luis and Isco visited Lucas the last time, they were surprised and at the same time delighted to see him so rich. Lucas did not know how to thank them. He gave a banquet in honour of these two men. After the feast was over, Lucas told his friends every detail of all that had happened to him, how he had lent the lead, how his wife had found the stone in the fish, and how a rich man had bought it for twenty thousand pesos.

Luis was now convinced that Lucas was honest, and had told the truth on former occasions. Lucas lived in his big house happily and in peace with his wife and children.

The Meeting of the Plants

ONCE UPON A TIME plants were able to talk as well as people, and to walk from place to place. One day King Molave, the strongest tree, who lived on a high mountain, called his subjects together for a general meeting.

Then every tree put itself in motion towards the designated spot, each doing its best to reach it first. But the buri palm was several days late, which made the king angry, and he cursed it in these terms:

"You must be punished for your negligence, and as king I pass upon you this sentence: You shall never see your descendants, for you shall die just as your seeds are ready to grow."

And from that day the buri palms have always died without seeing their descendants.

The Monkeys and the Dragonflies

ONE DAY, WHEN THE SUN was at the zenith and the air was very hot, a poor dragonfly, fatigued with her long journey, alighted to rest on a branch of a tree in which a great many monkeys lived. While she was fanning herself with her wings, a monkey approached her, and said, "Aha! What are you doing here, wretched creature?"

"O sir! I wish you would permit me to rest on this branch while the sun is so hot," said the dragonfly softly. "I have been flying all morning, and I am so hot and tired that I can go no farther," she added.

"Indeed!" exclaimed the monkey in a mocking tone. "We don't allow any weak creature such as you are to stay under our shelter. Go away!" he said angrily, and, taking a dry twig, he threw it at the poor creature.

The dragonfly, being very quick, had flown away before the cruel monkey could hit her. She hurried to her brother the king, and told him what had happened. The king became very angry, and resolved to make war on the monkeys. So he despatched three of his soldiers to the king of the monkeys with this challenge:

"The King of the Monkeys.

"Sir, as one of your subjects has treated my sister cruelly, I am resolved to kill you and your subjects with all speed.

"DRAGON."

The monkey-king laughed at the challenge. He said to the messengers, "Let your king and his soldiers come to the battlefield, and they will see how well my troops fight."

"You don't mean what you say, cruel king," answered the messengers. "You should not judge before the fight is over."

"What fools, what fools!" exclaimed the king of the monkeys. "Go to your ruler and tell him my answer," and he drove the poor little creatures away.

When the king of the dragonflies received the reply, he immediately ordered his soldiers to go to the battlefield, but without anything to fight with. Meanwhile the monkeys came, each armed with a heavy stick. Then the monkey-king shouted, "Strike the flying creatures with your clubs!" When King Dragon heard this order, he commanded his soldiers to alight on the foreheads of their enemies. Then the monkeys began to strike at the dragonflies, which were on the foreheads of their companions. The dragonflies were very quick, and were not hurt at all: but the monkeys were all killed. Thus the light, quick-witted dragonflies won the victory over the strong but foolish monkeys.

The Snail and the Deer

THE DEER MADE FUN of the snail because of his slowness, so the latter challenged the former to a race. "We will race to the well on the other side of the plaza," said the snail. "All right," replied the deer.

On the day of the race the deer ran swiftly to the well, and when he got there he called, "Mr. Snail, where are you?" "Here I am," said the snail, sticking his head up out of the well. The deer was very much surprised, so he said, "I will race you to the next well." "Agreed," replied the snail. When the deer arrived at the next well, he called as before, "Mr. Snail, where are you?" "Here I am," answered the snail. "Why have you been so slow? I have been here a long time waiting for you." The deer tried again and again, but always with the same result; until the deer in disgust dashed his head against a tree and broke his neck.

Now the first snail had not moved from his place, but he had many cousins in each of the wells of the town and each exactly resembled the other. Having heard the crows talking of the proposed race, as they perched on the edge of the wells to drink, they determined to help their cousin to win it, and so, as the deer came to each well, there was always a snail ready to stick his head out and answer, "Here I am" to the deer's enquiry.

The Spider and the Fly

MR. SPIDER WAS ONCE in love with Miss Fly. Several times he declared his love, but was always repelled, for Miss Fly disliked his business.

One day, when she saw him coming, she closed the doors and windows of her house and made ready a pot of boiling water.

Mr. Spider called to be allowed to enter the house, but Miss Fly's only answer was to throw the boiling water at him.

"Well!" cried Mr. Spider, "I and my descendants shall be avenged upon you and yours. We will never give you a moment's peace."

Mr. Spider did not break his word, for to this day we see his hatred of the fly.

The Story of a Monkey

ONE DAY WHEN A MONKEY was climbing a tree in the forest in which he lived, he ran a thorn into his tail. Try as he would, he could not get it out, so he went to a barber in the town and said:

"Friend Barber, I have a thorn in the end of my tail. Pull it out, and I will pay you well."

The barber tried to pull out the thorn with his razor, but in doing so he cut off the end of the tail. The monkey was very angry and cried:

"Barber, Barber, give me back my tail, or give me your razor!"

The barber could not put back the end of the monkey's tail, so he gave him his razor.

On the way home the monkey met an old woman who was cutting wood for fuel, and he said to her:

"Grandmother, Grandmother, that is very hard. Use this razor and then it will cut easily."

The old woman was very pleased with the offer and began to cut with the razor, but before she had used it long it broke. Then the monkey cried:

"Grandmother, Grandmother, you have broken my razor! You must get a new one for me or else give me all the firewood."

The old woman could not get a new razor so she gave him the firewood.

The monkey took the wood and was going back to town to sell it, when he saw a woman sitting beside the road making cakes.

"Grandmother, Grandmother," said he, "your wood is almost gone; take this of mine and bake more cakes."

The woman took the wood and thanked him for his kindness, but when the last stick was burned, the monkey cried out:

"Grandmother, Grandmother, you have burned up all my wood! Now you must give me all your cakes to pay for it."

The old woman could not cut more dry wood at once, so she gave him all the cakes.

The monkey took the cakes and started for the town, but on the way he met a dog which bit him so that he died. And the dog ate all the cakes.

Story of Ca Matsin and Ca Boo-Ug

ONE DAY A TURTLE, whose name was Ca Boo-Ug, and a monkey, Ca Matsin, met on the shore of a pond. While they were talking, they noticed a banana plant floating in the water.

"Jump in and get it," said Ca Matsin, who could not swim, "and we will plant it, and some day we will have some bananas of our own." So Ca Boo-Ug swam out and brought the plant to shore.

"Let's cut it in two," said Ca Matsin. "You may have one half and I will take the other, and then we shall each have a tree."

"All right," said Ca Boo-Ug; "which half will you take?"

Ca Matsin did not think the roots looked very pretty, and so he chose the upper part. Ca Boo-Ug knew a thing or two about bananas, so he said nothing, and each took his part and planted it. Ca Boo-Ug planted his in a rich place in the garden, but Ca Matsin planted his in the ashes in the fireplace, because it was easy, and then, too, he could look at it often and see how pretty it was.

Ca Matsin laughed as he thought how he had cheated Ca Boo-Ug, but soon his part began to wither and die, and he was very angry.

With Ca Boo-Ug it was different. Before long his tree began to put forth leaves, and soon it had a beautiful bunch of bananas on it. But he could not climb the tree to get the bananas, so one day he went in search of Ca Matsin, and asked him how his banana tree was getting along. When Ca Matsin told him that his tree was dead, Ca Boo-Ug pretended to be very much surprised and sorry, and said:

"My tree has a beautiful bunch of bananas on it, but I cannot climb up to get them. If you will get some of them for me, I will give you half."

Ca Matsin assented, and climbed the tree. When he got to the top, he pulled a banana, ate it, and threw the skin down to Ca Boo-Ug. Then he ate another, and another, throwing the skins down on Ca Boo-Ug's head. When he had eaten all he wanted, he jumped out of the tree and ran away to the woods, laughing at Ca Boo-Ug. Ca Boo-Ug did not say anything, but just sat down and thought what he should do to get even with Ca Matsin. Finally, he gathered a lot of bamboo sticks and planted them around the tree with the sharp points up, covering them with leaves so that they could not be seen. Then he sat down and waited.

As soon as Ca Matsin got hungry again, he went around to Ca Boo-Ug's garden to get some more bananas. Ca Boo-Ug seemed glad to see him, and when Ca Matsin asked for some bananas, replied:

"All right, you may have all you want, but on one condition. When you jump out of the tree you must not touch those leaves. You must jump over them."

As soon as Ca Matsin heard that he must not jump on the leaves, that was just what he wanted to do. So when he had eaten all the bananas he wanted, he jumped out of the tree on to the leaves as hard as he could jump, and was killed by the sharp bamboo points.

Then Ca Boo-Ug skinned him and cut him up and packed the meat in a jar of brine and hid it in the mud on the bank of the pond.

In the dry season the banana trees all died and the coconut trees bore no fruit, so a troop of monkeys came to Ca Boo-Ug and asked him if he would give them something to eat.

"Yes, I have some nice meat in a jar which I will give you, but if I do, you must promise to eat it with your eyes shut."

They were very hungry, so they gave the required promise, and Ca Boo-Ug gave them the meat. All kept their eyes shut except one, a little baby, and like all babies, he was very curious and wanted to see what was going on. So he opened one eye and peeped at a bone which he had in his hand, then he called out:

"Oh, see what I have found! Here is the little finger of my brother, Ca Matsin!"

Then all the monkeys looked, and when they found that Ca Boo-Ug had killed a member of their tribe they were very angry, and looked for Ca Boo-Ug, in order to kill him. But they could not find him, for as soon as he saw what had happened he had hidden under a piece of coconut shell which was lying on the ground.

The chief monkey sat upon the coconut shell, while he was planning with his companions how they should catch Ca Boo-Ug, but of course he did not know where he was, so he called out, "Where's Ca Boo-Ug? Where's Ca Boo-Ug?"

Ca Boo-Ug was so tickled when he heard the monkey ask where he was that he giggled. The monkeys heard him, and looked all around for him, but could not find him. Then they called out, "Where's Ca Boo-Ug? Where's Ca Boo-Ug?" This time Ca Boo-Ug laughed out loud, and the monkeys found him. Then they began to plan how they should punish him.

"Let's put him into a rice mortar and pound him to death," said one. "Aha!" said Ca Boo-Ug, "that's nothing! My mother beat me so much when I was little that now my back is so strong that nothing can break it."

When the monkeys found out that Ca Boo-Ug was not afraid of being pounded in a rice mortar, they determined to try something else.

"Let's make a fire on his back and burn him up," suggested another. "Oh, ho!" laughed Ca Boo-Ug, "that's nothing. I should think that you could tell by the colour of my shell that I have had a fire lighted on my back many times. In fact, I like it, as I am always so cold."

So the monkeys decided that they would punish Ca Boo-Ug by throwing him into the pond and drowning him.

"Boo-hoo!" cried Ca Boo-Ug, "don't do that! You will surely kill me. Please don't do that! Boo-hoo! Boo-hoo!"

Of course when the monkeys found that Ca Boo-Ug did not wish to be thrown into the pond, they thought they had found just the way to kill him. So, in spite of his struggles, they picked him up and threw him far out into the pond.

To their surprise and chagrin, Ca Boo-Ug stuck his head out of the water and laughed at them, and then turned around and swam off.

When the monkeys saw how they had been deceived, they were very much disappointed, and began to plan how they could catch Ca Boo-Ug again. So they called to a big fish, named Botete, that lived in the pond:

"Botete! Drink all you can of the water in the pond and help us find the bag of gold that we hid in it. If you will help us find it, you shall have half of the gold."

So Botete began to drink the water, and in a little time the pond was nearly dry. Then the monkeys determined to go down into the pond and look for Ca Boo-Ug. When he saw them coming, Ca Boo-Ug called to Salacsacan, the kingfisher, who was sitting on a branch of a tree which hung over the water:

"Salacsacan! Salacsacan! Botete has drunk all the water in the pond, and if there is no water there will be no fish for you to catch. Fly down now and peck a hole in Botete, and let the water out, before the fish are all dead." So Salacsacan flew down and pecked a hole in the side of Botete, and the water rushed out and drowned all the monkeys.

When Ca Boo-Ug saw that the monkeys were all dead, he crawled up on the bank, and there he lived happily ever after.

Tagalog Babes in the Wood

ONCE UPON A TIME there was a cruel father who hated his twin children, Juan and Maria, and drove them from the house on every occasion.

The children used to live on the grains of rice that fell through the bamboo floor, and such food as their mother could smuggle to them.

At last, when they were about six years old, their father took them off into the forest and left them without food or drink. They wandered for three days, being preserved by such fruits and leaves as they could gather.

Finally poor Maria said she could go no farther, but that she would die. Juan cut a mountain bamboo and from its hollow joints gave Maria a refreshing drink. Then he climbed a tree and in the distance saw a house. After much exertion they reached it and called out, "Tauo po." A voice from within said, "Come in, children." They went in and found a table set, but no one was there, though the same voice said, "Eat and drink all you want." They did so, and after saying, "Thank you, goodbye," they started to go away, but again they were bidden to stay. So they stayed on for a long time until Juan was a young man and Maria a young woman. From a great chest that stood in the corner they took out new clothing as their old wore out, and the chest was never empty, and there was always food in the magic dishes on the table.

The Three Friends: The Monkey, the Dog and the Carabao

ONCE THERE LIVED three friends: a monkey, a dog and a carabao. They were getting tired of city life, so they decided to go to the country to hunt. They took along with them rice, meat and some kitchen utensils.

The first day the carabao was left at home to cook the food, so that his two companions might have something to eat when they returned from the hunt. After the monkey and the dog had departed, the carabao began to fry the meat. Unfortunately the noise of the frying was heard by the Buñgisñgis in the forest. Seeing this chance to fill his stomach, the Buñgisñgis went up to the carabao, and said, "Well, friend, I see that you have prepared food for me."

For an answer, the carabao made a furious attack on him. The Buñgisñgis was angered by the carabao's lack of hospitality, and, seizing him by the horn, threw him knee-deep into the earth. Then the Buñgisñgis ate up all the food and disappeared.

When the monkey and the dog came home, they saw that everything was in disorder, and found their friend sunk knee-deep in the ground. The carabao informed them that a big strong man had come and beaten him in a fight. The three then cooked their food. The Buñgisñgis saw them cooking, but he did not dare attack all three of them at once, for in union there is strength.

The next day the dog was left behind as cook. As soon as the food was ready, the Buñgisñgis came and spoke to him in the same way he had spoken to the carabao. The dog began to snarl; and the Buñgisñgis, taking offence, threw him down. The dog could not cry to his companions for help; for, if he did, the Buñgisñgis would certainly kill him. So he retired to a corner of the room and watched his unwelcome guest eat all of the food. Soon after the Buñgisñgis's departure, the monkey and the carabao returned. They were angry to learn that the Buñgisñgis had been there again.

The next day the monkey was cook; but, before cooking, he made a pitfall in front of the stove. After putting away enough food for his companions and himself, he put the rice on the stove. When the Buñgisñgis came, the monkey said very politely, "Sir, you have come just in time. The food is ready, and I hope you'll compliment me by accepting it."

The Buñgisñgis gladly accepted the offer, and, after sitting down in a chair, began to devour the food. The monkey took hold of a leg of the chair, gave a jerk, and sent his guest tumbling into the pit. He then filled the pit with earth, so that the Buñgisñgis was buried with no solemnity.

When the monkey's companions arrived, they asked about the Buñgisñgis. At first the monkey was not inclined to tell them what had happened; but, on being urged and urged by them, he finally said that the Buñgisñgis was buried "there in front of the stove." His foolish companions, curious, began to dig up the grave. Unfortunately the Buñgisñgis was still alive. He jumped out, and killed the dog and lamed the carabao; but the monkey climbed up a tree, and so escaped.

One day while the monkey was wandering in the forest, he saw a beehive on top of a vine.

"Now I'll certainly kill you," said someone coming towards the monkey.

Turning around, the monkey saw the Buñgisñgis. "Spare me," he said, "and I will give up my place to you. The king has appointed me to ring, each hour of the day, that bell up there," pointing to the top of the vine.

"All right! I accept the position," said the Buñgisñgis. "Stay here while I find out what time it is," said the monkey. The monkey had been gone a long time, and the Buñgisñgis, becoming impatient, pulled the vine. The bees immediately buzzed about him, and punished him for his curiosity.

Maddened with pain, the Buñgisñgis went in search of the monkey, and found him playing with a boa constrictor. "You villain! I'll not hear any excuses from you. You shall certainly die," he said.

"Don't kill me, and I will give you this belt which the king has given me," pleaded the monkey.

Now, the Buñgisñgis was pleased with the beautiful colours of the belt, and wanted to possess it: so he said to the monkey, "Put the belt around me, then, and we shall be friends."

The monkey placed the boa constrictor around the body of the Buñgisñgis. Then he pinched the boa, which soon made an end of his enemy.

Truth and Falsehood

ONE DAY TRUTH started for the city to find some work. On his way he overtook Falsehood, who was going to the city for the same purpose. Falsehood asked permission to ride on the horse with Truth, and his request was granted.

On the way they questioned each other as to the sort of work they wanted. Truth stated that he intended to be a secretary, so that he might always be clean and white. Falsehood declared that he would be a cook, because then he would always have plenty of fine things to eat.

As they were riding along, they met a man carrying a corpse to the cemetery. He had no one to help him, and Truth, in his great pity for the man, jumped off his horse and helped him. After the corpse was buried, Truth asked, "Did you pray for the repose of the soul of the dead?" "No," was the reply, "I do not know how to pray, and I have no money to pay the priest for candles." Then Truth gave the man all the money he had, that he might have prayers said for the dead man, and went back to his companion.

When dinner time came, Falsehood was very angry at finding out that Truth had given all his money away, but finally proposed that they should go to the river and catch some fish for dinner. When they arrived at the river, they found some fish which had been caught in a shallow pool near the bank, and caught all they wanted. But Truth was very sorry for the fish, and threw his half back into the river. Falsehood murmured to him and said, "It would have been better for you to give them to me. If I had known that you would throw them into the river, I would not have given you any of them." Then they rode on. As they were going through a thick wood in the heart of the mountain they heard a noise as of crying, far away. Truth went forward to find what it was, but Falsehood, trembling with fear, hid himself close behind his comrade. At last they saw seven little eagles in a nest high in a tree. They were crying with hunger, and their mother was nowhere to be seen. Truth was sorry for them, and killed his horse, giving some of the meat to the young eagles, and spreading the rest on the ground beneath the tree, so that the mother-bird might find it.

Falsehood hated his comrade for having killed the horse, because now they were obliged to travel on foot. They went down the mountain, and entering the city, presented themselves before the king, desiring to be taken into his service, the one as secretary and the other as cook. The king granted both requests.

When Falsehood saw that his former companion sat at the table with the king and was always clean and dressed in good clothes, while he himself was dirty and had to eat in the kitchen, he was very angry and determined to do something to ruin the one whom now he hated so bitterly.

One day the king and queen went to sail on the sea. As they were far from land, the queen dropped her ring overboard. When Falsehood heard of the accident, he went to the king and said, "My Lord, the king, my friend – your secretary – has told me that he was endowed with magic powers and is able to find the queen's ring. He says if he does not find it he is willing for you to hang him."

The king immediately sent for Truth, and said to him, "Find the queen's ring without delay, or I will have you hanged early tomorrow morning."

Truth went down to the shore, but seeing how impossible it would be to find the ring, began to weep. A fish came near, and floating on top of the water, asked, "Why are you weeping?"

"I weep," Truth replied, "because the king will hang me early tomorrow morning unless I find the queen's ring, which has fallen into the sea."

The fish swam out and got the ring and gave it to Truth. Then he said:

"I am one of the fishes which you found on the bank of the river and threw back into the water. As you helped me when I was in trouble, I am very glad that I have been able to help you now."

On another day, Falsehood went to the king and said, "My Lord King, do you remember what I told you the other day?"

"Yes," replied the king, "and I believe you told me the truth, as the ring has been found."

"Well," replied Falsehood, "my friend told me last night that he is a great magician and that he is willing for you to hang him in the sight of all the people, since it will not hurt him."

The king sent for Truth and told him, "I know what you have said to your friend. Tomorrow I will have you hanged in the sight of all the people, and we will see whether you are the great magician you claim to be."

That night Truth could not sleep. About midnight, as he was in great distress, a spirit suddenly appeared to him and asked what was the cause of his grief. Truth related his trouble, and the spirit said, "Do not weep. Tomorrow morning I will take your form and wear your clothes, and let them hang me."

The next morning, just at dawn, the spirit put on Truth's clothes and went out to be hanged. Many people came to see the hanging, and after it was over, returned to their homes. What was the astonishment of the king and those with him when, upon their return to the palace, they found Truth there before them, alive and well!

That night the spirit appeared to Truth and said, "I am the spirit of the dead man for whom you gave your money that prayers might be said for the repose of his soul." Then it disappeared.

On another day Falsehood appeared before the king and said, "My Lord the king, my friend the secretary told me last night that if you would let him marry your daughter, in one night his wife should bring forth three children." The king sent for Truth and said, "I will give you my daughter to be your wife and if tonight she does not bear three children, I will have you buried alive tomorrow morning."

So they were married. But at midnight, as Truth lay awake thinking of the fate that was in store for him in the morning, an eagle flew through the window, and asked the cause of his sorrow. Truth related his tale, and the eagle said, "Do not worry; I will take care of that." Then he flew away, but just before the break of day three eagles came, each bearing a newborn babe. Truth awakened the princess and said to her, "My dear wife, these are our children. We must love them and take good care of them."

Then the king, who had been awakened by the noise of children crying, sent to ask what it was all about. When he heard the news he came into the tower where the princess was, and when he saw the children he was overcome with joy; for he had no sons, and greatly desired to have an heir to his throne. So the king made a great feast and gave over his crown and sceptre to his son-in-law, to be king in his stead.

Thus we see that those who help others when in trouble shall themselves be aided when they are in difficulty.

The Turtle and the Lizard

A TURTLE AND A BIG lizard once went to the field of Gotgotapa to steal ginger. When they reached the place the turtle said to the lizard:

"We must be very still or the man will hear us and come out."

But as soon as the lizard tasted the ginger he was so pleased that he said:

"The ginger of Gotgotapa is very good."

"Be still," said the turtle; but the lizard paid no attention to the warning, and called louder than ever:

"The ginger of Gotgotapa is very good."

Again and again he cried out, until finally the man heard him and came out of the house to catch the robbers.

The turtle could not run fast, so he lay very still, and the man did not see him. But the lizard ran and the man chased him. When they were out of sight, the turtle went into the house and hid under a coconut shell upon which the man used to sit.

The man ran after the lizard for a long distance, but he could not catch him. After a while he came back to the house and sat down on the shell.

By and by, the turtle called, "Kook." The man jumped up and looked all around. Unable to tell where the noise came from, he sat down again.

A second time the turtle called, and this time the man looked everywhere in the house except under the shell, but could not find the turtle. Again and again the turtle called, and finally the man, realizing that all his attempts were unsuccessful, grew so excited that he died.

Then the turtle ran out of the house, and he had not gone far before he met the lizard again. They walked along together until they saw some honey in a tree, and the turtle said:

"I will go first and get some of the honey."

The lizard would not wait, but ran ahead, and when he seized the honey, the bees came out and stung him. So he ran back to the turtle for help.

After a while they came to a bird snare, and the turtle said:

"That is the silver wire that my grandfather wore about his neck."

Then the lizard ran fast to get it first, but he was caught in the snare and was held until the man came and killed him. Then the wise turtle went on alone.